DEADLY WARNING

Jesse removed the paper clip and slipped the letter from its envelope. A tiny cross fell out and onto the bar.

You have before you the cross of Jesus Christ. It is on that cross that I swear to you that this is true.

This thing is dangerous. They will try to stop it. When the world knows, the greatest war of all time will result. You must never tell of this, for it would put you in great danger. They will kill you as I am sure that they are going to kill me . . .

Other Avon Books by
Jackson Collins

THE HIMMLER PLAQUE

Avon Books are available at special quantity discounts for bulk purchases for sales promotions, premiums, fund raising or educational use. Special books, or book excerpts, can also be created to fit specific needs.

For details write or telephone the office of the Director of Special Markets, Avon Books, Dept. FP, 105 Madison Avenue, New York, New York 10016, 212-481-5653.

THE VOTAN TREASURE

JACKSON COLLINS

AVON BOOKS NEW YORK

THE VOTAN TREASURE is an original publication of Avon Books. This work has never before appeared in book form. This work is a novel. Any similarity to actual persons or events is purely coincidental.

AVON BOOKS
A division of
The Hearst Corporation
105 Madison Avenue
New York, New York 10016

Copyright © 1989 by Jackson Collins
Published by arrangement with the author
Library of Congress Catalog Card Number: 88-92120
ISBN: 0-380-75509-2

All rights reserved, which includes the right to reproduce this book or portions thereof in any form whatsoever except as provided by the U.S. Copyright Law. For information address Cherry Weiner Literary Agency, 28 Kipling Way, Manalapan, New Jersey 07726.

First Avon Books Printing: March 1989

AVON TRADEMARK REG. U.S. PAT. OFF. AND IN OTHER COUNTRIES, MARCA REGISTRADA, HECHO EN U.S.A.

Printed in the U.S.A.

K-R 10 9 8 7 6 5 4 3 2 1

For my parents,
Paul and Pauline Collins

One

Emerson Wolfe watched the moon hanging low over the canyon rim. Beyond it, the great mountains of northern Mexico were blackly outlined against the sky, their peaks softened by the night.

Wolfe looked down the hill, at the sleeping village of Lengus de Cristo. Down there in the Catholic church, a man was dying. Here, in the cool sand, a man lay already dead. The only trepidation Wolfe felt was in the new and unsettling awareness that he felt nothing. An hour ago he had felt rage and disappointment, both of which were dispelled when Charleston Garman came from the adobe house and pleaded with them in his singsong preacher's voice. Now Charleston Garman lay dead at Wolfe's feet, his open-collared white shirt blackly spotted with his own blood. His murder was a no-nonsense malice-aforethought act and a marvel of brevity. From the time Garman had emerged from the house to his current position here in the sand, less than twenty seconds had elapsed.

Wolfe squatted beside the body and extended his hands, balancing his forearms on his knees. The waning moon gave an alabaster glow to his skin, reaffirmed his whiteness. Having spent the last few weeks in that hotel room in Hermosillo with Phillips and Garman, he had of late taken to passing the mirror to see whether his hair had begun to kink. Thoughts like that would finally stop now that things were beginning to happen, now that Garman was really dead, now that Wolfe was headed for Memphis and Phillips was headed for Connecticut.

Feeling his legs beginning to tremble, Wolfe stood and looked at the distant mountains, compared them to a tidal wave frozen in mid-lunge. That analogy was proper for the moment, since he and Phillips were themselves in mid-lunge toward one hell of a lot of wealth. This fuckup by Garman was but a minor setback, according to Phillips, but now little voices of fear and common sense began to sing a duet against the backdrop of his thoughts. Dammit, were they really going to murder a fellow agent and get away with it? Phillips had said yes, while Wolfe himself had opted for little more than a strong maybe. A yes and a maybe are pretty good odds when dealing with absolutes, but this thing was already going awry: the gold was gone, the Mexican farmer who owned this house was nowhere to be found, and, worst of all, two Catholic priests were dead. Sure, one of the priests was dirty, doing dope deals, but the Company had forever stressed that the best and the worst that could happen in the field usually had to do with the church. "Don't fuck with God," a wag had written on a restroom wall at Quantico years ago, following the lecture on churches. It was still good advice.

Phillips had told him to hide Garman's body, a thing that he found odious, especially in this strange darkness, and in this strange land. In his time with the Company he had become accustomed to death, but having shared living quarters with what was now a bloody heap of flesh was putting a new wrinkle on his sense of toughness.

He grasped his feet, pulled, felt a shoe come off in his hand. Grunting and wheezing, he backed toward the hog pen and heard the hogs doing their own grunting. Taking care not to soil himself with Garman's blood, he pulled the body up by the waist and heaved it over the wire fence. There were boomings and thumpings as the hogs rearranged themselves in the face of this intrusion. An old sow came from the little shed, looked at Wolfe and went back inside.

Wolfe was about to start back down the hill when he heard the unmistakable sound of someone running, the pounding feet making muffled cadence in the roadway.

"Don't shoot, Wolfie, it's me," Donald Phillips called. He ran to Wolfe and bent over, grasped his knees with his hands, inhaling raspily. "Gotta get in shape, baby. Gotta do it to it. How's Garman?"

"Compared to what? How'd it go in the village?"

Phillips raised himself and rubbed his sides with his hands. "Just like I said it would. We got one dead mackerel snapper and one dead Company brother. Any sign of Diaz?"

"No, and in one hour it will be sunup. We better come up with something funny real fast."

Phillips patted Wolfe's shoulder and said, "Man, you lost your balls overnight. This thing's gonna work."

Phillip's attitude was beginning to grate; it was not nearly as infectious as he would have wished. Wolfe said, "Now it's gotta work. We're in too deep for it not to." He looked toward the house, toward the hog pen. "Do we wait on the farmer or do we go?"

"We go. I'll tell you about it on the way to the airport."

They went down the hill and turned left into an arroyo. Their thirty-year-old Plymouth, a vehicle that would have been a collector's item in the States, was quite unextraordinary in Mexico. Wolfe slid behind the wheel and they rode in silence through the village. Neither looked at the church.

When they were on the main highway to Hermosillo, Phillips said, "The Company put me and Garman together because we're black. I was with the man quite a while—I know how he worked. That blonde will sooner or later turn up in Memphis—got to—Garman had an old uncle there who was his only living relative.

"That's one. Here's two: we gotta get those two letters to kill this thing in the cocoon. One was to a Mike Morton in New Haven, Connecticut, the other was to the old uncle in Memphis, Washington Clark.

"That's two. Here's three: we can do this thing within a week and be back and the Company will never be the wiser. As far as this Mexican Diaz, is concerned, well, he's an ignorant pig farmer. I say he'll panic when he sees Garman's body. There's time to take care of him when we get back off our little expedition to the States. Can't you drive this thing a little faster?"

Wolfe did not drive faster. His face was drawn, gaunt, introspective. "Two goddamned letters. We saw who they were to and did nothing about it. Two goddamned letters!"

"You're as guilty of that botch as I am," said Phillips. "We discussed this three days ago. Hell, if we had taken those letters he'd have known that we were in cahoots on the gold thing. We'll have those letters, just later than planned. They are the key to keeping this thing under wraps."

Wolfe thought for a moment and then said, "I say we go to Memphis together and wait for the woman in the Mercedes and to hell with the letters. And as far as the gold is concerned, all we know is that it was *some* gold. How much? How heavy? And why was it buried in a Catholic church?" He laughed, but it was a laugh of cynicism mixed with sadness. "Two weeks ago Charleston Garman started babbling about great hordes of gold and now he's dead and two priests are dead. And if Octavio Diaz had been at his pig farm, he'd be dead, too. And now I'm going to wander to Memphis while you trot off to Connecticut, and the Company will never be the wiser. Jesus, how'd I get into this mess?"

"Greed," said Phillips.

An hour later, Emerson Wolfe watched the ancient DC-7 lift off the runway at Hermosillo Airport, bank to the left, disappear in the sunrise. He walked back to the old Plymouth and drove into the heart of Sonora's capital city. Parking near a small café, he went inside and ordered a plate of scrambled eggs.

Maybe this was a fuckup, maybe it wasn't. Yesterday he and Phillips had drawn their savings from the bank, so for the moment money was no problem; Phillips' wary eye for contingency had been eerily on target in suggesting the withdrawals. And maybe, as stated, the Company would never be the wiser if they were gone for a week or so, their being out of the mainstream of international chicanery, buried as they were here in Hermosillo where nothing much ever happened. And, too, as Phillips, had said just last night, the death of Garman could always be laid at the door of Octavio Diaz, an insignificant fool who had come into the picture by asking Garman to do him a favor.

He noshed his eggs and biscuits but did not taste them. Adhering to the positives, he gave the thing an 80 percent chance of working, this 80 percent being composed of several absolutes that the pragmatic Phillips had all but inscribed in bronze: the blonde was brought into the thing hastily and was therefore probably ignorant of just what she was doing; Phillips knew Garman well and, as mentioned back at the hog pens, "knew how he worked." Another tacit positive was the element of secrecy; as far as the world or the Company or anybody else knew, this gold did not exist, had never existed. Dammit, why was the gold buried under a priest's bed? What was the Catholic church in Lengus de Cristo hiding? Whatever it was, it was enough to drive Charleston Garman mad. Yes, this was big, as big as Phillips had sworn all along it would be.

When he was back at his room, Wolfe sat on his bed and held the phone in his lap. All over the world he and his ilk were up to good that was no good, no good that was good.

Stonewall. Double deal. Diplomatic immunity. Fifth Amendment rights. Supreme Court reversals. Sandinista, Contra, foreign aid, Imelda Marcos's shoes, coups. Coups and shoes. This vocation gave him a ringside seat for this circus. He knew the headlines were right: the world was going to hell, and he might as well make a grab for his part of it.

He dialed, talked to the operator in Spanish, waited while she connected him with a number in Utah. The phone rang three times. A man answered.

"You remember that thing I called you about two weeks ago?" Wolfe asked.

"Yes."

"It finally came to pass. I'm going to need your help."

"To kill the nigger?" the voice asked.

"Yes, but not the same one. When can you be in Dallas?"

"I'm open. I just got in from a thing in Arizona."

"Oh? What business did you have in Arizona?" Wolfe asked.

"I'll tell you all about it. In Dallas."

"Tell me now. You're working for us now. Your code name is Cowboy."

"I like that. Cowboy. Sounds like me, don't it? As far as telling you about Arizona, that'll have to keep whether you like it or not. That's just the way it is."

"Okay. In the Galleria in Dallas is a restaurant called Bennigan's. I'll see you there in three days. Around noon. You'll be there?"

"I'll be there."

Wolfe replaced the phone, stood, went to the window. Hermosillo, Sonora, was sunny, smelly, and sinful. A flower vendor was down on the street selling orchids that he had picked in a nearby swamp. They were not his flowers, but he was selling them anyway, which made it theft. Multiply the sonofabitch by two billion and you had mankind.

But it was not the flower vendor that had his attention. What really perturbed Emerson Wolfe was the ease with which he had in the last two hours betrayed one accomplice and lied to another.

True, two weeks ago he had called Utah about the potential disposal of an Afro-American cohort, but at that time the person intended for liquidation had been Charleston Garman. Now that Garman was dead, the arrow of betrayal had come to focus on Donald Phillips. Let Phillips do the legwork on this thing, then kill him. Or, rather, let Cowboy kill him. And then it would be a simple matter to kill Cowboy. The gold would never be known to the Company, for who but himself would ever know that it had existed? Garman had been betrayed and was now dead; Phillips had been betrayed and was on a plane to New Haven; Cowboy would suffer betrayal when the time was right.

A covey of tourist ladies had stopped and were talking to the flower vendor. They were laughing, yelling back and forth in German. The vendor took their money and gave each an orchid and they went on down the street.

Emerson Wolfe turned and looked at the dismal room. Phillips had left his mojo behind. It was a good luck charm that had been acquired in Haiti, a small human hand of lacquered bronze.

Wolfe went across the room and rubbed the object. He needed luck.

Octavio Diaz awoke in the middle of his three-acre corn field. His throat was parched and his neck was burning from the sun's rays. Dusting himself off, he squatted on his haunches and looked at the intruding red ball in the sky and judged the time to be well past eight o'clock. This meant that he had been asleep here for about five hours. Yesterday afternoon he had walked over the hills and through the canyon to the village of Dos Palomas, whereupon he and his friends had drunk two bottles of tequila. They had begged him to stay but he had told them that he feared for his pigs, that one could not be too careful. They had laughed and waved him into the darkness. After a time of stumbling and cursing himself, the corn field had looked inviting, alluring, soft, the moon and the tequila doing for his crop the same things that they did for certain women.

Now he went up the hill and over it, saw that his little house and his pigs were undisturbed. He would water and feed the animals and then go inside for a nap. Pouring crushed corn and water together in a bucket, he placed the bail over the crook of his arm and went toward the sty.

An electric trill of terror ran down his back. The black American named Garman lay on his side just over the fence, and traces of blood and brain were sprayed over his shoulders and down his back. The pigs had rooted about the body, had even chewed on one of the hands; one of the fingers pointed skyward. Afraid to look around, Octavio moved forward and eased one leg over the fence and then the other, a ballet of movement that is peculiar to farmers. The pigs grunted and came toward him. He emptied the bucket into the old barrel that served as a feeding trough, turned, looked toward his house. It was silent and still and empty. He looked at his pigs and back at his house, aware that he was probably seeing both for the last time.

Octavio's heart pulsed wildly. With perspiration blinding him, he recrossed the fence and walked to the house. It was but one room and he instantly saw that nothing had been disturbed. They had left Garman as a warning, probably, or perhaps they had intended to kill Garman and himself. Garman had warned him that this might happen, had even given him two hundred pesos for emergency use. The money was hidden on a shelf beneath a coffee can. Octavio shoved the money into his pocket, went outside, looked at his animals and his house, then ran down the hill toward the village of Lengus de Cristo.

The church bell began to toll when he was halfway to the village. Octavio's anguish was instant, consuming, indescribable. He ran faster, his eyes blurred by tears, the village appearing to dance as his head bobbed, the mountains beyond moving as ocean swells. It was as though the bell accused him, isolated him from eternal salvation, shouted to the valley that he was at fault in the desecration that had occurred in the church.

Running with leaden legs, he recalled that this had begun by a whisper from the throat of Fate. Father Emiliano had told him that the black American might soon be coming to the village, had told him that Father Colon in Hermosillo had done an evil thing and had confessed to the black American that a strange secret was to be learned in the village of Lengus de Cristo, and Father Emiliano had told Octavio then of what the Holy Church had secreted in the church of Lengus de Cristo for generations.

Octavio had met the black man, had betrayed the Holy Church for his own purposes. But Octavio had not wanted gold—he had wanted freedom for a relative. Freedom, such a simple thing. The black American's warnings had begun to come much later. Now Octavio was overwhelmed by what his life had become in a matter of hours.

At the outer edge of the village was the Old One, Juanito, a village elder who had once been a seller of ducks and their eggs, but who now sat in a rickety rocking chair in front of his little hut and stared into the past.

"Why does the bell toll?" Octavio called, never breaking stride.

"They say it is Father Emiliano," Juanito called. "He is dead."

Octavio said nothing, but ran on with the certainty of one who has heard the shatter of brittle dreams and rushes to salvage their pieces. His miscalculations had been the stuff of poverty and ignorance, and he hated himself with that wordless hate that is ever the way of little men who strive and fail.

The villagers were clustered about the door of the church. Someone mentioned poison, and in the next second someone else remarked that the water had tasted strangely of late. Several mothers screamed and ran toward their houses. Octavio wanted to call them back, to tell them that it was not water but wickedness that had killed the priest.

Four young men carried the priest's body down the steps and all in the crowd crossed themselves. One of the carriers whispered something to the crowd and the word was passed quickly. A gaunt old woman walked past Octavio, her wrinkled hands wiping her eyes.

"What did he say, Madre?" Octavio asked.

"The good father's bed had been moved and a hole had been dug," she answered. "They will go for the *Federales*. Something was taken from the floor under the bed. They say that they believe the priest was murdered. This cannot be true: no one would murder a priest." She looked at Octavio as if for confirmation of this simple truth. When he said nothing she walked on toward her home.

At that moment the face of God, in the unusual form

of a watermelon truck, smiled on Octavio Diaz. He recognized the driver, Raul Rioza, and flagged him. The truck stopped to let the crowd pass and Octavio ran to the truck's cab.

"Mass so late in the morning?" Raul said, smiling.

"No. Father Emiliano has died," said Octavio.

Although he seldom attended church, Raul crossed himself and said, "May his sins remain in the dust."

"Where are you going?" Octavio inquired.

"To Juarez," said Raul. He pointed a thumb absently toward the staked and heavily weighted bed behind him. "Where else do I ever go? Cantaloupes one time, corn the next. The great stores in Texas now yearn for our early watermelons." He looked at the church with sad eyes.

"May I ride with you?"

"Gasoline is very expensive," said Raul. "The extra weight—"

"I will give you ten pesos," Octavio interjected.

"Get in," said Raul.

The villagers watched as the truck passed in the dusty street, and Octavio knew that some would wonder why he had decided to ride to Juarez with corn to be cultivated, pigs to be fed. But then they would realize that Octavio, a bachelor, had needs that would meet with censure in this tiny village where all knew everyone's business. Today, however, they would not laugh, and by the time they found Garman's body he would be hundreds of miles away.

The truck groaned and shimmied up the hill that led to the main highway and Octavio hung his head out the window and looked at his village for what would be the last time. Ten minutes ago he had been afraid, but not sad; now he was sad, but no longer afraid. The wind whipped his dark hair over his eyes as he looked beyond the village and toward the hill where his house stood. The tin roof was as tiny as a needle point in the tan swells and dips of the hills, and he imagined that he could see vultures circling.

Two

The girls downstairs were laughing as the man called Chief stepped from the room onto the second-floor balcony. He looked out across the decrepit place that called itself Ciudad Juarez. City of Juarez. To the north and slightly to the east he would see El Paso, a place of electric lights and flush toilets and people who did not wipe their asses with their fingers. Someone put on another record downstairs and the girls laughed again. For some reason Mexican whores always grouped and laughed while their American counterparts usually worked singly and laughed not at all. Were it not for the probability of some exotic crotch rot he might go down and pay two dollars for a hunch crib of his own, but there was work to do. He looked across the darkening mass of hovels once more and shook off the feeling that old Juarez would not be proud of what he had wrought. For that matter, Chief himself had nothing to be proud of, certainly not on this night.

Octavio lay on a table in the center of the room. He was naked and his hands were tied behind his back. A single light bulb hung from the ceiling and Octavio squinted against the light. Both of his jaws were darkening from the recent slapping.

"Any luck?" Chief said as he stepped in from the balcony.

"No sir," said one of the two white men who flanked the table. "But I think this young man wants to cooperate. You do want to help us, don't you?" He smiled down at Octavio.

The Chief closed the balcony door and said, "Well, it has taken us a couple of days, but here we are. It's quite a jaunt from Sonora to Juarez. You are quite a fellow, Diaz. Wouldn't you like to get back to Sonora? To Hermosillo? Why don't you tell us about the two black men and the white man? Cooter here didn't mean to hurt you, only to get your attention. Those other three were bad fellows and we want them." When Octavio continued to squint at the galling light, Chief said, "Tell us about the bad *norteamericanos*, hokay?"

"He speaks English, Chief," said the white man who had been silent to now.

Chief looked up with a dull vehemence. "Oscar, keep the fuck out of this. I know this greasy little fuck speaks English." He looked down at Octavio and said, "See, I know a good deal about you. More than you might imagine. I know, for instance, that three Americans came to your village from Hermosillo last month. The two black ones were named Phillips and Garman. The white one was named Emerson Wolfe. Phillips and Wolfe have disappeared and we will find them. But Garman bothers us. He went nowhere, yet he is gone. It makes us insane." He pointed at his head and drew air circles. "Please help us." Shrieks of laughter emanated from downstairs and he said, "You can be with the girls in a matter of minutes. Would you like that?" He made a loose fist with one hand and poked it suggestively with a finger, waggling his eyebrows.

"Chief, please, for God's sake—"

"Oscar, get the hell out of this room right now! Go stand in the hallway! Do it!" He watched as Oscar went out and closed the door. Now he looked at the dingy yellow wallpaper, at the three torn chairs, at the old sagged mattress on the wrought iron bed. "I got enough shit on my neck doing this in this place, and I don't need Oscar to give me any goddam sermons. You trust him?"

Cooter nodded. "Yes sir, I do. Oscar knows where his bread is buttered even if he does occasionally have an attack of conscience. He just doesn't like . . . ." He looked at Octavio.

"Tie his ankles and come out here on the balcony," Chief commanded. A minute later Cooter joined him outside and they stood with their backs to the city facing the doorway and Octavio. "You know what we gotta do here, don't you, Cooter?"

"Yes sir, I do."

"Are you up to it?"

"Yes sir."

"Have you done it before?"

"Yes sir. Twice in Tehran, once in Tegucigalpa, once in Guatemala."

"Does it bother you, Cooter?"

"No sir. This one might a little, mainly because I don't know what in hell is going on."

"That makes two of us. Tell me what you know."

Cooter spat off the balcony and wiped his lower lip with the back of a hand. "I know that I was on assignment to lay out some covert stuff against a vice president of the Bank of Mexico. Sometime this weekend I get the word to go to Sonora and find out why three of our people ain't responding to any messages, three lost sheep, two of which happen to be black, Garman and Phillips. The white one, Emerson Wolfe, I knew slightly. Why the Company ever kept him, I'll never know. Anyway, they smell a rat and send me and Oscar up. We got onto this Octavio right away; he had been dealing with one of the blacks, according to the other villagers."

"Dealing? In what?"

Oscar pursed his lips and shook his head slowly. "They didn't say. And I think they didn't know. A funny thing, the priest in that hogtied Mexican's village was found dead last week and that's when our boy on the table in there took off."

Chief turned and looked at the darkened city. Abutted in its shabbiness against the near-far El Paso, it symbolized evil touching good, confusion mocking logic, vulgarity nursing at the breast of propriety. He realized that he did not hate third-worlders, he was merely tired of being among strangers. The disposal of one Octavio Diaz would not stand the world on its head, but having

Cooter do so within sight of El Paso made it somehow different. Chief had once watched a Montagnard warrior stick shit-soaked spears into the belly of a Cambodian boy. That was brown doing it to brown, and he had ordered it. But ordering white to do it to brown, and right here where the Great Eagle might look across the border and see it being done, well, there was something about it that was distressing, noxious, desecratory. He thought of Thomas Jefferson, who had brought a purity out of chaos, and of Sergeant York, who had committed chaos to preserve purity. Somewhere between then and now the logic had failed. "Jesus," he said.

"Jesus what, Chief?" Cooter asked.

"Jesus everything and Jesus nothing. We got a dead priest, a Mexican pig farmer and three company men who were into something that was apparently for their own good instead of the common good."

"But we don't know that for sure, sir. I mean, the fact they're missing does not mean they were on the take. Not necessarily."

Chief looked at Cooter as a matron might look at a maggot on a banquet table. "Dammit, Cooter, *think!* If this was three garage mechanics it wouldn't mean shit. But these were not garage mechanics—they were . . . Company men. They belonged to the biggest invisible lightning bolt that exists. Take my word, when three of *ours* disappear, heads turn—*big* heads."

Cooter looked at his superior, started to speak, did not. From below came the sound of another song. It was "This Magic Moment" by the Drifters and Cooter whistled along with it. When the man beside him appeared to have cooled a bit he said, "Okay, Chief, let's say they were up to something and they have lit out; we can always disallow any . . ."

"No, we can't," Chief interjected. "One we could disallow, but three is a goddam dangerous number, four if you count our buddy on the table in there. It's not the body factor; it's the mouth factor. One person disappears because he's wacko or he's defected to the bear's camp or he's got a piece of ass on his mind that he has to take care of." He shook his head. "But three, no. I don't like the smell of this one. I'm gonna get yelled at and I don't even know why." He watched as a small Mexican boy rolled a tire down a street and into an alleyway. "You said something about our white man, Emerson Wolfe, something about why the Company ever kept him on. What did you mean?"

Cooter said, "Well, sir, you'd have to know Wolfe yourself. I don't know if I can explain him."

"I got all night. Give it a shot."

"Mealy-mouthed as hell, lethal as hell. And, probably, crazy as hell. He'd cut a baby's throat without batting an eye and then lend its mother a Kleenex to wipe her eyes with. Know what I mean? Shake a black man's hand, tell him a joke, and then tell the next white man he saw about how bad he hated goddam niggers. Knows passages of the Bible by heart and might quote them to some Indian whore he had just screwed in the ass. But he's a political animal from the word go, a sharpie. Psychiatrists have a word for his sort, but I don't know what it is; the kind of a person who's thinking one hundred miles an hour and always uses any situation to his own absolutest advantage. He does not make mistakes. He's damned good at getting other people to do shit details for him, and when the work is done there he is glowing like a Gucci watch, taking the credit and picking up the marbles."

"Sounds like you knew him pretty well."

"Slightly, like I said. Remember when that oil well blew in Guadalajara and killed those twenty Mexicans? I was in with him on that one, us and about four others. The oil company was shut down for the investigation and went into receivership six months later. Exxon or Texaco or somebody took them over, which was what the Great Eagle wanted, I guess. Anyway, the whole thing from start to finish only lasted about a week and he went to Nicaragua, I think it was, maybe Honduras. He could have helped start the shit that's going on down there."

Chief had listened carefully to this biography of Emerson Wolfe but had taken no solace from it. He looked at the naked man on the table and saw that he appeared to be at once sleeping and crying. "He's about to crack, Cooter. I've seen it before. I'm going to take a walk. When I come back in about two hours I'll expect it to be all over. See that cantina over there?" He pointed to an orange facade halfway down the block. "I'll meet you and Oscar out in front of it. By the way, how did you get this room?"

Cooter smiled. "Gave the madam one hundred pesos. She thinks Oscar and the Mexican and I are queers. Ain't that a hoot?"

"Well, don't do it until you're sure you've sapped all he knows. There's something *major* going on here, I just feel it. See you in two hours."

Chief walked past the crying, grimacing brown man and went out into the hallway. Oscar was leaning against a wall and came halfway to attention, started to speak or to smile, but was unable to do either.

When Chief was on the street he walked ploddingly, deliberately, unhappily; it was one of those moments known by all who brood wherein the objective is to walk beyond oneself, out of oneself. A girl of about nine stepped from an alley and said, "Hey, meester, blow job?" He raised a hand theatrically as if to strike her and she darted into the alley as suddenly as she had emerged.

Chief did not stop walking until he came to a small bridge that wedded the banks of a dry creek, beyond which was a paper-strewn park. He sat on the bannister and stared down at the umbilicus of brown water. Once, in his boyhood, he had sat on a creekbank in Missouri and had watched as a turtle devoured the body of a perch, and the order of things, cruel as they were, had made sense to him then, much more so than now.

A laughing couple approached the bridge. When they saw him they became silent. When they were past the boy whispered something to the girl and she giggled.

Whatever it was that he had sought was not on the bridge and he stood and walked away. At a nearby highway the lights of a car laser-lit a drunken woman. She staggered and shouted obscenely as the car swerved and moved on. He wanted to go over and kick the shit out of her, but he did not. Hell, she was having a good time; let the bitch go.

He retraced his steps toward the bridge. Someone giggled off to his right and Chief was able to discern the unmistakable act of lovemaking. The couple who had walked past him some minutes before were writhing together a few yards away beneath a stand of short bushes, her naked thighs encircling the young man's naked hips. Some six blocks away, in a room over a whorehouse, one was dying; here under a stunted growth beneath a stunted moon, another was being created. Mesmerized by his own confusion, he walked on.

The bleat-honk of an ambulance came from the vicinity of the hotel and Chief knew that Cooter had done his work. This did not cause him to run, nor did he even walk hurriedly; a career as one of the waving cilia in the gutwork of bureaucracy assured that whatever report he filed at whenever time would itself be filed by filers, analyzed by analyzers, contemplated by contemplaters. Hell, truth be told, the men of the Company had disposed of a good fifty or maybe seventy-five Octavios around the globe in the last thirty days. Maybe when this tour was over he could wangle a hitch in Japan; damned little ever had to be done in Japan, which was odd, considering what the polite little motherfuckers had done at Nanking and Bataan.

He neared the cantina and looked beyond it to the whorehouse. An ambulance was pulling away slowly. Cooter had done his work well: slow ambulances are for dead people. He only hoped that Cooter had gotten all the information that was necessary to tie this hog to the fence and leave it to rot.

"What's going on?" he asked a sweating old Mexican who was barefoot and clad only in Duck's Head overalls.

"Someone say a man fall from the whorehouse and break hees neck. I hope he alive."

I'll give twenty to one he isn't, Chief was thinking, but he said, "Oh, how did he fall from a whorehouse?"

"Who know?" the man said, shrugging. "They stay

drunk a lot so maybe he drunk. Who can sleep in such madhouseness? Is it such in your country?''

Chief just smiled and watched the Mexican go back to his small dark shop.

"Madhouseness," Chief whispered. "An adequate summation."

As the small crowd began to disperse into the darkness he saw Oscar and Cooter standing near the alleyway that sided the cantina. A soft wind rose and a bit of newspaper blew against Cooter's leg and he cocked his head sideways as if to read it in the mauve light from the neon sign.

"Save me the sports page," said Chief.

"Yessir, I will," said Cooter.

"Oscar, go have a drink. I'll send Cooter for you later." As Oscar walked disconsolately into the cantina, Chief motioned for Cooter to follow him into the alley. When they were a few yards from the street Cooter unzipped and pissed noisily against the concrete wall.

"They'll call you an ugly American if you get caught doing that," Chief said.

"I been called an ugly American before," said Oscar, shaking it off, zipping up.

"So how did it go?"

"Weird," said Oscar.

The word hung between them. It was almost as if a third party had joined them in the darkness.

"There's a lot of words I like to hear in an oral report, but *weird* isn't one of them. It always triggers something that makes me think I'm not gonna get much sleep. So how was it weird?"

"Garman, our black man from Memphis, is dead. Our Mexican in there left him in a hog pen. He paid the man who drove him here to Juarez to go back and bury the body. But it wasn't him that killed Garman; that was done by either Wolfe or Phillips."

"Our own men killed Garman? Was he talking to the Bear?"

Oscar laughed. "No, that's just it: that's where the thing gets goofy. Garman and the Mexican had become good buddies. The Mexican says that over the last month or so Garman got sort of nervous, so much so that he wouldn't mail his own letters, got the Mexican to do it for him. Letters to Memphis, where he was from, and New Haven, Connecticut. Garman went to school there, New Haven. Went to Yale to be a preacher; bombed out somehow. Garman, Phillips, and Wolfe were in it together, but Garman got cold feet, apparently, and wanted out."

"Hold it. They were in *what* together?"

"I'm not sure," said Cooter. "The three of them went to work in Hermosillo about three months ago. Our dead one, Charleston Garman, got to neglecting his duties, started hanging around the Mexican's village, a little place called Lengus de Cristo. Pretty soon the other two, Wolfe and Phillips, got as interested in the village as Garman was. From the smell of it, they had decided to go into cahoots on the deal at Lengus de Cristo, whatever the deal was."

"Sure," said Chief morosely, "whatever the deal was. So what was it that lured them to this village, this . . . ."

"Lengus de Cristo. Means 'words of Christ.' I don't know, and neither did Octavio Diaz, our friend from the table. He told me about his conversations with Garman, how bad he felt when he found Garman's body. He was talking fast to save his life, but I still got the feeling he was holding something back. One thing I did gather, though, whatever it is, it's big."

"You mean big sizewise?" Chief asked.

Oscar shook his head. "No, I mean big . . . *importance*wise. See, they were in Hermosillo doing a covert deal and Garman got friendly with a priest, a Father Colon. Father Colon is dead and now the priest in Lengus de Cristo is dead, both, Diaz believed, by poisoning. Diaz was just more or less an errand boy for Garman, and when he found Garman's body in his pig pen he lit out. One thing about Garman I did learn: one of his letters went to a guy named Washington Clark in Memphis."

Chief thought of these things for a moment and then

said, "So we got three company men in Hermosillo and all of a sudden they bug out to a small village. A priest is killed in Hermosillo and then a priest is killed in Lengus de Cristo. And none of our three tells his superior what is going on." He rubbed his nose harshly as if trying to get an answer to fall from his head. "Jesus."

Cooter chuckled and said, "Now are you ready for the biggie?"

"You mean I haven't already heard it?"

"Nope. So here it comes: whatever it was they were after was buried under the priest's bed in the church in Lengus de Cristo. A hole about two by two by three deep. Diaz said that he was sure that Garman had removed the thing, which was why the other two killed him and put him in Diaz's hog pen. Wolfe and Phillips were warning him."

"Warning him of what, for chrissake?"

"Who knows?" Cooter said with despair. "One of the last things Diaz said was that Garman was a man of God, that Garman's last work was the work of God." There was a pause and then Cooter concluded, "Sounds crazy as hell, I know, but that was what the man said."

Chief said nothing. They walked out of the alley together. Beyond the dingy windows of the cantina they could see Oscar arm wrestling with a burly lad of about fifteen. A cluster of drunks stood about the table cheering and betting.

"Okay," said Chief, turning to Cooter, "I want you to write all this down just as you've told it to me and give it to me in the morning. Don't even let Oscar know what you're doing. Until I figure this shit out I want a heavy lid on it."

"Sure, Chief. But if you can make bat sense of this, you're a better man than I am by a mile." He waited for Chief to take the bait and share his thoughts, but the only sound was the cheering from inside. "Okay," he said, "you'll have it in the morning."

Chief started to walk away but suddenly turned. "By the way, how did you do it to Diaz?"

"Fist on the neck, untied him, dropped him. Whole

thing took thirty seconds. It was clean. No tracks to me and Oscar."

"That's what I wanted to hear," Chief said. "Orders should be followed properly.

Chief saw a pair of very drunk American soldiers hailing a cab and he went over and stood with them. They collapsed in the back seat and Chief sat in the front seat with the driver. No words were spoken, as words seldom have to be spoken in a border town, and the driver headed them toward the Rio Grande and Fort Bliss beyond. The border guards had seen it all before and waved the cab on through. He got out in downtown El Paso just as one of the soldiers threw up in the lap of the other. The driver took his ten and cursed in Spanish and drove off into the night.

An hour later, lying in his motel bed, showered, shaved, his attitude adjusted slightly, Chief examined the day lazily, allowing the babel of seemingly unrelated words and incidents to form a dubious logic:

Three Company men, Wolfe, who was white, and Phillips and Garman, who were black, had been working on something in Hermosillo but had gotten sidetracked to a village called Lengus de Cristo. Words of Christ. That smelled not of defection to The Bear, but of something else: greed. But greed for what? Not pussy—that was available in spades in Mexico. No, it had to be money. But what money? And, certainly, what money in a poor mud and grit and hog-pen village in the impossibly poor state of Sonora?

That was part one; this was part two: Garman had been murdered and his corpse left as a warning to Octavio Diaz, who, thanks to Cooter, was now also dead. But Garman being dead and left as a warning suggested that Phillips and Wolfe were in cahoots, as Cooter had speculated, and a black man and a white man in cahoots against a black man was neither common nor sensible in Chief's experience so it meant that all three had probably fallen out over the deal, which meant, ergo and eureka, that it had to have been Garman himself who dug up whatever it was from beneath the bed of the priest in Lengus de

Cristo. And whatever it was was still out there floating around somewhere.

"Help me, Lord," Chief said, looking at the outline of the square light globe above his bed. He waited for a minute and the Lord sent no messages through the light. This was one he would have to do himself, and the Lord was going to fuck over him because he was a sinner.

I'll be better next week, Lord, but right now I got some thinking to do. Part three: Priests. Two dead priests, a Father Colon and a Father Somebody Else, one in Hermosillo and one in Lengus de Cristo. One priest might have Communist leanings but two, never—the Vatican was reliably pro-West. So that ruled out politics and brought the whole mess back to one five letter word: greed.

Thank you, Lord, it's getting clear and easier, I think. Which brings me and You to part four: Denouement: Either the priests were on some kind of take, which is unlikely, or they were hiding something that involved the Church. And if one hides something that involves the Church, one does so because it is detrimental to the Church. And what could be detrimental to the Holy Catholic Church? An old Mayan document fraught with evil? Evil Hideth From The Light, the Bible says, and if the Bible is right, then why would priests, people certainly conversant with the Bible, hide something?

"Oh, shit, Lord, you're doing it to me again, making me crazy with guessing," Chief said, rolling over onto his side so that he would not have to look at the appointed icon over his head. He began to tick off what he felt were the absolutes:

Two priests and a black operative were dead. That made it, as Cooter had said, "big, importancewise."

It was something that was important to the Catholic Church, important enough to be hidden. Something evil.

Garman had been the one who dug it from beneath the priest's bed and the other two had killed him for being greedy. And they did not know what he had done with it, hence their warning to Octavio Diaz. Yes, they had thought that Diaz would lead them to it and he had foxed them.

But Garman would not have entrusted the thing to Diaz, which meant that he had probably sent the thing somewhere for safe keeping. And the safest place in this goddam crazy world was still the United States of America.

Having run out of fingers, Chief used his thumb for the fifth tickoff: The thing had been sent either to New Haven, Connecticut, or to Memphis, Tennessee, the two places Garman had contacts he felt he could trust.

To hell with it all—Chief had done his part. Whatever this thing was, it was on its way to Memphis, probably. And Memphis was a good eight hundred miles to the northeast, out of Chief's jurisdiction. Let the others take it from here was his last thought before he slept.

Three

Six hundred miles to the southwest of where Chief lay in his motel bed, Ellen Harrison Rogers Talbott lay nude on a bed in the Grand Beachcomber Hotel waiting for the boy and his friend. After having showered, douched, brushed her hair (fifty strokes up, fifty down, just as her mother had forever commanded), she had unlocked her door, turned out the lights and had studied herself in the mirror's pewter-dark refraction. Her long blonde hair had become, in this strange light, pale, almost milky. And so had her pubic hair. She had touched herself and shivered near orgasm in anticipation of having, for the first time, not one man but two.

Now she arose, walked to the great windows, drew the curtains back. Here, from the ninth floor, she could see peripheral slices of Acapulco ranging either direction, the hemispheric line-break of color in the distance that separated night sky from night sea. This was her seventh night on the road, her first night in Acapulco. Until now she had had only one man, but if her plan began to materialize, to take energy from its own erotic volition, she might have as many as ten before she returned to Michigan. Somehow, from whatever computer the inverse and converse of the raging mind employs to calculate its gains and losses, she knew that nine men were too few and that eleven would sound like too many, would sound like a lie; she could stand anything from them except being thought a liar, certainly this time. Yes, she would make it ten. Ten exactly. She would tell them the truth about the number and, if they pressed her, the truth about their races. She would tantalize by saying non-Caucasian, a thing that would make her mother gasp, possibly faint, and then if they asked *Was it a . . . nee-grow*, she would smile and rise as if to pour delicate tea into a delicate cup of Petite Fleur (by Villeroy and Bosch, sold in the finest boutiques), and then she would delicately back to the delicate table where her mother would have delicately and genteelly fainted and slumped sideways in her American Drew dining chair (the Cherry Grove Collection of American Drew, of course, available at Carriage House or the better of the better stores). And, of course, her fat husband, the good doctor, as her mother had referred to him since the sweating, square-headed, lard-assed bastard was in his first year of med school, would rush over and say something delicate and genteel like "Let's get Mrs. Harrison onto the Oriental rug," making sure to say Oriental rug as if even in admission of niggerfuck there had to be allusion to gentility, a showing, as it were, of the shovel with which the Best People shore up their world against the Common Herd. (Yes, Mrs. Harrison passed out, but it was, admittedly, nay, *boastfully*, on an Oriental rug.)

The best and the best and the best. Two words, best and finest, had governed her life. Only the best people. Only the finest china, finest diamonds, best girls' school, best women's university (Smith, dear; Bryn Mawr is so . . . well, déclassé, so . . . 1930s).

At twenty-two Ellen had married Brinton Cullison Rogers, of the Grosse Point Rogerses, and *Town and Country* had "done a do" on them. Her mother had said that she hated the fact that those reporting people had come, then had promptly bought ten copies of the magazine. Her mother had also seen to it that she and Brint were ensconsed in a more fashionable townhouse in Gross Point and that a series of postnuptial parties stretched on for three months, three months in which Brint made love to her twice. Brint had attended Exeter, Choate, Harvard, and Princeton, had graduated from none, had stayed drunk on Chivas Regal, an avocation whose demands on the young man the marriage had done nothing to lessen. There was talk of his getting a position in PR at Ford or Chrysler, but it was merely talk. It lasted two years, and she got the linen and stemware while he got his Chivas. He also got the muscular Italian named Torello with whom he had spent a great deal of time, but such things were not mentioned. Two years ago mother had matched her with Dr. Schuyler Talbott (of the Chicago Talbotts), and on their wedding night he had bitten down on her nipple viciously and had offered to tie her up and pour perfume into her vagina. Divorce, certainly divorce twice, was out of the question, and his week-long stints at the hospital were what had made it work. The arranged marriage is the gracious world's manner of selective breeding, her mother had said a dozen times, and commonness finds its own way. Mongrels, her mother had called factory workers, sales clerks, newsboys, carpenters, mankind whose misfortune it had been not to be born into her own realm.

Ellen was glad to be among the mongrels for the first time in her life. The Mercedes that Schuyler had bought her last month had not been washed in two weeks, and she had even found it rather pleasant to talk to gas station men and discount store rabble. But, God, if they found out what she was really up to, what she had really been doing, well, hell would not have it!

The black man in Hermosillo had been the third man in her life. He had been good, the way sex should be, but there had been a strange manner about him that had clouded her enjoyment. True, he had been well-fixed, and his equipment had worked admirably, but it was obvious that his mind had been . . . well, elsewhere. It was a deliciously frivolous thing, her having met him while she shopped for a proper handbag to complement a pair of snakeskin shoes. He had seemed nice, pleasant, even fawning, and at first she had taken this to mean that he was simply hungry for the sound of an American voice. (It would not have done to have talked to a black man at home, servants notwithstanding, but here it was acceptable, even desirable; let the coloreds know that to the north black and white were as one, show them that brotherhood from sea to shining sea was more than a song lyric.) His name was Charleston Garman, and seven hours after their meeting in the shoe store they were in her hotel bed. She had been a bit queasy about his touch, at first; queasy about kissing him, at first; downright incoherent with passion as his muscular and naked black bulk had loomed over her at the moment of entry. The mirror over the dresser had afforded her a view that could not be his, and she had become enamored of the "other" couple therein, the hard-charging black man exquisitely violating the blonde goddess with the uplifted and seeking thighs. It had been a voyeuristic episode, and she felt guilty not of fucking but of watching; she hoped fervently that the blonde woman in the mirror-movie was not pregnant or diseased.

The clouding of enjoyment had come after they had.

"You're all I got. We're going to do a Huck and Jim. This is very important; you'll never know how important. It must be exactly as I say. My uncle lives in Memphis and you must deliver it to him. Votan lives, and the word must go out, but the others don't want the word out. And I can't emphasize this strongly enough: you are not to look."

Gibberish.

She had been aswirl in eddies of wickedness and counterthought and mindless lust.

That had been four days ago. Or was it five, or three? She could not remember.

Votan lives. What did it mean?

We're going to do a Huck and Jim. What did it mean?

The word must go out, but the others don't want the word out. What did it mean?

She returned to the bed and lay down, the coolness of the sheets offering counterpoint to the slight mugginess of the tropic night. From that part of the human brain that is never at rest came an answer: a runaway slave wouldn't run south, would he, Jim?

Of course. That was what Charleston Garman had meant. They were looking for the thing to be sent immediately north; she had told him that she was en route to Acapulco, to the south. Shrewd.

She wanted to go to the car and at last look at whatever it was, but she fought down the urge, buried it, allowed it to steep as the sweetener in this fortnight cup of wicked tea from which she was blissfully drinking. Somewhere far to the north her husband, who had granted her this vacation, was performing surgery. Somewhere in her purse was the name Washington Clark and an accompanying address in Memphis, Tennessee. Somewhere two or ten or perhaps a hundred people were looking for a thing that was at this minute in the trunk of her Mercedes. How sinister it all was! How exciting!

The door opened slowly. A spear of light came from the hallway, widened, dropped behind two male figures, blinked out as the door closed. The young Mexican bellhop and his promised friend came to the bed and sat on either side of her, mute bookends to the tome of voluptousness that she had become. The bellhop leaned slightly and fondled her pubic mound, his dark hand caressing in slow, circular motions. The friend leaned from the other direction and tongued one of her nipples.

Ellen Harrison Rogers Talbott extended an arm, caressed a pillow, lifted her body slightly, and placed the pillow under her hips.

Four

Jesse DeVaron awoke with a devilish hangover. His neck was bent at an unseemly angle and his left cheek burned. As if this were not enough, someone had thrown him out at an airport. He lay on his side staring into a vacant hangar whose floor was carpeted and whose ceiling had been masked in a dark fabric. The agony on his cheek became unbearable and he lifted his head. Something fell from his face and rolled to the front of his nose. He saw that the offending article was the cap from a whiskey bottle. He waited for it to detonate, and felt disappointment when it did not.

Now he saw that the hangar's ceiling was actually the underside of his couch, its empty floor the living room of his apartment. It had been a good Sunday night, probably, but now it had dissolved into Monday.

Like a sea lion flippering onto a strange beach, he hauled himself toward the couch and pushed himself upright. The apartment had suffered no major damage. Mostly furnished in what he referred to as "garage-sale Gothic," it would have been hard for a casual observer to determine whether the previous evening had been one of mayhem or of sedentary drunkenness. His twin bookshelves still held his war books, his novels, his terribly superannuated encyclopedias, and the coffee table exhibited that bachelor's mélange of objects that were forever begging to be straightened or put away: old magazines, a cluttered ashtray, a screwdriver handle that was too good to throw away, a bill from American

Express. Across the room on another coffee table was a television set bracketed by two stacks of old *National Geographics*. He recalled that of all the thousands of magazines in the world, *N.G* were hardest to throw away. It was a bit of weirdness that he would ponder at another time, maybe.

But rising above this substructure of unkempt jetsam was a wall filled with photographs, documents, plaques, and it was these that caused him immediate bother. A photograph of himself and James Oliver "Ollie" Colbert on their graduation from the Memphis Police Academy, another photograph of himself and the long-gone Rhonda on their wedding day, a photo of the squad in front of a bunker in Vietnam. Honorable Discharge, U.S. Army. Certificate of Merit, City of Memphis. The staring at this wall-hung memorabilia—and the memories that came with them—had become a ritual over the past few weeks, and now, with head throbbing, shirttail out, stiff in back and arms, Jesse DeVaron admitted to himself that his impending forty-fifth birthday had a great deal to do with these reconnaissances into the past. Forty had meant nothing, nor had forty-four. But forty-five was three fifths of the way There, if the actuarial tables could be believed.

Asserting itself into his visage like an egocentric child interrupting a formal gathering, the empty George Dickel bottle glinted from sun rays filtered through the curtain. It had been three-fourths full last night when he had sat down to watch TV, and somewhere between then and now its contents had evaporated. It was booze that was responsible for his current estrangement from Janice, his lady love of the past two years. It was booze that had finally sent Rhonda out the door nearly a decade ago. It was booze that had caused him to make a brag in a bar nearly a quarter of a century ago about how he would yes-by-God join the goddamn army in the morning. And, though it had been couched in euphemisms about "medical retirement," it was booze that had removed him from the Memphis Police Department three years ago.

He went to the bathroom, showered, shaved, stared at himself in the mirror, took two aspirin. The morning looked warm outside and he dressed in black pants, white shirt, houndstooth sport jacket. The shoes that he chose were black and scuffed, but it was because of this scuffing that they were selected; they gave him an excuse to go over to River Towers and get a shine and to get out of this goddam apartment and into the real world of Monday.

Memphis was already baking when he got down onto the street. Heat waves shimmered from the pavement and the pale blue skies arching upward from Arkansas were cloudless. He went into the parking lot behind the building, saw that his two cars were unmolested and breathed in happily. The green 1968 Ford convertible was unlocked and he looked under the seat. The pint of Dickel was there, just as ordered. Last night, in the middle of the muddle, he had called Toby Lang at the bar down the street and had asked that a pint be put in the convertible. Old Toby was as good as gold, as usual. Although Jesse never drank at Toby's place—it was bad for business to drink in one's own neighborhood—the "emergency-supplies" understanding that Jesse and Toby had was a thing of two-years running. Jesse tried to imagine how many bottles Toby might have slipped under the seat over the last two years and guessed the total to be near a hundred. Maybe more. He slammed the door, patted the hood, promised the old heap a wax job in the very near future and went over to the white Caprice Classic. The Chevy was two years old when he had floated a bank loan and bought it at an auction four months ago, but it still smelled and acted like new. The only problem with it was aesthetic; the goddam thing was totally devoid of class or pizazz; it smacked of PTA meetings and Sunday drives in the country or church picnics. Someday, if the fates smiled on Jesse DeVaron, he would indulge himself two frivolous items: a Cadillac and an M-1 rifle. But what the shit, he said to himself as he started the Chevy's engine, you'll be lucky to make payments on this sonofabitch. At this moment he had eight hundred dollars in savings, a little over two hundred in checking. But the rent was paid and he had groceries in the apartment. Not only that but the old Ford was long paid for and he was two months ahead on his rent and on the Chevy payments. And the good doctor across town owed him twenty-five hundred. Not bad, really, for a person who had been a private investigator for a little over two years. A bar fly had once told him, "If you can drink when you want to, fuck when you want to, and sleep when you damn well please, what else is there?" It was the best sort of question, one that answered itself.

Jesse drove west on Poplar, fought his way through downtown, broke free of the city's confines onto Riverside Drive. Off to his left and standing high on a bluff was River Towers, its twelve stories looking out at the great Mississippi. It had originally been a luxury hotel, but five years ago it had "gone condo." Truth be told, it did not know what it was, for some of the specialty shops that had served its lobby in its hotel days were still thriving. Jesse liked it because it was a city within one building, a place where one might arise from his bed, take a look at the river, hop an elevator down to the lobby for breakfast or a shoeshine. If he ever had enough money for the Cadillac and the M-1 he might even have enough left over to locate at River Towers. It was a transient fantasy, but one that gave him a glow as he drove into the parking lot that faced the river.

A hulking black man opened the door for Jesse. His name was Hip Willis and he wore a doorman's coat and cap of electric blue with gold trim. Jesse touched one of Hip's epaulettes and said, "Hip, you're either a drum major or an admiral in the Rhodesian Navy. What's with the comic opera getup?"

"Fuck you, Jesse. They decided to give this place some class. I didn't mind havin' to wear a black suit every goddamn day, but this is somethin' else." An old lady came out and Hip touched the tip of his cap smartly. When she was gone he said, "That kind of shit. See what I mean?" Hip looked at the circle on Jesse's face but didn't comment.

"I'm pissed. I didn't get a salute."

"You don't live here, either, you asshole. And where

did you get that sport coat? You tryin' to play Rockford Files or somethin'?"

"Or somethin'. Anything going on that I might need to know about?"

Hip was suddenly serious. "On the way out, get with me. It's Popper."

"What about him?"

"Later," Hip whispered.

For a year he had been asking Hip whether there might be any news that would lead to a case, casual banter that had forever led nowhere. But now Hip had indicated that at last Popper, who was possibly the last of the old black shoeshine men who could pop a pre-civil rights cloth with great spirit, was the source of something sinister. It did not figure. Certainly it did not mean money in Jesse's pocket. But if Popper had a problem he would be glad to advise him, for he loved Popper and he loved Hip Willis, loved them enough and was close enough to them that such devastating words as nigger and honky passed in their conversations with nary a break in stride. The swapping of sartorial insults with Hip was not a thing that would erode their friendship; it was the cement that held it together, an openness of verbiage that made the New South one hell of a great place to live.

"Hey, Jesse," said Donkey Baby, Popper's assistant. "Old Popper he ain't here." He looked at Jesse's shoes. "Man look at them mothers. You either been pickin' cotton or killin' pigs shoes that bad."

Jesse crawled up onto the shine chair and said, "Donk, I wish you'd learn to talk with commas. Where's Popper?"

"Been actin' weird kinda couple days. He come in he go out he cry sometimes."

"Sounds like he may be suffering from senility."

"My sister had that when she were a baby I think. Man these shoes need it I don't mean maybe."

As Donk bent to his buffing and polishing, Jesse picked up a paper from the next chair and saw that the president still had his ass in a bind over the messes in the Middle East and Central America. When the shine was finished he stepped down, handed Donk a dollar and scooted out to avoid further inanities of Donk's patois.

Hip Willis loomed near the doorway holding his new blue cap in his hand. He eyed it as if it were a strange bird that might be about to peck him or shit on his wrist.

"You hear about Popper?" he asked.

"Only that he's been acting weird," said Jesse.

"It's heavier than that, Jesse. The old man is scared. Follow me." Jesse followed Hip outside and down the walkway to a copse of shrubbery that fronted the building. When Hip was satisfied that they could not be seen, he handed Jesse an envelope. "Don't open this until you are away from here, Jesse."

Jesse felt something small and hard inside the envelope. Placing it in his coat pocket he said, "What's this all about, Hip? Are you putting me on again?"

"Not this time. We bullshit a lot, but this time it's for real. Old Popper is scared like I never seen a man scared. He gave me that letter to give to you early this morning."

"Any idea of what's in it?"

"No, but he' doin' a lot of warbling about Jesus. Maybe he's just cracked up, like Donkey Baby thinks."

"Yeah, Donk just advanced that theory to me, too," said Jesse.

"How would Donk know?" Hip asked. "He's crazy himself. Talking to him is like bein' whipped through hell with a buzzard gut."

"So I've noticed. What do you think I should do?"

"I don't know," said Hip. "He's such a likeable old turd, I just thought if he was in some kind of trouble you might look into it."

"Free, of course," said Jesse.

"Well, he shines shoes for a living, so it ain't like you're gonna go on a retainer. You gonna help or not?"

Jesse looked out at the river. A barge was sloshing up the river toward Saint Louis. He wished that he were on it. "Yeah, I'll look into it. I show up at the damnedest places at the damnedest times. How'd Popper know I'd be here today?"

"He figured you'd tie one on over the weekend and show up for a shoeshine on Monday. You generally do."

Jesse felt stung, humiliated. "Yeah, I guess I have become a creature of habit."

"I gotta go," said Hip. "Just remember, whatever's in that letter is mighty important to an old man." He moved out of the shrubbery and ran up the walk.

Jesse went to his car feeling a burning sensation in his temples. By the time he was back on Riverside the slow burn had become a dull spear of rage that held firm in his guts without moving. Long ago he had learned that certain triggering mechanisms in the human soul were ever present, and just now the deadliest of these was insult dressed in the finery of truth. He had suffered insult as a boy, the hopelessly grinding life of being born to a sharecropper being what it was, but he had mostly forgotten the feeling of helplessness that had been the major part of it. The Presbyterians who had brought winter clothing to the shack for his sister Rosa and himself at Christmas some thirty-five years ago had meant well, but now he recalled their sidewise glances at the wood stove and the cracked linoleum. In his adolescence there had begun a round of parties where "kissing games" were played, but he had never been invited, a thing that hurt and puzzled him until one day when he happened to overhear a girl say that the DeVarons forever smelled of beans and bacon, the foods that were in fact the mainstay of the family during the bitter months of a sharecropper's winter. Having endured these insults, and a hundred more, Jesse DeVaron was able early in life to relate to the black race not as a threat to be patronized but as a bolster to his own powers of human endurance. Thus it was that rage and compassion were forever at war within him, and thus it was that Hip's words, delivered from Popper's sense of the inevitable, were the stuff of absolute irony.

By the time he had driven halfway through the city he had regained control of the day and of himself so that he could think logically. He would beat the booze, he would get Janice back, he would perhaps even try to establish contact with Rosa, his only living relative, the sister who had wandered in and out of his life.

As he paused at a traffic light, a great church hovered in serenity on a distant corner. Without really knowing why, and with a sneer in his voice that was a votive to paradox, Jesse said, "God, get on my side for a change. Give me a sign."

Nothing happened. Jesse began to laugh. He looked about to see whether anyone in the other cars had been watching. None had.

The light changed and he drove on. By the time he was two blocks from the church he felt better. Popper's insult delivered secondhandedly by Hip had been forgotten, Popper's letter had been forgotten, and the impromptu prayer had been forgotten.

He looked down at his shoes. Donkey Baby had done a good job.

Five

In the old section of Fort Worth, Texas, there is a cocoa-colored edifice that bears the name Stockman's Hotel. With rooms smartly remodeled in Victorian *cum* Wild West, it offers the visitor a foray into fantasy at reasonable rates. To the left of the registration desk is a bar that meshes with a small eating area that contains ten tables, but they do not mesh so much as they abut, for the former is a garish affair of buffalo heads, steer horns and saddle stools, while the latter is a no-nonsense place of pictureless walls and yawning waitresses.

Cowboy sat at one of these tables and read the *Star-Telegram* while his right hand toyed with his fork over a concoction that the menu had called a "Trail Drive Omelet." He had not bothered to remove his gray felt western hat, a bit of headgear that coincided with his faded blue jeans and dusty brown cowboy boots. But it seemed quite out of place with his shirt, long-sleeved Oxford cloth with button-down collar. His onyx-black sideburns set into the sides of a leathery, sun-darkened face, he reminded one of the waitresses of Elvis Presley with a trace of Rock Hudson added for good measure, except for the fact that he was taller.

"More coffee, sir?" she asked, noting that, indeed, his eyes were blue. He nodded and she filled his cup and went back to the kitchen wherein her temporal world was eggs and smoke and her love was a stack of movie magazines.

Cowboy put the fork down, turned the page and found what he had been seeking:

Phoenix Police Still Baffled

Phoenix (AP) Police in this Arizona city are still puzzled at the lack of clues in the heinous slaying of two Mormon missionaries Wednesday night. Oletta Bishop, 56, and Mayann Johnson, 55, were found by friends who had gone to a small apartment complex where the ladies lived together. Police say that both had been dismembered. Neither had been sexually assaulted, according to Det. Robert Snellgrove of the Phoenix Police Department.

"Phoenix has the largest concentration of Mormons outside Salt Lake, so we don't think that this was a religion-related thing. It was just two nice old women who happened to get in the way of a crazy," the detective told reporters.

Cowboy placed the paper on the table and turned to his omelet. The police had lied. It was getting so that none could be trusted anymore. As a boy he had trusted everyone, and God and the flag and the president were good and noble. And now even the police had become liars. They were saying shit about J. Edgar Hoover being a garden-variety crackpot, about JFK being an ass wolf, about maybe someday the possibility of a Jew or nigger or woman president. When Kate Smith sang "God Bless America" he had hidden in his bedroom and cried. His childhood was a time of crying jags and fist fights. They had not understood then in their small numbers, and they did not understand now in their ever-growing numbers. But he would help to change all that; indeed, change was coming and he was proudly at its spearpoint. When Wolfe had assigned him the code name Cowboy a few days ago, he had gone home and cried, but it was one of those good cries, a God-and-glory-and-stars-and-stripes cry that swore vengeance against those who were anti-Christ, non-Caucasian congestions in the heart of American greatness.

"I mean, Jesus H. Christ, come on," a puffy-fat man at a nearby table was saying to the waitress. "I can take

a lot of things, but a fly in my coffee, Jesus H. Christ."
The waitress removed the cup and said nothing. When she was out of the restaurant the two men were alone.

Cowboy stood and in his boots he was five inches over six feet, monstrous, lean, expressionless. He ambled over to the fat man's table and said, tonelessly, "Stand up."

"Oh, who the hell are you—"

Cowboy leaned in and grabbed the man by the lapels of his suit coat, the tiny hardness of a Rotary Club pin digging into his palm. Now the man tried to open his mouth but Cowboy slapped his cheek hard and then backhanded him from the other side, the fat face lurching first this direction and then that. A chair fell over on the Navajo-design carpet. Cowboy pulled the man to his feet, pushed him onto the hardwood floor near the bar, picked him up again, and laid him belly down over one of the saddles that served as bar stools. Lifting the man's coat, he saw that the man wore beltless pants. He hit the man in the spine and the heavy body rigidified as if stung by an electric shock. Now Cowboy pulled the waistband downward and exposed the soft, hairy, pimply buttocks. He swung evenly and fast five times, his hard palm stinging painfully even as he smiled at the welts on the ugly hips.

"Now you say you're sorry," Cowboy whispered.

"I'm sorry," the fat man blubbered, snot and tears intermingling on his mouth.

"Say you love the Lord and you apologize."

"I love the Lord and I apologize."

Cowboy backed away and shrugged, his massive shoulders filling out and stretching the fabric of his shirt. He lifted his hat, ran his stinging hand through his black hair, and looked to his right. Three open mouths stood at the kitchen door, held there by two waitresses and a black cook.

"You ladies should avert your eyes," he said. When they did not move he said angrily, "Nigger, you get back in that kitchen." The black woman squealed and hurried away. He reached into the pocket of his denims and placed a ten-dollar bill on the bar. Tipping his hat, he said, "This should cover it. Good morning, ladies."

When he was outside he blinked at the morning sun and walked four doors down and entered a boot shop. "11-D," he said to the clerk, a blonde-haired youth who wore tennis shoes, jeans and a T-shirt with TCU stenciled across the front. "Black or navy blue."

The lad smiled. "Yessir. What price range?"

"I don't care."

The young man went into a back room. Cowboy looked at the interior of the place, his nostrils filled with the invigorating scent of leather. Against a back wall someone had taped a small sign: IF GOD HAD NOT MEANT FOR MAN TO EAT PUSSY, WHY DID HE SHAPE IT LIKE A TACO? He went over to the sign, pulled it down, tore it to shreds, dropped the pieces on the floor.

Twenty minutes later he handed the blonde lad six one-hundred-dollar bills and accepted twenty-eight dollars change.

"Thank you, sir. Now I'll box your old boots and—"

"Keep 'em," Cowboy said.

"Uh—and do what with them, sir?"

"Christ said, 'The poor ye always have with ye.' Give 'em to the poor. You promise?"

The boy's mouth moved strangely. It was as if he were about to smile or vomit. "I . . . promise."

Cowboy went outside. He placed his change in his wallet alongside nine one-thousand-dollar bills. The navy blue square toes felt good and he did an impromptu tap dance. Two teenage girls saw this and giggled at him and quickened their pace. His eyes locked on their soft little rumps until they were down the street and around a corner. "Forgive me, Father, for I will fornicate soon," he said to himself, and to the Father who understood and always forgave.

The parking lot was filling with tourists, and his chromeless blue Ford pickup stood forlornly among the shiny Chryslers and Buicks like a pig at a poodle show. Mounted in the bed just behind the cab was a heavy steel receptacle that bore the name TRUK-BOX. He put his key in the lock and lifted the strong, lightweight lid. His two suitcases were intact and undisturbed, as were the holster-encased Colt Diamondback and the thirty-inch machete, this last object encased in a U.S. Army canvas cover of olive drab. Making certain that no one was nearby, he slid the machete from its cover and looked it over for what must have been the tenth time in two days. The blood and shit of those two old Mormon women had been scalded and polished away to perfection, and God's Own Swift Sword was beautiful and ready once again.

Six

A pallid and cheerless sky enshrouded the city of New Haven. The sun had surrendered at mid-morning and even the irises and tulips that bordered the walkways were of lessened complexion.

From his second story window at Yale Divinity, Dr. James Ellmon Wagstaff recalled colors that of late had been so much a part of his life. At Maureen's funeral in February the world had been sleet white and oak black. When they had met thirty-six years ago all that had existed within the romantic spectrum were lavenders and pinks and yellows. Her wedding dress had been powder blue with white lace; her casket had been powder blue with white padding. God gave us thirty-six green years and then turned it all to gray, veiled it for His own purpose, he reflected. Green to gray, Alpha to Omega.

"The mail, sir," said Mike Morton.

Dr. Wagstaff turned from the window and smiled at the speaker, but it was a practiced smile that contained no happiness. Short, fat, bearded, balding and divorced, thirty-four year old Mike Morton was one of those academic nobodies who had somehow finagled a berth whose imposing title was Coordinating Specialist, Divinity Department. For eight years Dr. Wagstaff had never seen Morton do a great deal more than he was doing at this moment, which was to stand in the doorway and hold the mail until it was taken from his hand. True, Morton had an office, and a copy machine, and occasionally "turned out pamphlets" that were mostly ignored, but were he not ambulatory he might as well have been one of those stone lions down on the common.

"Is there something else, Mike?" he asked, suddenly realizing that he had been staring for several seconds.

"It's about a letter, sir."

"Yes?"

Morton came into the room guardedly, radiating self-effacement. "It's a letter from one of your old students. Charleston Garman. I'm sure you remember him."

Dr. Wagstaff nodded. "Yes. A black student from . . . somewhere in the South. A good student. A bit too intense, perhaps, even radical in some of his viewpoints about religion." Now his smile was real. "He sent me a letter?"

Mike Morton shrugged and smiled idiotically. "Yes, sir, in a manner of speaking; he sent you a letter, but it was inside another envelope that was addressed to me." The two men stared at each other for several seconds and then Mike said, "Something strange about that, wouldn't you say?"

Dr. Wagstaff pursed his lips, nodded, took the letter. The envelope was incredibly thin. Whatever this long-past student named Garman had to say, certainly he had minced no words. Too, it had to be very good or very bad; idle chitchat is forever of portly nature.

"Thank you, Mike. That will be all." He watched as the disappointed Morton went out of the office and closed the door behind him.

Prepared for either a pleasant hello or a brief vituperation from a disgruntled ex-student, Dr. Wagstaff sat at his desk, opened the letter that bore his name, unfolded a single sheet of yellow paper. Perhaps it was his imagination, but a slight odor came from the paper and then dissolved into nothingness; it was almost as though something evil had waved a warning banner at him. He tried to dismiss it as a foolish thought, but even as he donned his reading glasses he was aware beyond conscious thought that iniquity had come into his hands.

April 12

Dr. Wagstaff:

Votan lives!
Much danger here. Only three of us know. Herrmann was right. They do not want it out for fear of the obvious chaos it would cause. Old Joe Smith was not as crazy as they thought. The other two do not trust me. The Company will want to destroy it but I will not do so. Danger even in your having this letter, hence my mailing it to Morton. More later if possible.

                                                          Garman

The professor placed the letter on his desk, picked up his phone, and touched Mike Morton's extension number: 86. "Mike, would you bring me Charleston Garman's student file? And would you hurry, please?" He replaced the phone and read the letter a second time, a fifth time, a tenth time. At last he slid the folded yellow missive under an ink blotter that bore a drawing of the crucifixion, stood, walked to the window. He felt ashamed, confused, angry. And afraid. A line from an Emily Dickinson poem slithered around in his head like a blind snake that must move but knows not where it is going: *Much madness is divinest sense, to a discerning eye.* He wanted to recall the rest of the poem, but could not. He had stared out this same window and had felt this same way on hearing of the assassination of John F. Kennedy. That day had been murky while this one was sundappled, but then, as now, his nerve endings had gone on hold and his soul was nowhere to be found. Soul. Such a strange little word. He had used the word a million times in his life, had always defined it as the inner self that is the part of humanity that belongs not to humanity but to God. Words, phrases, sermons, lesson plans, ministerial conferences, sabbaticals to the Holy Land. What a worthless pile of shit his life had been! Soul. Yes, when you came right down to it, the soul was all that counted, and every black dope pusher in Queens and every sharecropper in Georgia had one. A simple thought came to him: the soul may be the essence of love, but it is activated by fear, thus the need for ministers, rabbis, priests. Scared people love the Lord.

"My God," he whispered, leaving the window, returning to his desk. He recalled the smell of hill dirt from his Kentucky boyhood, his first fright-riddled sermons to wild-eyed coal miners when he had felt the call, the scholarship board's decision and his saying "Yale" because he had seen a portrait of Eli in an encyclopedia somewhere, his shame at the way they had made fun of his accent, his marriage to Maureen, his decision to stay on and earn a doctorate. Life is what happens while you're making plans, said a currently popular saw, and it was right on target. "My God," he said again.

He had stared at the picture of the crucifixion for a long time when he became aware of Mike Morton standing over him. Morton's chubby hands held a common file folder, and his eyes wore the dull-yet-explosive look of someone who might or might not be on the verge of great trouble. "Is this . . . anything, sir?"

Dr. Wagstaff smiled, took the folder, shook his head. "No, Mike. It simply has to do with the workings of a person who wishes to remain anonymous. We can keep a secret, can't we?"

Mike brightened and rubbed his beard thoughtfully. "Yes, sir. Consider it closed, for my part." He turned and left the room with the exuberant haste of a student who has passed a questionable test.

Dr. Wagstaff spent thirty minutes on the file. It amazed him for what must have been the hundredth time in his career that a person's emotional states were so perfectly reflected by a transcript. First semester, five A's, one B; second semester, four B's, two C's. Botany, history, American literature, gym. The stuff of college, some of it in Garman's own handwriting, some in the precise and no-nonsense ruminations of a computer's printout. A young black man from Memphis, Tennessee, had come to the great university in the northeast, had become disillusioned, had settled in for a spate of mediocre grades, had graduated, had taken his place in the great faceless work force. One of millions from hundreds of universities all over the world. Garman had flirted with journalism, leaned toward the ministry in his sophomore year, eased toward law in his junior year and had at last emerged with a B.S. in Social Studies. A checkered career at Yale; at best, the unsure gropings of a man whose skin hue had clouded and at last obliterated whatever dreams he had brought with him from the South. This was made palpable by certain of Garman's own writings, painfully scripted with slantings and harshly crossed T's that varied from semester to semester, but always with a reference to his race. It was race, or racism, that had left Garman with but one living relative, a shoeshine uncle in Memphis; it was race that had caused the federal government to allow a young black man to be "quotaized," as Garman had written it, to Yale; it was race that had caused him to write in his senior year on a makework bureaucratic form: "I will enter government service as it is the government that has revealed to me that I am an entity to be contended with, not because of myself but in spite of myself." Garbled English whose only sense was anger.

Now the professor leaned back and endeavored to fit the student that was with the man who had written the letter, an act not unlike building a new house on an existing foundation. "Votan lives," the letter had said. But the letter had also said, "real danger here." Part acquiescence and part paranoia, perhaps, or perhaps a mixture of these and other parts that were the workings of a diseased mind too long steeped in the black experience.

No, Garman was not insane, he concluded. The letter was real and its message was *true*. Dangerously true.

He closed the file and went to his bookcase, a tall and overstuffed oaken warren wherein stood the tomes that had been the signposts of his life. He reached up to the fifth shelf and took down *Conquest of Man*, read the author's name, Paul Herrmann. Within a minute he found the passage that he was looking for and had strangely hoped that he would not find, memory mocking him all the way because he knew that the passage was there: ". . . carefully considered, this leaves no other conclusion open than that the Light God Quetzalcoatl was a real person, that he was neither an invention of Spanish propaganda nor a legendary figment of Indian imagination . . ."

"No other conclusion," Dr. Wagstaff whispered. He went to his desk, placed the book and the yellow letter in the file folder and placed the bulkiness under his arm. Before he left his office he turned and looked at it for what he felt might be the last time. If Garman were indeed not a madman, then what he had shared with his old professor was indeed wonderful, indeed dangerous.

Seven

Jesse sat in the doctor's waiting room and listened as the Muzak from the hallway offered a violin rendition of "Aquarius." He had always liked the song and wondered what it had to do with naked people. He had been in a prowl car in the late sixties when he had first heard it, and his partner had said that the song was from a play about naked people. Now he never heard the song without helplessly thinking of Lee Remick running naked in slow motion across a field of flowers. Like all who have such thoughts that are triggered by old songs, he wondered whether he was just a little weird.

"The doctor will see you now, Mr. DeVaron," said the lady at the desk.

Jesse left his fantasy and his two-year-old copy of *New Woman* in the waiting room and went down a hallway. Rooms on either side smelled of alcohol and suffering. He entered the doctor's office and closed the door behind him. The cardiologist was a gray man in a white coat who sat behind a huge desk and did not bother to get up, nor did he even nod. As Jesse sat in a chair to the front of the desk the doctor lit a Bel Air and placed it in an ashtray made of bronze and shaped like an alligator.

"You shouldn't smoke," said Jesse. "It's bad for the heart."

"You shouldn't drink. It's bad for the liver."

"Everything's bad for everything," said Jesse. "How'd you know that I tipple?"

"An educated guess. Skin and eyes, mostly. What did you find?"

"You want the ten-dollar spiel or the ten-cent spiel?"

"The ten-cent one will do." As the doctor picked up the cigarette Jesse noticed that his hand quavered slightly.

"Your suspicions were on target. While you were addressing the ladies' group Saturday night she was at the Admiral Benbow, room 202." He watched the smoke from the doctor's cigarette curl into an anvil. Possible there was symbolism there, but he couldn't figure what it was.

"That about it?"

"It's what you wanted to know. Ten cents worth."

"Okay, you've been on this for three weeks. Now give me ten dollars worth."

"His name is James T. Rhoden. He's a junior accountant in the firm of Weldon and Greene, CPAs. They do your taxes, so that's got to be how she met him. Rhoden is married, thirty-seven, two kids, wife's name is Barbara. Your wife isn't the only one he's screwing; there are at least two others."

"How do you know that?"

"Because when your wife was at home I spent some time following him. He's the classic sort who tells his wife he's got to work late at the office. He's probably got more pussy juice on his desk than he's got debit sheets."

The doctor did not smile. "A motel is bad enough, but to think of my wife with her thighs open and her skirt up on a desk is so . . ." He dragged hard on the cigarette as if to pull out the correct word.

"Commonplace?" Jesse suggested. "Human? The words are interchangeable. You learn that in my line of work. There are no good people; there are only people who haven't yet been found out."

"You're a cynic, DeVaron."

"Nope, I'm a realist. A cynic is merely a realist who hasn't gotten his degree in human studies yet."

"A philosopher, too," said the doctor. "A man of many talents."

"Save the applause for later. You owe me thirty-one hundred bucks." Jesse wondered where the figure had come from. It was even more than he had planned to gouge from the good doctor.

The doctor's eyes widened, then almost closed. He stubbed out the cigarette in the alligator's back and lit another. "I thought that the agreed amount was twenty-five hundred and expenses."

"It was. But it took longer than I thought. Besides, I had to pay some folks to run some interference for me." Jesse was lying, albeit only slightly. He had given a college boy fifty dollars to follow the doctor's wife to the motel, but it would do little for his own cause to admit this. All else that he had said was true; still, he found himself wanting to scratch his nose, an act that he feared might undermine his credibility at this moment.

The doctor opened his desk, took out a checkbook, thought better of it, replaced it. He opened another drawer and removed a small plastic folder. Jesse saw that it was a packet of American Express traveler's checks. The doctor signed three, tore them off, handed them across the desk. "Three thousand. Does that make us even?" he asked.

"I guess it will have to," said Jesse with a pained tone; actually, he was rejoicing. "Not everybody keeps that kind of traveler's checks lying around. Going someplace?"

The doctor did not answer, but looked at his watch. "I think that should about do it for us, DeVaron."

"Aw shit, and just when I was beginning to like you, too." He stood and started for the door. "Call when you need me."

"No way in hell will I need you ever again," said the doctor. "Three thousand dollars. Why do I feel that the specter of blackmail is hanging in this room?"

Jesse smiled coldly. He started to let it pass but a hot coal of rage dropped out of his head and landed heavily in his guts. "I worked three weeks for this three grand and you begrudge me. You probably did surgery this morning that made you eight or ten thousand dollars. Three weeks against three hours. We're both in our rackets for the money. Blackmail is telling a patient he's gonna die without a bypass and he doesn't get the bypass without the money. That, friend, is blackmail."

The doctor looked flustered, indignant. "How dare you compare what I do with what you do. I save lives. It's my calling."

Jesse took the doorknob gently, opened the door and looked at the hallway. It was empty. *What the hell,* he was thinking, *go ahead and sink the bastard.* "I'm going to throw in a bonus, Doc. That redhaired sort that you were going to fly away with for the weekend to . . . where? Vegas? The Bahamas? Makes no difference. At any rate, she's playing you for a fool. She's screwing the guy who has the apartment next to hers."

"You're a lying bastard!" the doctor roared.

"Ask her. Better yet, watch her. I just saved you about a half million in this divorce and the next one you might have had. I'm a humanitarian. It's my calling." Jesse winked theatrically and closed the door behind him. When he was in the street he was overcome with a sense of euphoria. He had three thousand dollars, he had just deflated an overstuffed ass by helping the overstuffed ass out of impending difficulty, and he had done it all smoothly. Schiller had written somewhere that opposition always inflames the enthusiast but never converts him. Getting into the Chevy, driving toward his bank, Jesse felt that the adage applied here. The good doctor had certainly looked inflamed; maybe the conversion would come later.

He deposited the checks except for three hundred dollars pissoff money. As he went to the car it amazed him once again how awkwardly horrible life could be with no money as compared to how incredibly beautiful it could be with a pittance such as this. Because his lifestyle was so low key, three thousand dollars guaranteed him at least sixty days of hassle-free existence. He knew people who had need of six thousand dollars every thirty days to keep their creditors in abeyance. Absorbed in that bliss that only the recently destitute can ever know, he drove down the street to treat himself to a steak, happily unaware that this would be his last calm moment for many days.

Eight

The city of New Haven, Connecticut, was entombed by a late afternoon drizzle when Mike Morton left the great Georgian-Gothic building and ran toward his car. Some of the lesson-plan notes for next week slipped from his grasp and fell wetly onto the pavement. He cursed, looked up to see whether anyone had heard, grabbed the papers and ran toward his yellow Toyota. Leave it to the weather to screw up things for next week when this week had hardly begun. He got into his little car, laid the papers in the passenger seat, raised up, and fumbled for his keys. He had once been told by a caustic acquaintance that there were two kinds of people in the world: those who had their keys out before they entered a car and those who looked for them after, the latter being that grotesque group into which Mike Morton fell. It was at times like these that he put his fantasies of beautiful women and yachts and lavish homes on hold and admitted to being the fat, insignificant gargoyle-toad that he was. He was hemmed in by life just as certainly as Yale was hemmed in by New Haven, and he, too, was like the great university in that he was staid, pompous, deified, and quadrangular, the quadrangular part of his self-analysis becoming in his mind "square," as a female student had referred to him some years back. In his sadness he ticked off the names that had meant so much when he had come to this paragon of American culture—Branford College, Davenport College, Pierson College, Memorial Quadrangle—and now he wondered when they had become so removed from the reality of life. He ran the names by again and they settled dully and slightly malodorously in his thoughts, like ashes from a pile of burned gym socks. Glory found, glory lost. There was goddammed little that was divine about being a glorified office boy at Yale Divinity.

He drove to that part of the city wherein the architecture was of a more utilitarian sort, a mirthless place of apartments and garbage cans and persons who walked huddled against a coldness of the soul on even the most pleasant of days. He parked the car, grabbed up his papers, and went inside a three-story apartment building to the dankness and despair of his two-room-and-bath existence. After placing his burden on an impromptu bookshelf made of stained boards and bricks, he slipped a cassette into his stereo and smiled as Stevie Wonder sang "Overjoyed." Maybe Stevie wasn't Mozart, but one did have to give heavy credit to his way with a song.

The knock at the door was in perfect cadence with the lilt of the song and at first Mike was puzzled about whether he had actually heard it. Now it came again, off-tempo. He opened the door and found himself looking at a blue suit, white shirt and paisley necktie, his only thought being that whatever it was, it was well dressed. The handsome black man was smiling down at him from a head that was well over six feet off the floor, a handsome head overtopped with a glossy, straightened hairstyle that glistened even in the dark hallway.

"Phillips, U.S. Government," said the man. He held up a small wallet with an identification card encased in glassine. "May I come in?"

"Uh, sure," said Mike, moving out of the way, feeling vaguely accused, threatened, wary. He thought of his tax return and wondered whether his white lies here and there had become as large and dark as thunderstorms whose lightning from Washington was now jeopardizing his freedom.

Phillips seated himself on the couch's slickened and fading fabric and looked about the room. Cocking his head slightly sideways, he read some of the titles in the bookcase and saw that most were oriented toward things accepting God and questioning God.

"Hope you'll pardon the place," said Mike, seating himself across the room. "No need to spend money on good stuff here; thieves, you know."

Phillips nodded. "Yes, I could tell that the Audicrowdy didn't frequent the area." He did not smile.

Feeling scorched, Mike said, "So what can I do for you?"

"I'll come to the point: this conversation has never occurred. Gravest consequences if the wrong people were to know of it. Do you know a person named Charleston Garman?"

"The name is familiar," Mike answered, a hoarfrost of apprehension covering his neck and shoulders. "Seems there was once a student, or maybe a teacher here by that name. If I recall, he was a . . ." The word *Negro* died in his throat.

"Black?" Phillips smiled. "It's all right; I've heard it before. Now, what do you recall about him?"

Mike was thinking, Only that he sent the professor a letter through me, and why am I *sweating*? But he said, "Quiet. Average height. Usually at odds with the system here. But that's no big deal: this is Yale—we expect recalcitrance. I'm not sure whether he ever took a degree."

"Do you know an Emerson Wolfe?"

Mike answered quickly, "No, I honestly don't."

"Does the name Popper mean anything to you? How about Washington Clark?"

"Neither one," said Mike.

"Popper is a nickname used by Washington Clark. But that's neither here nor there. You used the word *honestly* when I asked about Wolfe. Why did you do that?"

"Do what?" Mike felt his folded hands flutter apart and come to rest on the arms of his chair. Even as he did so he watched Phillips taking his ineptitude in, weighing it, preparing it for dissection.

"Never mind, for now. Have any of these people ever been in contact with you in any form? Phone? Letter?"

Mike stuck out his lower lip in parody of a child's puzzlement and shook his head. "Noooo," he said slowly, "not that I can recall. I'm just more or less an office boy for certain professors in Divinity."

Phillips looked at him without expression. Ten seconds passed, twenty. Mike heard the ticking of something from somewhere and at last realized that it was the Stevie Wonder tape.

Phillips nodded at the stereo and asked, "You like nigger music?"

Mike started to smile but something told him to refrain. He nodded instead.

"Does that mean yes?" Phillips asked.

"Yes," Mike said.

"Yes what?"

"Yes, I like . . . that kind of music."

"What kind of music?"

"Nig . . . ro music. Bobby Blue Bland is one of my all time fav . . ."

"Tell me about Charleston Garman. This time get it right."

Mike sensed a furnace blast at his veracity, at his safety, at his career. This man meant business, whatever his business was. Phillips sat across from him, melting him with those dark eyes. In less than two minutes, he had been able to reduce Mike to a quivering behemoth of self-doubt and defensiveness. Up to now it had been words; he wondered whether the black man meant to get physical.

"What is it that I haven't gotten right?" Mike asked, stalling.

"Are you denying that Charleston Garman wrote you a letter at some time in the past week?" When Mike did not answer he pressed on: "He is a sly one, I know him well. If he has gotten you tied up in this there might still be time to extricate yourself."

"Frankly, I don't know what in hell is going on!" Mike said.

"I wish that I could believe that. I really do."

"Well, you're going to have to believe it, because I

really don't know. Yes, a letter came to me yesterday. But there was another letter inside the envelope. Garman requested that I give the letter in the envelope to someone else. That's it! That's the truth! That's all that I know about any of this! I don't know who you are or what you are or what the hell any of this is about." Mike's guts felt as if they had become steel springs. Enough of this shit was enough.

Phillips leaned forward, started to speak, instead looked out a window at the casual wavings of an elm. The drizzle had become a general rain and the afternoon was darkening.

"This person who got the letter, was he one of the faculty?"

"I'm not at liberty to say who he was, not until I know more about this," said Mike.

Phillips held up two fingers. "Two letters. Two people. You can help to stop this thing now."

Mike looked at Phillips sternly. "Stop what thing? I'll help if you'll let me."

"What do you know of Quetzalcoatl? Does the name mean anything to you?"

It was now that Mike's years of study crosslatched with his memory and illuminated this previously unlighted labyrinth of words. Now they had led somewhere. He said, "It . . . sounds like something Spanish. Maybe I've read the name somewhere."

"Let me ask it this way, then. What of Votan? Did you ever hear of him?"

"Him? No, not that I . . ."

"Okay, what about Wixepechocha? Anything occur to you, anything come back?" Phillips' words were coming faster now, and there was accusation and threat in them.

"Aren't those volcanoes in Mexico? I've heard of Popocat . . ."

"Cut the shit," said Phillips. "You know who they are and what they mean and you're lying about everything. Now, who got the letter?"

Mike lunged forward, trying to escape the chair, but his larded body fought itself and by the time he had half arisen Phillips had jumped atop the coffee table, a death glare in his eyes.

Mike Morton's last thought was, *This is craziness and weirdness and madness and I hate it and I am going to die and I hate to die not knowing what in hell is going on.*

Less than two seconds had passed.

Phillips leapt, his left leg extended, his right aimed at the floor for counterweight, ballast, pedalpoint in the graceful act of murder. He had judged correctly, had known all along that this fat, bearded, lying blob of Caucasian shit would be unable to rise in time to save itself. The heel of his left foot caught Mike just at the juncture of right eye and nose cartilage and there came the unmistakable flesh-deadened sound of traumatized vertebrae as the fat man's neck snapped. Like a viper slithering away even as it extracts its fangs, Phillips went on over the backside of the chair just in case he had missed.

The room was soundless, motionless. The back of Morton's head hung sidewise and at a most unnatural angle. There were sweatbeads at the back of the fat neck.

As he came up off the floor, Phillips rubbed his elbow. A pain, but nothing major. It had been a good kill. A minor rivulet of blood ran from Morton's nose, evaded his lips, changed course and moved in perfunctory trackage toward the chin. Odd, how white people looked in death, as if they had forgotten something and were trying to remember where they had left it. Black people merely looked dead, but honkies were something else. He smiled at the body, looked about the room, wiped his hands with a white handkerchief. Now all there was to do was to see which of the professors for whom Morton had played office boy took it on the lam, then follow the bastard. This thing was going to be a piece of cake. And fun.

Nine

In the Memphis bar called Segregarious, Jesse DeVaron was nursing a salty dog and eyeing a redhead who sat with a fat and fatigued salesman-type.

"Who her?" he asked Muley, the bartender.

"Her new," said Muley.

"Her gottum nice buns," said Jesse.

"Her maybe gottum herpes and clap, too," said Muley. He rubbed his white cloth absentmindedly around Jesse's glass.

"Colbert been in lately?"

"Nope." Muley scratched his bald head morosely.

"You're a million laughs today, Muley."

"You must have made a big hit on somebody, Jess. Usually it's *me* trying to keep *you* from going into your tent and falling on your sword."

"I got my bills paid and dough in the bank," said Jesse. "What more could a body ask?"

"My old lady is giving me hell. You own a house?" When Jesse shook his head, Muley went on: "She's wanting to sell our little white frame, now that the kids are gone, and buy a goddam big place with trees. Figure it if you can: five people sleep on top of each other in something the size of a Cream of Wheat box for twenty years, and then three of those people move out, so that there's finally enough room, and now she wants to sell and get something bigger. God, I hate women."

"Yeah, me too. A woman is a life support system for a prick, Colbert says." He watched as Muley went over to wash his hands and delve into a jar filled with Polish sausages. Dropping two of the obscene objects onto a napkin, Muley brought them back and placed them in front of Jesse. "What's that for?" Jesse asked.

"For Thursday night. You don't remember?"

Jesse felt sheepish. "Can't say I do."

"You bet me two weenies you could spell segregarious in ten seconds. You were jack-daffy on George Dickel so I took you up on it."

"And I won, huh? I been coming in here for two years and never asked: what in hell does 'segregarious' mean?"

"The guy that owned it before hated niggers. He built this place during the freedom rider stuff, way back. When I was buyin' it from him I asked the same question. He said, 'Human beings are gregarious but segregate themselves, so they are segregarious!' Sorta cute in an evil way, don't you think?"

Jesse nodded. "In an evil way." Something suddenly gnawed his memory and made him feel oddly insecure. It was as though this almost-perfect day were a new coat that he had donned and worn in public only to find that he had failed to remove its price tags. Dammit, what was it? Was he supposed to be somewhere, to call somebody, to . . . what? Well, piss on it.

". . . and I'll be damned if I'll pay that for a house," Muley was saying. "You want another?"

Jesse nodded, licked the last of the salt from the rim of the glass, swallowed the mixture of melted ice, gin, and grapefruit juice. As Muley turned to make him a fresh one Jesse said, "Be right back. The plumber is knocking."

He walked the length of the place, noticed that the redhead was a good twenty years older than he had thought, dismissed her as a prospect. It wasn't that her age was a turnoff—bad ass can be twenty, good ass can be seventy—but she had buck teeth and bad skin. Like all adult males, his sexual computer had billions of counterbalanced diodes and whatnots; the process of evaluating and filing her had taken no time at all.

As he relieved himself he felt a minor nagging at his

left nipple, leaned forward to let his shirt adjust itself, shrugged. A bit of graffiti on the wall caught his eye: *Something is about to happen, something is going to happen, I can't figure what's about to happen.* He wondered who had written it. Whatever the man's problem, Jesse could only hope that it was by now resolved. Unaware that the message could have been written for him, or by him, he zipped and went back to the bar. As he sat and picked up the fresh salty dog, the chitinous presence in his shirt touched his nipple again. He looked down, and saw that it was the letter from old Popper. He had forgotten the thing until now.

Age and illiteracy were evident in the spider-leg handwriting, and there were traces of shoe polish at the edges of the paper. Attached to the note with a paper clip was yet another letter.

Mr. Devairn:
My nephew write this and it scare me. I know him and I raise him from a baby when he mama die, so I know him not to lie. This is serios, for I know him not to lie never. I think he need help but I haven no money and need you if you can to see me on this. Popper.

Jesse read it again and tried to establish a remembered face that would superimpose itself over the word *nephew.* Yes, now he recalled old Popper's nephew, a tall and serious young black man who had sometimes shined shoes with Popper on Saturday. And it seemed that the youth had gone off to a big university—Stanford? Harvard? Yale?—some ten or twelve years ago. He was but one of those myriad humans who had come and gone in the sight line of Jesse's life, whizzing by like the cars of distant neighbors, and just as unremarkable. He removed the paper clip and withdrew the second letter from its envelope. A tiny cross fell out and onto the bar. Without really knowing why, Jesse picked his drink up and put it on the little bit of metal, the back of his neck bristling at this blatant sacrilege.

Uncle Popper:
You have before you the cross of Jesus Christ. It is on that cross that I swear to you that all herein is true.

Do you remember when we laughed at the name Cowdery? You were reading to me and called it cow-dairy. It was our private joke, and still is. The truth lay there, but we did not know it.

This thing is dangerous. They will try to stop it. When the world knows the greatest war of all time will result. You must never tell of this, for it would put you in great danger. They will kill you as I am sure that they are going to kill me.

You once said that the only white man who never let you down was the policeman named DeVaron. I trust your judgment, as I always have. Talk to him on this, and no one else. Never admit to anyone but him that you ever saw this letter.

I must go.

Jesse moved the drink, put the cross and the letter back into the envelope, folded Popper's note, placed it all in his shirt pocket.

"Anything wrong, Jesse?"

"Uh . . . no . . . Muley."

"Why didn't you eat the weenies? You look kinda sick."

"You hungry? You eat 'em."

"Thanks." Muley grabbed one of the sausages and walked down to the other end of the bar with the thing hanging out of his mouth. He picked up a five left by a departed customer, placed it in the cash register and came back to Jesse's perch. "What's her name?"

"Who?"

"The woman who wrote the letter that you ain't too happy with."

Jesse frowned and shook his head. This was not a problem one shared with a bartender.

Jesse went outside to gray streets and a red sky. The cool of the lounge was overwhelmed by the warmth of sunset. There was something down and dirty in this letter from Popper's educated nephew that bore looking into. A nebulous feeling of danger fell over him as he got into the Chevy, for he knew beyond the realm of logic that he was about to get into something that would pay him nothing, could get him killed, or get his ass kicked. But these thoughts were in open conflict with a deeper emotion, that being the thrill of the chase. Popper's nephew was *schooled;* something was up.

"Oh, shit," he said. "Here I go." He found himself driving toward Popper's shack over on Alabama Street.

To know the whole of the South in microcosm one should merely come to Memphis, he was thinking as he parked and got out in front of Popper's little yellow house. To the west, where the sun was bleeding purples, there was Arkansas with its flat rice fields and cotton patches and dog track, a pastiche of antiquity and neapolitanism. Twenty miles to the south lay the kudzu jungles of Mississippi, a state whose accents were as definable as the state line itself. And to the north and east was rolling-hill Tennessee, walking-horse Tennessee, rockabilly-but-country-club Tennessee. Craziness and beauty coexisting: this was Jesse's Memphis.

He went up the grass-cracked concrete steps and knocked at an ill-hung screen door. There was no reply, nor was there that feel of almost-indiscernible movement from within that a visitor feels from without. He went around to the back, mounted the dark wooden steps that led up to a tiny back porch. The back door was open and the house was dark. He used his elbow to push the door aside, his cop experience already warning him that Popper was dead.

Popper lay on his couch and something was sticking out of his head. It was very hot in the dark room, and all that Jesse could at first delineate was the rectangle of window that stood above the couch. He fumbled in a pocket of his jacket and took out a matchbook. The room yellowed gaily and then whitened sadly. The blade of a small hand axe was buried in Popper's face horizontally, the handle standing out from the head like the lever of an ancient yard pump. Whoever had done it had been very good or very lucky, for the metal was buried two inches deep right at the top of the old man's nose. Both eyes were bulged, what was left of them, and there was very little blood.

Jesse blew the match out, dropped it onto the linoleum, touched the letter and note in his shirt pocket.

Questions came: Who would kill an old illiterate shiner of shoes? Who was Cowdery? What was the nephew involved in that had gotten Popper killed?

Whatever it all meant, it had come to rest right in the middle of Jesse DeVaron's life.

Ten

"Jess, you are the lyingest sonofabitch I've ever known, bar none. I hope you die face down in pig shit." Having said this, Detective James Oliver Colbert of the Memphis police department went over to the window and pulled back a curtain. "What do you pay for this filthy hellhole anyway?"

"Two hundred a month."

"You're getting fucked."

"I know, but I call it home."

Colbert raked a finger across a window sill, looked down on the street and grunted. "Funny how much dust there is in a city. Who'd 'a thunk it?" He turned back to Jesse and said, "Now, asshole, are you gonna tell me?"

"I would if I could, Ollie, but I don't know what to tell."

"Don't call me Ollie, dammit, you know how bad I hate that. Now, let's start over: last night a black man was murdered with an axe and somebody calls and says they saw a white Chevy with part of your plate number to go with the description." Colbert adjusted his tie and lifted his chin. "You can comprehend why we might be just a little interested, can't you?"

Jesse shrugged and faked a yawn. "No." He was loving every second of it. Soon Colbert would go into his exasperation strut. He loved to watch Colbert do it. Since they were rookies together twenty years ago he had seen it probably thirty times and it was the best free show in Memphis.

"No? Why no?"

"The oldest reason of all: I'm not guilty of any goddam murder. That's not saying I haven't thought of killing you a few times."

"Very funny. Let's just delve into what we have here," said Colbert, beginning to strut, unaware that Jesse was snickering inwardly and thinking, *Here it comes.* "You are Jesse DeVaron and you are forty-four years old. You were married for six of those years to a woman named Rhonda and you and she fought and she took off. You now see a woman named Janice, a doll who could have her pick but she's got to be stupid because she only screws you. You and I joined the Memphis cops twenty years ago together and made it through by the skin of our teeth, mainly because we were hung over or crotch-raddled most of the time. We spent seventeen of the last twenty mostly together until you got mad at department policy and told them three years ago to shove it. You never do anything without a reason and you'll lie at the drop of a hat. You ain't getting rich in the private dick business but you're paying your bills, sometimes. You drink too much and you keep a bottle of George Dickel in your old green Ford convertible for emergencies. You are six-two, have jock itch and athlete's foot and brown eyes and brown hair." Colbert was walking up and down between the couch and table as he chanted, like a hillbilly having a religious experience. "Which all brings us to last night. You also have a white Chevy whose last three license digits are B-12, like the vitamins. The computer tells me that there are only eleven cars in the state of Tennessee with those last three digits and only four of them are white. The other three are way to hell and gone over around Knoxville or wherever. You and I both knew the dead man whose name was Popper but it will read Washington Clark on his tombstone." Colbert stopped in the middle of the room and looked both redeemed and persecuted. "Now do you see why I am taking a shit in your mess gear, Jesse? Do you want to go on lying to me, your dearest pal, or do you want to besmirch me at the department by association?"

"I want to besmirch you, Ollie!"

Colbert sat down heavily on Jesse's couch and looked about the apartment. "No wonder you drink. This place depresses me."

"Everything depresses you, Ollie. How are Hazel and Jimbo?"

"Hazel is fine and Jimbo is a junior at Memphis State."

"Jesus, just last week I held him on my lap and he pissed all over me. Remember?"

"Yeah, but last week was twenty years ago and why were you over at Popper's last night?"

Fun had been had with Colbert but now it was time to get serious; the cops knew damned well that Jesse had killed no one and Colbert was just doing some digging; this was certainly no time to go too heavily into the note from Popper or the letter from Popper's nephew; Colbert was right when he had said that Jesse would lie, and now was the time for a bit of . . . well . . . chicanery.

"I was over there because Hip Willis told me that Popper wanted to see me," he said.

"When did Hip tell you this?"

"Yesterday, noonish."

"And from there you went to Segregarious and had salty dogs and Muley raised hell because his wife wants a new home. Don't ask, I called Muley and he told me the same shit."

"So there you have it," said Jesse. "It was just dusky dark. I went in the back door and Popper was holding an axe up with his head bone. I left the same way I came in and drove around town thinking about it and came home around twelve."

Colbert hunched forward and held his chin in his palms. "I should have gone to optometry school like my parents wanted," he said. "I have a weird feeling that you're about to lie, but, idiot that I am, I'm gonna ask: Do you have the softest idea of what's going on?"

"No," Jesse said.

"See, I knew you'd lie. Maybe you don't know what's going on, but you know more than I do, right?"

"It had something to do with Popper's nephew, the one that used to shine shoes on Saturday and went off to Harvard or someplace." He felt warm inside; he had said just enough.

"Yale," Colbert corrected. "The kid's name was Charleston Garman. I used to kid him about Charlton Heston and he'd say, 'The difference between Charlton Heston and Charleston Garman is only skin deep.' I guess it was a race thing he was referring to. A sharp kid, went to Yale on some kind of government thing, if I recall. You think he did it?"

"No."

"Then you know who did?"

"That's a dumb question, Ollie."

"Yeah, I guess it was." Colbert stood and started for the door. "Just one more murder that'll be filed and forgotten, I have a feeling," he said.

"Stay in touch," said Jesse.

"Bet on it," said Colbert. He went out and closed the door behind him.

Jesse locked the door, took the letter from a copy of *From Here to Eternity* and reread for the tenth time the phrase ". . . the greatest war of all time will result."

Popper's nephew was a madman. Yale had blown his mind out the window, or racism had, or poverty had, or superstition had. Certainly *something* had.

". . . the name Cowdery . . . you called it cow-dairy . . ."

Jesse went to his bookshelf and pulled down volume six of *The American People's Encyclopedia,* Cost of Living to Dynamometer. About Cowdery there was nothing. He got sidetracked and read about William Cowper. He wondered if old William Cowper ever had jock itch. Probably not.

Maybe Cowdery was a misspelling. Maybe it was a code word. Maybe it really was "cow dairy." Maybe and maybe and maybe.

"Jesus," he said aloud, "I need a drink." But something newly born and heavily muscled and vehemently implacable in him answered, *No you don't.*

"Maybe I've cracked up. Maybe I'm an alcoholic, like some have said." *No you are not.* What you are is *bothered* because you know damned well that there is no such thing as triplicate in coincidence, "co" being the prefix that means *two,* not three. You have a frightened old man who is now murdered and you have a letter that you know damned well was written by a lucid mind and you have the little cross of Jesus Christ that fell from Charleston Garman's letter yesterday and immediately put on hold your urge to drink. He is speaking to you, Jesse. Listen.

Late in the afternoon the storm began to break up and the sky was suddenly yellow. It was that strange pastel yellow that always follows a day of rain. James drove toward the sunset and knew that very soon he would be very tired. The long drive and the constant rain had beaten him and his bones ached. Too, the Great Question had tortured him all day and he knew that he would have to think of it tonight, although he was aware that there was no answer.

He checked into a forgettable little motel at the edge of a forgettable little town. Because his room smelled of ancient cigarette smoke he left the door open and walked up the circular driveway that led back to the highway. By now the sunset was but a thread of oleander that delineated that part of America that was called Appalachia, and beyond that he believed that he could see orange touches of lightning.

An old couple walked a dog along the driveway and James wanted to talk with them, with anyone. The dog growled and the woman whispered to the animal. James watched them as they walked toward their room, and he felt alone. The highway was alive with night traffic and he imagined that all the cars held people who were going to untroubled homes where there was conversation and much love. Because he knew that the greatest torture to those who are lonely is to be near those who are not lonely, he walked off the driveway and down to a grove of small elms. He leaned against one of the trees and prayed in the darkness for all those Mormons who were about to die because Votan lived.

When he had finished his meditations he went down the hill to a fenced pasture. The daytime aromas of cattle and hay were heightened by the night air and he recalled the innocence of his boyhood, yearned for those ignorances of youth that are life's only blessed and unencumbered moments. He had once helped an uncle in a pasture such as this, an athestic and alcoholic uncle who had smelled of snuff and bourbon. The uncle had often said that had religion never existed then probably war would never have existed, a thing that had disturbed the young James, had caused him to pray often for the uncle's soul. But over the years the certainties of ignorance had become slandered by the certainties of learning, the resulting index of it all being confusion.

James looked beyond the pasture and saw that the second front was coming fast; what had been orange puffs in the dark sky were now definite veins of lightning. All this misused heat and energy gave recall to writings that spotlighted the anus of religion.

". . . the children were led to the flaming and were thrown in one by one. Most did not scream until they had landed among the embers and were being consumed. The pile in the pit grew so that by midafternoon one little Jewish girl attempted to step from the pile directly onto the cool earth at the edge. She was shot in the head, most of her face being blown away. The screaming went on well into the night. Babies, swaddled in gasoline-soaked rags, were the last to go, their infant shrieks causing one of the SS men to comment that they were as tin whistles. Jewish workers with lorries cleaned the ash and bone from the pit the next day, some three hundred kilos of the gray material yielded by the pit. . . ."

Auschwitz. Treblinka. Ravensbruck. Chelmno. Belsen. Buchenwald.

"The Spanish Inquisition was a tribunal, modeled by Ferdinand and Isabella on the medieval Inquisition. The chief inquisitors were always clerics approved by the Church. Those who were convicted of heresy were

paraded before the community in a ceremony called auto-da-fé. Usual punishment was death by burning; however, other forms of punishment were the forced drinking of molten lead, gouging out of eyes, hacking off of limbs, bodies stretched and broken on the rack. Pregnant women were impaled on long spikes, and some were in such advanced state that their infants were expelled and hung from the womb crying until death by exposure or starvation . . ."

The Holy Catholic Church at work in Spain in the fifteenth century.

". . . as they Confess'd not their Transgressions and Treaties with the Satan that were the Source of their state of Witcherie, they were taken to the hill on the Common and were Hanged for Alle to see, the Hangman being in his Craft certain the Deathe of each was resulte of Suffocation so that the Gravity of Offense against the Creator was Amended and Atoned in manner foresworn as desired by Himselfe, Almighty God. Thus the Wailings and Groanes of the dying Witches was applauded by those Righteous souls who gathered to observe the Dispatch of those who had enleagued with Satan. . . ."

Salem, Massachusetts, America, seventeenth century.

". . . as the chained Negroes were thrown onto the log pile a service at a nearby Pentecostal Church was ending. Some of the church members called across the field for the fire to be postponed until all at the church could be notified. When the assemblage had taken place, the Negroes and the log pile were liberally doused with gasoline. The flames and the screams of the dying Negroes rose as one and were greeted with shouts of 'Huzzah' and 'Hosannah' from the crowd. One of the Negroes rolled from the flames, his trousers burned away, and several of the Church elders complained that the man's body was exposed and they went about holding their hands over the eyes of sisters of the Church. The minister shouted for them to let the children draw near to the fire so that they might see in their youth the wrath that God might invoke should they embark on evil paths in their adulthood. The shackled hands of one of the

Negroes were undamaged by the flames and were cut off and preserved in a glass jar by one of the churchmen . . ."

Gurdon, Arkansas, 1916.

The first winds of the coming storm touched James' face and he walked up the hill to the dimly lighted motel and went into his room. He closed the door and found that most of the smoke stench was gone. A Gideon Bible lay on his lamp table and he lay on his bed in the darkness with the book on his chest. His life had been modeled on an absurdity, a duplicity, a paradox; indeed, the paradox would now have to grow a beak with which to devour itself once again, this time in the form of intercession by the United States government. Yes, if Votan lived, if the letter was correct, then the FBI or the CIA would certainly be onto the potential for war against the Mormons, the absolute disruption of religion in America. It would be an interesting thing to see, to be a part of. His thoughts rested on a couplet from a Christmas song: "Said the drummer boy to the mighty king . . . Do you know what I know . . ." The government would stifle this because they *had* to. He wondered whether they would kill him. Possibly. Just now he didn't care.

There came ten minutes of great thunder and lightning. As the rain began James thought of Beirut, the Gaza Strip, Londonderry, of the hatred between Muslim and Sikh, of the hatred between preacher and Pope. Hundreds of books read, hundreds of lectures given, seminars attended, all the learning, so called—what had it been for? Shema, Torah, Talmud. Jain, Dietrich Bonhoffer, Niemoller, Billy Sunday, Billy Graham. Shinto shrines, the temples at Angkhor Wat, Theoglossolalia, snake handling, Koran, Shroud of Turin, Miracle at Fatima. And on and on. Now it would end or begin again with a holocaust that must consume Salt Lake City, and all because Votan was alive.

Dr. James Wagstaff threw the Bible across the room. He heard it hit the wall and flutter almost soundlessly to the floor.

Eleven

The largest indoor shopping arena in the world is in Dallas, Texas. Calling itself The Galleria, the structure is a half mile by a quarter mile of stone and bricks overtopped by twin glass arches. The interior contains hundreds of shops, dozens of restaurants and the exact center at the ground floor features that strange and trendy necessity of all great malls, an ice skating rink. Strutting young men with accents from Rome, New York, and Paris can be seen conversing and haggling with dusty and cowboy-booted men whose accents are as grainy as lespedeza hay. Stores with names like I. Magnin and Saks Fifth Avenue shoulder shops that dispense cheap T-shirts and fake Navajo jewelry.

Pondering this cosmopolitan atmosphere from beneath a potted palm at a restaurant called Bennigan's, Emerson Wolfe took a final bite from a French fried potato and shoved his plate to the center of the table. Yet unsatisfied, he ordered a chocolate milk shake and dabbed at his mouth with a napkin. In the last hour he had ordered a burger and fries, followed up with another burger and fries, followed by an order of fries. The waiters had begun to look at him oddly. But Wolfe did not mind; American food had been very much on his mind for the last few months, and he had promised himself a moment of gluttony. Nobody anywhere south of the Rio Grande had the goddamnedest notion of what a French fry was supposed to taste like, and like all who have deserted their native environs for extended periods, his taste buds had begun to rant like rats on a garbage sack as soon as he had entered Mexico. That was more than ten months ago, but God, it seemed longer.

A black man walked by wearing sunglasses and Wolfe thought of Don Phillips. A childhood chant echoed in Wolfe's mind: two on one is nigger fun. Now Garman was having nigger fun, even from the grave.

It was that sonofabitch Garman who had really queered the deal. Garman, with his weepy eyes, his way of whining to the Lord about this thing. This piety was an aberration in Garman's character that neither Wolfe nor Phillips had been aware of at the onset of the caper. Garman had begun to speak in tongues at the last, had become a spouter of theoglossalic idiocy, using words like *Quetzacoatl, Wixepechocha, Votan, Gucumatz, Hystus, Sume, Bochica, Kukulcan*. And then he would shift gears and roll on the floor sometimes with yet another set of verbal infirmities: *Tongaroa, Kane-Akea, Lono, Kane, Kana, Contici*. And then he would rise up, sit on his bed in silence for as much as an hour. One night he had nodded off to sleep saying, "It cannot be, but it is. Oh, cow dairy. Oh, Uncle Popper, be not lost, spread the word." Wolfe knew all this to be exact, for one night he and Phillips had recorded it; they had planned to play it for the man with the fuzzy nuts in Washington if Garman should become violent or compromise national security. CYA. Cover Your Ass. Funny, he had not thought of the phrase since it had been said by a lieutenant from the Screaming Eagles during Reagan's invasion of Grenada. The fresh-faced young officer had shot three spics in the back of the head just for the hell of it. When Wolfe had asked why, the paratrooper had said, "You cover your ass, easy money, and I'll cover mine."

CYA. Cover Your Ass.

It had started with that goddam priest, Father Colon. The Power Up North, those pot-gutted and overpaid bastards who carried briefcases in and out of that little nondescript house in Reston, Virginia, had filtered the word down that dope was now very much on the public mind, that something had to be done as a sop to the TV

Dinner set. *Time* Magazine was doing a cover story on cocaine at least once every three months, and her vainglorious sister, *Newsweek*, was squawking about how the border patrols were poorly manned and underfunded, about how the Coast Guard needed more AWAC spotter planes, and on and on. Emerson Wolfe had been bored with Hermosillo, with its shores and its beer, and with the two niggers who had been sent there more or less to get them out of Oaxaca, where the supervisor was a man who hated niggers but would not admit it, such admission being a bad career move. Wolfe had liked them both, Phillips especially, who could regale him with tales of fast cars and white pussy, and Garman pretty well, although Garman had a way of sleeping late and meditating a lot that was disconcerting to his Company brothers.

"You ain't gonna believe this shit, but I know a priest who's dirty," Phillips had said some three months ago.

"So? It's Mexico. The whole country smells like bean farts and mule shit," Wolfe had replied. It had been a Sunday morning and he had been hung over.

"No, I mean dirty dirty. He's on the track where the white horse runs."

Wolfe had stirred at this. "Cocaine? A goddam priest is dealing in cocaine?"

Phillips had nodded and beamed. "The way I got it figured, we ain't doing a damned thing now. I hate Mexico, you hate Mexico, and sleeping beauty over there, he hates Mexico." He pointed to Garman, whose bed was flush with the hotel room's window and whose dark foot was pointed out over the sill at the adobe city. "So we bust this priest, so to speak, and it gets us out of here. I'm gonna ask for Germany this time. There's blonde ass over there that—"

"Yeah, yeah, I know about all that, but I don't follow you on the priest thing."

"Simple, Wolfie baby. I been doing some thinking. I got a pal who did a tour in Northern Ireland. Belfast. The IRA has been getting some of its weaponry from the Bear. John Q. America doesn't know this, but you can bet that the Quantico Ear has picked it up. Now, we can't seem to hate Catholics, and we can't seem to be siding with the Protestants either, but we can't ignore those weapons. Right? You follow me?"

"A word now and then."

"Well, you know how the Company works: have it if you need it, use it if you have to. The unwritten word is that if we ever need a news leak that breaks open this Belfast-Moscow tie with the weapons, that leak should be tandemized with another leak that will bend the Catholics over and shut them up. Hell, you know how it works; you've been around a long time."

Wolfe had raised up on one elbow. Even in his tequila-fogged state, the thing being proposed was making sense, partly. "So we get the goods on the priest, file our report for the Eagle to use if he needs it, get stars on our report cards, and get to ask for a transfer. How'm I doing so far?"

Phillips had stood and done a soundless, barefoot tap dance on the worn carpet. "There was a man named Machiavelli, and he wrote a book about us, baby. We may be just the waving cilia that moves the shit out of the gut of the Great Body, but we are necessary. And who says that cilia should not be rewarded?"

"What the hell is cilia?" Wolfe had inquired.

"Gut-flushing hairs. I took a biology course at Howard. But that's neither here nor there. Do you like the plan so far?"

Wolfe liked the plan and so had Garman, although the latter, groggily pulling in an overheated foot from the noon heat, had questioned activity that would bring the glare of discredit upon the Church. "You ain't even a Catholic, mister, so shut the fuck up!" Phillips had explained.

So it was that by the following Thursday night they had made their approach to the priest, had confronted him, had agreed that Phillips should remain outside while Wolfe and Garman did the inquisition.

"This cannot be," the old man said. A palsied hand toyed with his clerical collar. It was very quiet in the little office at the back of the church and the low-wattage bulb in the desk lamp offered praiseless and bloodless glow to the scene.

"But it is, Father," Wolfe said. "What we cannot understand is, why?"

The old priest touched his brow with light-yellowed fingertips. "Two years ago a man offered a great deal of money to the Church if I agreed to perform a wedding for his sister. The woman had confessed that she was twice divorced, a thing that her family did not know, a thing that her brother wanted to be a secret. I did this thing for the money; I violated the edicts of the Holy Order. The money I gave to the poor. But the man did not stop there. He now saw that the Church would make an inviolable place for his evil trade: narcotics. He warned me that I would be disgraced and excommunicated if I refused his evil demands. I shamed God, I shamed the Church, and I shamed myself. All these things I have confessed to Father Emiliano at the parish of Lengus de Cristo. My ears have penance, but my soul mourns. I am glad that you have come. Now it has ended."

"This other priest, Father Emiliano, is he . . . involved?" Garman had asked.

"Not in this matter. Although he sleeps over the ultimate truth, he is a good man. I am very old, and I have been a man of truth, but I have also aided in the suppression of truth. All my wisdoms now hover above me and whisper that one word: truth. I ask myself whether I am good or whether I am evil. Did I do evil to perform good, or did I perform a good that was evil? Would the Church survive truth? Is the Church not itself truth? What would God have me to do?"

Wolfe and Garman had looked at each other, each wondering if the other was aware of coherence in the old man's babblings. It was Garman who had spoken: "Surely God would forgive you a wedding and some dirty money, Father."

The priest had looked at Garman kindly and said, "I am aware that you are a godly man. Forgiveness and charity are written in your eyes."

"Enough of this revival meeting," Wolfe had said angrily, glaring at Garman, who had apparently gone over to the priest's side in the wash of deified pap that was sloshing about in the room. "The good priest here is into dope, Charleston, so let's get him to write it down and get out of here."

Here the priest had wept, collapsed onto himself in the pallid light, shuddering and reeling in his chair, his head rotating in his agony as though he were beset by invisible birds that clawed at his scalp. Wolfe had sat bemused; Garman had at last reached forward and touched the old man's shoulder, a movement whose calming effect was instantaneous.

"I . . . must . . . tell you . . . something," the priest had said at last. Looking at Wolfe and then back at Garman he had groaned, "You . . . alone."

Wolfe had arisen and gone outside the church where Phillips half stood and half lay against the wall.

"Are we home free?" Phillips had asked.

"Sure. One thing about a mackerel snapper, they love to confess. Stake you to a beer?"

"I guess. Think it's okay to let Garman do this alone?"

"Sure. How could he fuck it up?"

The answer to that one had soon become apparent in spades. He and Phillips had gone for a beer, returned to the hotel well past midnight, collapsed in their beds. It was past three in the morning when Garman had returned. His weepings and moanings, the first of what were to be many, had awakened them.

"What's going on?" Wolfe had asked, pulling a pillow from his beer-bludgeoned eyes.

"Don't know. He keeps talking weirdness. 'Votan lives.' That kind of shit. Come listen."

They had listened until well past sunrise. At last Garman slept. They went through his clothes and found the priest's confession, a terse bit of sobbery scrawled on a wood-grainy bit of notebook paper; the old man had done little more than admit that he had sinned against the Church and that he was sorry for it; however, it bore his signature, and that was all that was needed in the first place, for the Company had ways of ascribing messages over signatures. Garman had slept on through the day and into the darkness, and Wolfe and Phillips flipped a dime to determine which would kill the priest. Phillips won (or lost, depending on one's viewpoint of such things) and left the hotel with the syringe at about nine in the evening. (The potion was untraceable after two hours and an injection just inside the anal sphincter would do nicely. "The ultimate suppository," Phillips had called it.)

Now that Phillips was gone and the priest soon would be gone and the confession was in hand, Wolfe had stared across the room at the awakening Garman, pondering what must be done with his newly crazed compatriot. Killing was allowable, but ill-advised at this time: too many questions, too much paperwork. Since it was the session with the priest that had mushed his mind, and since Phillips was out of earshot, it was time to go to work. (Dictum One: Always be ahead of the opposition.) Strange, up to then he had not thought of Phillips as the opposition.

"Want to talk about it?"

Garman had rubbed his eyes. "Yes. Votan lives."

"Let's cut the shit. Who's Votan, and where does he live? Here, in Hermosillo?"

"The greatest treasure known to mankind, Wolfe." He continued to stare at the ceiling. "We who sought have found, yet we who thought we had found have lost. I now know of grandeur that portends agony, and in the end of the agony there is the grandeur."

"Yeah, sounds downright scriptural, but what has it got to do with anything?"

Charleston Garman had then looked at Emerson Wolfe with a soft, distant look in his eyes that frightened Wolfe, and left him annoyed with himself for being afraid.

But the feeling had changed by the next day, a day that began a diffuseness of occurrences that had led him here to Dallas: Garman's sudden obsession with the village of Lengus de Cristo, Garman's letters to New Haven, Connecticut, and to his old uncle in Memphis (crazy letters, gibberish letters that said things like "cow-dairy" and, as usual, "Votan lives"), Garman's friendship with a pig farmer named Octavio Diaz (whereupon Wolfe and Phillips had become aware that there were too many cooks in the kitchen and that Garman was going to keep the "treasure" for himself, for whatever nuthatch reasons he might be considering in his now godmaddened state, a state in which he had promised to "share this wonderful thing" with them, whatever the thing was, a promise on which he had reneged when Wolfe and Phillips had begun to openly discuss the whores and cars and boats that might be bought with the proceeds of the three-way "split"). Toward the end of it Phillips had begun to regard Wolfe's actions as strange and, of course, Wolfe had seen this activity on Phillips' part as strange and, since what *looks* strange *creates* strangeness in the observer, within two months Wolfe and Phillips were as crazy as Garman had been in the beginning.

In the final two days they had all flown their true colors, Garman stepping out of character completely and spending the night with a blonde doll who drove a white Mercedes with Michigan tags, Phillips screaming that the whole thing was about to blow up in their faces, Wolfe sending his letter to a psychopath named Vernon Cameron. Cameron, a jack-Mormon, was crazy as hell, but might come in handy as muscle in this matter. (Let "Cowboy" Cameron eat the shit, do the dirty work, take the heat—this was how Wolfe worked, and he was pleased with himself, elated, jubilant.)

Except that it had not worked.

He bridged the phrase now, amended it to *it has not yet worked, but it will.*

Sipping his milk shake, watching the nice ass stroll by just beyond the wrought-iron fencing that separated Bennigan's from the promenade, Emerson Wolfe was happy to be in America again. Hell, maybe the Company had not missed the three of them at all. Maybe he would concoct a cock-and-bull story about how Garman had told him to go to Dallas and do . . . what? Except that Garman was dead. *We just missed connections all around, and I still don't know the nature of just how much treasure there was, except that Garman had said that it was gold. And how did I know that Phillips was going to panic and fly off to Connecticut?*

God, what a fuckup.

But if he played his cards right, the Company would forgive him, believe him, keep him on. Hell, all sorts of folks sneak out for some time off—it's the American way. He wished that he knew what was going on in New Haven.

"Hey, Wolfie," said Cowboy.

Wolfe was shocked from his remembrances and worries by the greeting. Cowboy walked on past the wrought iron, entered the door of the restaurant, and came back sashaying through the maze of tables. It gave Wolfe plenty of time to size the man up, to figure whether Cowboy was as crazy as he remembered him, if not crazier. Cowboy was a handsome sonofabitch, there was no getting around that fact; even now several female glances were magnetized; Cowboy hat, Levis, Oxford-cloth shirt and fancy boots, Vernon "Cowboy" Cameron was probably being fantasized by the ladies as a rich rancher from down Waco way, and not at all the psychotic, murderous, religious fanatic from Utah that Wolfe knew him to be.

Cowboy sat down. He did not offer to shake hands. Although the men had not seen each other for the better part of a year, Cowboy drifted easily into conversation.

"The Lord has been good to you, Wolfie."

Wolfe was slightly embarrassed. He hated having to toe dance amongst the apostles when talking with Cowboy, but it had to be done. Just now Cowboy was a damned important person to him, crazy or not. "Yes he has, Cam . . . er, Cowboy." Now he recalled why he had ordered the shake; beer would have been unthinkable. Had he just cut a baby's throat, Cowboy would have understood—but a beer, no.

"I like my code name," Cowboy whispered. "I've always hated my name. Vernon Cameron. Sounds like a car dealer with a lot of those little triangular flags." He looked away from Wolfe and out at the great expanse of shops. "The Jews are working like maggots today, Wolfie. Just look at 'em."

Wolfe looked. He saw no Jews, just people. "Yes they are, Cowboy. Their day is coming."

"In that letter you wrote me you said that the Catholics were up to something. You didn't say what."

"No, I didn't. But it's serious. That's why I needed a man like you—somebody who understands and appreciates the flag and God. There's a time coming, Cowboy, a time when men like us can breathe free in America the way God intended."

Tears clouded Cowboy's eyes as he looked away from the roiling hordes of Jews that his mind had perceived in the marketplace. He said, "My brother was lucky to have a friend like you."

"Correction: I was lucky to have a friend like him. Jordan Cameron was a prince among men. I'd even go so far as to say a prince of peace." Wolfe watched as Cowboy nodded and touched his eyes with his fingertips. He yearned for the nutty bastard to take off that goddam cowboy hat. A black youth walked by carrying a chromium-colored radio the size of Oregon, and the sounds of "I've Got a Woman," by Ray Charles, whumped and boomed across the restaurant. Wolfe hoped that the sound did not pervert this sacred moment for Cowboy.

It did not.

"Their time is coming. The Covenant has special plans for the Afros," said Cowboy.

"I'm glad you feel that way. One of the people who is involved in this is an . . . Afro. His name is Don Phillips. He is an evil man, very dark skin, very dark soul. He wants to . . . do it with white women."

"They all do, Wolfie. You show me a nigger and I'll show you a mongrel dog that stinks and lusts. They're all on welfare. They undermine what the Constitution meant for the white race to be. Where is this Phillips? Is he in Dallas? My sword is mighty."

"My feeling is that sooner or later he will be in

Memphis, Tennessee. That's why I needed you. The one man in the world I can trust, Cowboy, is you. There are Jews in this thing, and Afros. It is their desire to betray us to something godless. I'm not sure, but I think the Reds may be in it. Remember that family of spies in our own Navy some time back, the ones who got documents from the aircraft carrier John F. Kennedy? See what I mean? Who can one trust nowadays? Your country needs you, Cowboy."

"John F. Kennedy. There was a man for you, even if he was under the godless edict of Rome. I say the Bay of Pigs was his finest hour."

"You may be right, but don't forget the blockade of Cuba. Kennedy was our last truly great president."

"If only he hadn't been a Catholic," Cowboy said. "That's why I hate him."

"Yes," said Wolfe. "I've always hated him, too. He was rotten to the core, and no great shakes as a president."

"But he stood toe to toe with the Reds, and there was his greatness as a president."

"He had greatness, no doubt about it."

"I think I want one," Cowboy said.

"What? A Catholic?"

"No. One of them." Cowboy pointed at Wolfe's milk shake.

Wolfe was happy that this *Who's On First?* palaver had ceased for a while. Each time Wolfe spoke with Cameron he found it easier to pick up on his cues and echo the big man's catch-phrases with a facility that alarmed him. As Cowboy drifted off on a private lunacy that required no talk, Wolfe studied him. Vernon "Cowboy" Cameron would never have looked proper in a tuxedo, and his massive shoulders and sunblasted face would have a hard time adapting to the starkness of a businessman's suit, but on a golf course or a cruise ship he could get laid ten times a day. It was a paradox that Wolfe planted directly at the door of the God that Cowboy worshiped mightily, the God for whom Cowboy would kill at a moment's notice.

Emerson Wolfe had met Cowboy at the funeral of Jordan Cameron, a Company man who had died of a heart attack in Mexico City last year, his demise brought on in part by the four packs of Lucky Strikes with which he scorched his gullet on a daily basis. The funeral was attended by fewer than twenty people. After having spent a few hours with the deceased's brother Vernon, Wolfe understood the sparsity of mourners: Vernon Cameron was, well, different. Scions of a nine-thousand-acre cattle and mining empire, the Cameron brothers were typical of certain westerners whose great holdings make them wealthy while isolating them in the center of houseless and treeless largesse. And it was in this isolation that the Camerons came to *know* the truths that the winds of the desert and the wandering ranch hands and miners spewed forth: God is good, Jews run the world, there is evil threatening the land, beware and beware. Beware of blacks, beware of that man because he is from another county or another state, beware of Methodists and Baptists and Pentecostals and politicians with unpronounceable names. Jordan Cameron had joined the Company to escape the tedium of ranch life, and to ensure that the ranch stood forever in its lucrative loneliness, unthreatened by Jews and blacks and politicians with unpronounceable names. And he had joined to get away from his brother Vernon who, even as a young boy, had suffered excruciating nightmares and who once was found speaking to God in a rose bush. Oddly enough, Vernon's only interlacement with organized religion had been an acceptance of the Mormon Church, an allegiance that lasted for two years, long enough for him to believe that the Mormons were crazy, and for the Mormons to *know* that he was. And so it was that three weeks ago Wolfe had felt the thing in Hermosillo beginning to get heavy and he had sent a letter to Vernon Cameron asking for his assistance, show-bizzing the thing up by assigning Vernon the code name "Cowboy," since such a name was a reflection of all the things that psychos like Vernon imagine themselves to be: independent, patriotic, virile, capable. Yes, any way one chose to study it, this gold that had run Garman to dementia was as good as in the greedy hands of Emerson Wolfe. He almost hated to kill a unique specimen like Vernon Cameron, but knew that when all the brush was cleared away and the treasure was in his hands, that kill him was exactly what he must do.

"Want to share?" Cowboy asked.

Emerson Wolfe drifted down from his aerie of lethal intention and said, "Share? Share what?"

"You been looking away for almost five minutes. The waiter brought me my milk shake and asked if you wanted something and you didn't even answer. Want to share your thoughts?"

"No. Why don't you share your own thoughts?"

"I've been doing some things that would make you proud that you chose me to help," Cowboy said happily.

"Oh? Such as?"

"Did you ever hear of an organization called the Covenant and the Sword and the Arm of the Lord?" Cowboy whispered.

Wolfe nodded.

Cowboy tapped himself on the chest and said, "You're looking at a member."

"That's good," said Wolfe. But it was not good. The FBI would have found Cameron sooner or later, and joining extremist groups would bring them to his door very quickly. And if they were watching Cowboy, they were also watching Wolfe himself. "When did you do this?"

"Three weeks ago. I know what you're thinking. Don't. It's safe."

"You're sure?"

"I'm sure. Remember that big shootout in Arkansas a couple of years ago, the one where they got Gordon Kahl and that sheriff got killed? That got me to thinking. Then about six months later they arrested the others and broke up the camp they had established up on the Arkansas-Missouri line. Well, they didn't get 'em all. I got a friend who was a sympathizer, but the FBI don't know about him. He brought me in. The Jew tax conspiracy that has worked its way into the federal government had better look out."

"This sympathizer friend, who is he?"

Cowboy shook his head and smiled enigmatically. "You don't need to know. Let's just say that he's somebody that hates Jews and niggers and Mormons and all the other parasites the way I do. He asked me to do something for proof of my loyalty. I did, and it scared the gee-whiz out of him."

"Oh? What did you do that scared the . . . gee-whiz out of him?"

Cowboy smiled again, and this time it was a smile of triumph. "Here's the part you're going to like, the part that proves you made a good choice in getting me to help you, the part that proves God sent me and you to each other at this moment of Armageddon."

Wolfe waited. His throat was closed, numb, nonexistent.

"I went down to Phoenix. And in Phoenix I chopped two old Mormon missionary women into dog meat. I cut their snatches out and stretched them over their heads."

Emerson Wolfe said nothing.

Twelve

In Trenton, New Jersey, Dr. James Wagstaff knelt in a synagogue and prayed. The Star of David on the leaded glass windows had beckoned to him and he had stopped the rented Olds Cutlass on impulse. When he stood he noticed that a young rabbi was watching him.

"May I help you?" the rabbi asked.

"No, thank you," said Dr. Wagstaff pleasantly. "Stay with it. You're right on target."

The young rabbi watched with bemusement as the man who had prayed went to his car, whistling all the way.

In New Haven, Connecticut, Don Phillips was dancing with a newly acquired friend named Marla. She was a green-eyed redhead. The song was Bobby Bland's "Turn On Your Love Light," a tune rich with trumpets of elation and guitars of ascension, a good rocker with which to give one's dancing partner shameless hunches. Two hours ago, by simple process of elimination, he had come to the conclusion that Dr. James Wagstaff was his prey and that the good doctor was en route to Memphis. Phillips had four beers under his belt and he was deliriously happy to be out of Mexico. Too, he knew beyond question that whatever the gold thing that Garman had fucked over him with, well, it was doubtless on its way to Memphis also. Find Wagstaff and Garman's uncle in Memphis and wait for them to come together and there, like the crosshairs of a fine surveyor's instrument perfectly quartering a circle of light, there would be the gold. He wondered what kind of gold and how much gold, but wonder is not necessarily worry; right now he was wondering whether Marla's pubic hairs were also red.

It took him only four more dances and a trip to a motel to achieve the answer.

They were.

In Alexandria, Virginia, in a sparsely furnished office over a garage, a CIA coordinator named Vaughn Biddle accepted a collect call from El Paso, Texas, listened for ten minutes, hung up. On a piece of paper he wrote the names *Chief, Cooter, Oscar,* grinning as he did so. The grin faded as he wrote *Don Phillips, Emerson Wolfe, Charleston Garman.* He added several notations to himself, and for others, and picked up the phone. Dialing 1-901-387-0808, he waited until the third ring.

"Yes?" a male voice said.

"Biddle here. How's things in Memphis?"

"So-so."

"They're about to get so-er," Vaughn Biddle said. "Get a pen and write this all down."

Ellen Harrison Rogers Talbott watched the sea off to her left. Porpoises were arcing in pairs, disturbing the Pacific's sunglitter. Wonderfully, by disturbing it, they enhanced it. The richness of ocean air came in the open window of the Mercedes and the intermingled scents of kelp and spray and salt were invigorating; she was at one with nature. In spite of her eleven-hour northward drive from Acapulco she was not at all fatigued.

At Mazatlan the great federal highway trunks northward and extends an arm eastward. Tomorrow she would take this eastward highway to Durango, Torreon, Monterrey, on into McAllen, Texas; but just now Mazatlan beckoned.

She checked into the Sunset Palms Hotel surrounded by bellboys who saw the car as the source of perhaps a thousand-peso tip. Strangely, the beautiful *gringa* opted to carry her own bags. And even more strange, the woman was being coquettish with the three vacationing

Korean businessmen who eyed her from the lounge. From somewhere came the sound of Itzhak Perlman's violin and her mood welcomed the music and the flirtations of the Asians. She had never had even one Asian, let alone three. She wondered how long it would take her to shower, change, and get back down to the lounge.

On the day wherein he was to become a Rich Man, Jesse DeVaron awoke and screamed. A great vulture had landed at his face and was about to peck out his eyes. The goddam thing's right foot was clutching the white earth at the front of his vision and its toenails were going to rip out his throat. It would carry his limp and wind-waved body back to its nest and the baby vultures would look upward and blink their little beady eyes and whack and nibble at his guts and buttocks until he was gone. Then they would kick his skeleton out of the nest and the wolves would gnaw at his poor bones. He screamed and waved his arms.

Someone banged and thundered. There came a door-muffled query: "Hey, what the fuck! You all right in there?"

Without really knowing why, Jesse shouted back, "Yeah! Who is it?"

"This is a goddam respectful place. You wanna D.T., get the hell into the street, f'r chrissake!"

Jesse waited until he heard the man walk away down the hall. Then he raised up on one elbow and looked about the room. It was a bathroom with a white tile floor. The eagle's feet supported an ancient, mostly yellow porcelain bathtub. Of all the shitty things in American culture, eagle feet on a table's or bathtub's legs were the most open to question. Having assured himself that his dignity and sense of refinement were intact in spite of his current circumstances, he pulled himself off the floor and looked in the mirror. He still wore the gray pinstriped suit, white shirt, and dark blue tie that he had set out with the night before. There were red and burgundy spots on the tie, and these he licked. Ketchup? No, barbecue sauce.

Now he remembered. Blues Alley on Front Street. Twelve mixed drinks, Dickel and Coke, followed by a plate of ribs. They had done a lot of Howlin' Wolf and Lightnin' Hopkins songs last night and the whole place had huffed and flourished under the warm cloud of Delta blues. God, he had loved it. On "Key to the Highway" the whole crowd had joined in, stood in their chairs, and waved beer steins and rib bones and whatever else was handy. Memphis flexing its vocal cords in the blood pride of its unquestionable heritage. Rock on.

Feeling like a cedar that had just been debarked, he left the hotel room and went downstairs to the seedy lobby. Reading the gilting on the outer windows, he found that he had spent the night, or a portion of it, in the Arcade Hotel.

"How much for the room?" he asked the desk man.

"What room? Where's your key?"

Jesse felt his pockets. "I don't know."

"You the one was yellin'?"

"Yeah. Sorry about that."

"You was 226. Here." The man thrust a wad of bills at Jesse. It turned out to be twenty-four dollars. "You give me a fifty last night. The rooms is twenty-four plus the tax. We're square. You wanta sell that Ford convertible?"

"No. How'd you know I have a . . ."

"You was pretty muchly zonked when you came in at about three. Kept sayin' you didn't need that bottle under the seat of that Ford convertible, that you was gonna sell the whole goddam thing. So? What model? How much? I got a kid crazy for a convertible."

Jesse shook his head. "It isn't for sale." He smiled sheepishly and walked into the street. A clock inside a steak house informed him that it was 9:18. His car was two blocks away, and as he passed Blues Alley the place was dark and empty and soundless, and he felt very lonely.

There was nothing on his door when he got back, and nothing in his mailbox, except for a thing from Ed McMahon telling him in computerized letters the size of pygmy tracks that he might have already won a million dollars. Like all who grunge and sweat through life trying to eke out enough to pay their rent and utility bills, a million dollars was, to Jesse DeVaron, nothing more than a fantasy numerical entity that was a one and a group of zeros and commas attached, a thing like nuclear holocaust or women's equality that people thought about or discussed, and then did little to fertilize so that they might rise from the dreary muck of common occurrence. Unaware that forty percent of a million dollars was almost on his doorstep, he threw the packet from Publisher's Clearing House in the waste basket, shucked his clothes, and got into the shower. He had dried and put on clean shorts and lathered his face when he heard a knock at his door.

"Yeah?"

Someone yelled something. Disgusted at the interruption, Jesse went to the door and again said, "Yeah?"

"Are you Jesse DeVaron?" the male voice inquired.

Jesse unlocked the door and opened it slightly. The man was handsome and stocky and he wore a dark suit. Beneath salt and pepper hair there was a face that was part impishness and part sadness.

"I'm Randall Hood, Shelter Insurance Company," he said. "May I see you for a moment?"

"Sure. Come on in." Jesse showed the man the couch and sat down in the chair that faced it. He didn't want any goddam insurance, and the lather that was drying on his cheeks would serve as a stop-loss for the agent's sales prattle. He wondered how many people old Randall Hood had interviewed in their shorts.

"You have a sister named Rosa Leigh DeVaron?"

Jesse felt his heart lurch. Even as he nodded he knew what was coming. "We . . . aren't very close. Is something wrong?"

Now it was Randall Hood's turn to nod. "Were you aware that she was killed last month in Omaha, Nebraska?" He looked down and away.

"No, I wasn't," said Jesse. The words hung over the room like obscene birds seeking a nest of shame in which to alight. "We weren't close. Some . . . family things. You know?"

Hood nodded and set to work with the efficiency of one who had seen it all in the insurance business. Pulling a thin sheaf of folded papers from his pocket, he said, "Our agent in Omaha contacted the home office in Columbia, Missouri. Rosa had a two-hundred-thousand-dollar life policy with DI—er, double indemnity. The death certificate is on file. All we need here is for you to sign a beneficiary statement and the money will be yours in a few days. Have you considered options?"

Jesse's brain was boiling, his body was numb. Hood asked questions: name in full, Social Security number, relationship to the deceased. Jesse heard himself answering, but his thoughts were in the past. He remembered a tire hanging from a rope, the oak from which it hung being the only shade in a sharecropper's yard. The little girl with the sunpeeled nose was laughing as he pushed her. He remembered them standing in the back of a truck, wind whipping their hair as they rode to town to get a stand of lard. He remembered her crying as she wore a pair of his old and faded overalls to the country school that they had attended, the smell of the yellow and dusty school bus being that unmistakable smell of dirt road poverty. He remembered her going to the bus station with forty-one dollars and saying, *There's got to be something better than this.* Rosa Leigh Devaron Hill. So there had been a marriage at one time, he mused, a brush with decency and convention that was set against a backdrop of prostitution, barmaidery, God knew what else. Five years ago, after receiving word that she had been hauled in by the Cleveland cops for hooking and dealing in coke, he had written her a letter canceling any blood tie, a thing done in a moment of pique, rage, chagrin. She had taken him at his word. Somewhere, someday, somebody would write a book about the real America, about families who work their guts out and then die flat broke and unsung, about sisters who have to prostitute themselves, about the shacks on the fringes of factory towns and the bent and toothless old men who sit at the back booths of nameless bars and cry into their beer, about the despair that forever lay over the richest country in history. Some make it, some don't. Except for himself, the DeVaron family was now gone.

"Options?" Jesse asked dully.

"Lump sum, partial, total left at interest. There are dozens of ways that this can be handled." He handed over the paper headed "Beneficiary Statement," and Jesse signed it. Replacing the paper in his coat pocket, Hood said, "I called the man in Omaha. Our agent. I was aware of your . . . distance from your sister." He reddened slightly; *distance* was not the word that he had wished to use. He spoke again: "She was married to a man named Olan Hill, but they were divorced last year. He was a car dealer. She got a heavy divorce settlement. She was just about to go into a ceramics business. She was a fine lady, according to our man in Omaha. She sure took care of you."

Jesse nodded. "Yes. Yes, she did."

"My suggestion is for lump sum. Insurance companies are sturdy, but they are notorious for paying low interest; however, it's your choice."

Jesse felt something in his left hand. It was the plastic razor, a yellow and white Bic. It looked small, ridiculously shaped, superfluous, mocking. He was rich; he never again had to shave himself. Such a strange thought. "Lump sum," he said. "Do it lump sum."

Hood arose and smiled, extended his hand, which Jesse shook lamely. "I'll get this in the mail this afternoon. These things usually take about a week, sometimes less. Do you have any questions?"

"Only one: does this kind of thing happen often?"

"What kind of thing?"

"If I've got this straight, and I'm not dreaming, you just told me that the amount is four hundred thousand dollars!"

Hood smiled. "Yes. And you're undergoing what I call the 'life-claim stupor.' I've seen it probably forty times. People think life insurance is a phrase that means nothing;

they can't comprehend the real impact it has on other lives. You're a rich man."

When Hood was gone Jesse rinsed the dried shaving cream from his face, started the shaving process over again, and found himself dressed and sitting on his couch without realizing that he had crashed there. He looked at his clock radio, saw that it was just after noon. He wanted to cry but could not, wanted to laugh but dared not. It had *happened* but he *believed* it not. Hood was right about life-claim stupor—it depressed, it addled, it was a sweet dream swaddled in death or it was death that was the origin of a sweet dream. He was a beneficiary. He toyed with the word: *beneficiary*. Eleven letters, a sound, an entity in the English language that neither his mind nor his ear had to now attributed to himself. Somewhere out there in the city there were people in luxurious automobiles, and now he was free to join them in their Cadillackery, the Mercedery, the Jaguary. The world of sharecroppers, grocery clerks, meter readers, and all the other drudging ilk was behind him now. He was rich, but he did not *feel* rich; relieved, yes, but rich? No.

Rosa Leigh DeVaron was gone forever. He felt nothing about it, just as he did not feel wealthy. Truth be told, he admitted to himself, there was one side of his brain that was sighing with relief that Rosa's twisted and tawdry adult existence had ended. It occurred to him that he had asked Hood nothing about the accident. He almost wished that it made him feel lonely to be alone in the world, but this, too, was an emotion that was asleep just now. Asleep, or, it was to be hoped, dead.

Today was the day of Popper's funeral. He had not planned to go, preferring, as was his custom, to remember the deceased as he had been in life. In the forty-eight hours since Popper had been murdered he had drank a bit and goofed about a bit with that wondrous but unproductive ease of existence that only an unmarried and self-employed man with money in the bank can know. But here he was dressed, here he was rich, here he was with an afternoon to kill, and here he was alone in the world. What the hell, a funeral might prove to be a social upper.

While going out to the Chevy, he pondered whether he might be too callow in his views of humankind. He had not given a real damn about anything in a long while, and it disturbed him.

When he got to the church, a place of stark white shiplap overtopped by a mosque-like dome, they had already taken Popper in. The hearse stood at the side of the building and fewer than twenty cars were parked in front. Jesse heard the minister saying, "The Good Book says we have to love one 'nother, but nowhere does it say we have to like 'em." Smiling to himself, Jesse went inside and sat on a back row. His first impression was that of having free-fallen into a tropical garden, such was the array of flowers about the place and the scents that were interminglings of roses, carnations, and perfume. He was not the only white person there, so he relaxed and rolled with the flow of the minister's words, words that went on to say that Popper was not only liked but loved as well. Jesse drifted off on this and tried to remember where the distinctions of love and like had made themselves apparent and then he recalled that the play *Death of a Salesman* had dwelt on such. He thought of the money, of Rosa, of Popper. A large black woman in a florally overladen dress had swooned and had to be carried from the nave. So swift was her removal, so choreographed, that he wondered why white people did not have passion prancers in their own churches.

After thirty minutes the service ended and Jesse walked with the other mourners past the coffin. The undertaker had done excellent work and Popper's features were but slightly distorted from the work of the axe.

Suddenly it all fell on him—Rosa, Popper, the money, life in general—and he moved quickly to a side exit shielding his eyes from the gaze of several dark men who gave him only perfunctory notice. He sat in his car and sobbed heavily until the procession was gone. He felt awake at last, aware at last, and, somehow, cleansed at last. Starting the car, he looked at the little white church and whispered, "Old man, rest easy."

He drove past a liquor store, slowed, sped on.

Somehow booze poured on this day would have given it the wrong color, and without analyzing this strange new feeling of not wanting a drink, Jesse looked for food. A place called Coco's lay just ahead, and its blue shutters and balanced shrubbery impressed him. Inside, the tables were overladen with white cloths and the flatware had the heft and balance of fine dueling pistols. He felt a little saddened by it, the newness of the place, the radiation of hope and expectation on the faces of the owners and waiters, for he knew that within six months to a year it would be closed and boarded and that weeds would be growing in the parking lot; good restaurants survive in the South, but fine and fancy restaurants never do, and, as this one was fine and fancy, it would not. He had a good steak on Spode China, was too hungry to relax and savor the luxury. He guessed that would come as he grew accustomed to being a rich man.

Having paid and gone out to the car, he admitted to himself that there was but one thing that would keep him sober tonight. Wheeling over onto the six-lane expanses of Poplar Avenue, he drove fifteen blocks, hung a right on Highland and drove through the guts of old Memphis, an area that had not lost its 1930s gentility. It was a route that he could have driven in his sleep, for during the past two weeks he had driven it twenty times, usually in the wee hours, usually drunk. He wondered whether Janice had ever driven past his own apartment, studied the lighted windows in pain, studied the darkened windows in even more pain, as he had her own. Probably not. Women don't suffer like men do, he assured himself, for their suffering is an ethereal thing that finally evolves into self-righteous masochistic martyrdom, while males undergo something much more tangible, something akin to an invisible wolf gnawing at the balls and the heart with teeth as hard and as cold as ice cubes. Muley down at Segregarious had once said, "My wife wants some money to go to Florida for a few days. She don't smoke and don't drink and she's got her own pussy, so what the hell does she need money for?" It had elicited laughter from Jesse and the others, but there had been a grain of homegrown truth in it; in that statement was an attitude, an enigma, an accusation, a plea. The sexes would forever need each other, and hate each other for that common need.

Janice's white Chrysler was in its standard place at the apartment complex, and he drove in off the street and parked beside it. As ever, he counted the eleven bric-a-brac steps up to the second level and the old anticipation was still there. *Just be cool and don't say anything stupid,* he warned himself, aware that hundreds of millions of men over hundreds of years had been, and were now, and forever would be, approaching doorways with the same thought in mind: *Just don't do anything stupid.*

"Hey, kid. I came for the Coniff album," he said, feeling stupid.

Janice smiled, said nothing, waved a hand inward toward the living room. As he entered, Jesse regarded this as a good sign, this silence and these hand signals that were anything but the rage that had ended their last meeting.

"Speak of next year and the devil laughs," Janice said. "That's an old Japanese proverb."

Jesse sat on the couch and ran his hands over the puffy corduroy material. God, the good times that they had had on this couch.

"I guess the old Japanese who said it knows what it means," he said.

"When you left here screaming two weeks ago you said next year would be damned well soon enough to—"

Jesse lifted a hand, palm outward, a call for peace. "You want me back or do you want me to go?"

Janice felt the upper portion of her bodice and touched a button. For a moment it appeared that she might be about to undress there in that belovedly bitchy and taunting way that she had done when they were new and fresh and exciting with each other, when they might have sex in a department store dressing room or, as had once happened, in a used car lot in the back seat of an unlocked Cadillac. He knew that above those white high heels, caressed by the white summer frock, there was one of the most magnificent and flawless bodies that he had ever beheld, fondled, licked, kissed, filled with all the passion that one man could offer one woman in a lifetime, a body whose alabaster smoothness was the paragon of a billion fantasies of a billion males, a body so made for love that he had at times felt infamous for doing to it some of the things that he had done, desecratory things but things desecratory in the irrational lunges and slaverings of ardor.

The memories hung there between them for the greater part of a minute. Her hand did not leave the button; his eyes did not avert from her own.

Jesse stood, went to the door, blew her a kiss. She smiled at him. He went outside and down the eleven steps. It had been a heavy moment and he was happy that they had not blown it. Like all who love, they both knew that the invisible rope that tethered them to the core of another being was unbroken. She would be there for him, but not tonight; he would be there for her, but not tonight. From somewhere came the thought that there are times when love transcends sexual need. It was a new thought for him, and he was slightly puzzled by it.

When he got back to his apartment the phone was ringing.

"Hello."

"J? O. RB 20."

"Sure."

He had not had time even to turn on his lights. He went outside, started the Chevy, and was back in night traffic less than four minutes after having left night traffic. God, what a day this had been! What a day it was yet being! Rosa, riches, Popper's funeral, Janice, and now Ollie Colbert with something staple to chew on. As he drove up Union and turned left on Parkway it came to him that maybe this day was but a panic opera whose music was a mélange of threnody, symphony, and delta blues. Music? Oh, Jesus, he had forgotten the Coniff album at Janice's, which was a good thing, since it would forever be there as an excuse to go back, which was why he had left it there in the first place, a wise lover always secreting a go-fetch in the abode of the beloved. His mind ticked and tocked like a timepiece that registered the occurrences of a secret cosmos, and he knew again that each human is a secret cosmos that cadences within, due to forces from without. Tick and tock. Now old Ollie Colbert, his pal since eons ago when they had rookied together, had called him with the code that they had devised, a sort of pig Latin that was mostly initials and numbers. "J" meant Jesse, "O" meant Ollie, "RB 20" meant meet at the old red and blue porno house in twenty minutes. JORB20. That was gibberish to any but themselves who might have been listening, ergo, Ollie was at a place wherein he might have feared being overheard or maybe he thought the phones were bugged. One thing was certain, it was not a frivolous matter. Ollie was on to something important, something that would not wait.

Red and Blue was now dun colored and had been for five years, but this bit of camouflage on the part of the owners had made Jesse and Ollie even more secure in their code chat. It was a natural, for who would ever suspect that police would conduct exchanges of information in a place that was the heart of depravity itself? Jesse and Ollie Colbert, that was who.

He chuckled as he parked the Chevy, eyeing the usual slitherings of queers, night crawlers and unfulfilled husbands who moved like erratic moths in and out of the light and shadows of the theater's exterior. He went in, past the rubber dong case, past the rows of twisted-flesh books and down the long hallway that resembled a barely lighted cellblock, the wooden doors on either side bearing a number or the inevitable handscrawled sign "Out of Order."

"Hey sailor, want a hot time?" Ollie Colbert whispered from number 19.

Jesse went in and Ollie locked the door behind him, the rasp of metal gonglike in the tiny confines of the booth. Ollie dropped a quarter into a slot and the white pasteboard square on the door flared to life. A blonde was swimming in a pool whose waters had become tainted by leaves from a nearby bush; alas, she was motioning for a muscular youth to remove said leaves.

"Same old shit," said Ollie. "You'd think the grocery boy and the plumber and the swimming pool cleaner would have been replaced over the years. How's it going?"

"It's been a weird day."

"It's about to get weirder. You been up to anything Alcatrazzy?"

"Such as?"

"You tell me," said Ollie.

"I thought I just did. Dammit, Ollie, this is twice in two days you've—"

Colbert interrupted: "Yes, it's twice in two days that I've tried to be your goddam friend. I ain't gonna stay here long, so let's get some shit straight—you hold out on me and friend or no friend, I'll consider it torn. You got that?"

Jesse looked at the movie on the door. The pool cleaner had the woman's bathing suit off and he was going down on her in a closeup. Her tongued area was iridescent with the man's spittle. "You're serious about this. I can tell," he said.

"Damn right. What's with you and Popper?"

Jesse looked away from the movie and tried to make out Ollie's face in the pornoglow. All he could discern was that Ollie was not smiling, was not even close to it. "I was a customer of his, and I went to his funeral today. What else do you want to know?"

"What I want to know is what you had on Popper or he had on you. Were you doing a job for him?"

"Maybe."

"Yeah, sure. But it's a *maybe* that might be of some consequence. Here's an old black shoeshine man that never had five hundred dollars in his life, so he gets murdered with an axe and good old public-spirited Jesse DeVaron goes to his funeral. You're shitting an old shitter, Jesse baby, and I don't like it."

"Can I make you a deal, Ollie?"

Ollie nodded. "If it's a two-way street, we'll deal."

"Okay, give me two days, and then I'll give you what I got, if I've got anything. Fair?"

"Fair enough."

Jesse felt relieved. The simple truth of the matter was that he hadn't given Popper or the letter or the cross a great deal of thought in the last couple of days. Business-wise, he had gotten two calls from disgruntled spouses who did not want to give their names just yet, opting for what they called "time to think it over." One was a husband over in Germantown who suspected his wife of playing hide-the-sausage with someone, the other a wife from Whitehaven who was saving from her household money in order to pay two hundred down to have her husband followed.

"You didn't call me here to ask why I went to Popper's funeral, Ollie; the word *Alcatrazzy* got my attention. What gives?"

Ollie smiled lopsidedly and stood. The projector's light was now taken from the door and imposed itself on his chest. He was the only cop in Memphis who had a couple going at it dog fashion on his shirt front.

"Give me forty-eight hours, Jesse. The same forty-eight I got from you." With that he snapped the lock and left the booth. The movie went off and Jesse found himself alone in the darkness. Those porno-booth smells of cleaning fluid and cardboard and semen-soured floors assailed his nostrils. He felt very alone, very confused. Two weeks before, during their fight, Janice had told him that he was selfish, cold, unfeeling. He searched his psyche now to determine whether it was true. The tears shed today in the car after the funeral had been real enough, but what had they really been for? Himself? Perhaps the Ollies and Janices of the world were but the bees of compassion flying around the petals of his ego after all. Hell, some eight or ten hours ago he had been told that his only living relative was dead and he had promptly gone to a funeral, had a steak, visited a lover, chatted in a porno movie booth with a cop; any way one viewed it, he wasn't exactly prostrate with grief. Maybe they were right—maybe Jesse DeVaron was just a self-serving sonofabitch. It would be a good thing to brood over, but some other time. Right now he wanted a drink.

When he got back to his apartment he took off his jacket, threw it over a chair and was in the small kitchen making a Dickel and Coke when the doorbell rang. He thought of Janice, ran through the living room, and opened the door.

"Mr. DeVaron?" one of the two asked. He was young, blonde and fair while the other was dark, acne-pitted of face and mostly bald. Both wore suits, white shirts, and conservative ties. They might have passed for conventioneers at the night of the big banquet to an untrained eye, but Jesse saw something else in their demeanor, and he did not smile. "Sure. What can I do for you?"

They flashed ID cards and Blondie said, "I'm Agent Reeder; this is Agent Riggazi. May we have a minute of your time?"

A minute of your time. Jesse fought the urge to laugh. These officious bastards from the FBI always made a roust sound like a high tea at the Hasty Pudding Club. He stepped backward and ushered them in. Reeder looked a bit like a male version of Cybill Shepherd, while Riggazi's drollness conjured up images of a dark Don Rickles without the smartass. A perfect pairing, good cop and bad cop. Jesse tried to imagine how many suspects the two had charmed and intimidated with their angel food and razor blade appearances. Hundreds, probably. But he wasn't about to be one of them. He told them to sit, offered them drinks that were refused almost by rote, and sat down to face them.

"Mr. DeVaron, we are conducting an investigation that has no portent of threat to yourself. If you would prefer to have an attorney present it can be arranged. Having said that, I will ask this: is all that I have said clear to you and do you wish to have an attorney present?"

"No. You people do good work. I've got a J. Edgar Hoover badge from when I was ten. True blue." He waited for them to smile. They did not. "Okay, ask me your questions," he said, somewhat cowed, embarrassed.

"Very well, Mr. DeVaron. Recently a man named

Washington Clark was murdered. We would like to know just what you knew about his activities prior to his death."

"He shined shoes."

There was a silence. Everybody looked quizzically at everybody else. "Very funny," said Riggazi. His voice was like iced blood being scraped from a bayonet.

"Funny? No. I'd hate to shine shoes for my daily bread. I don't bend over so well. Hurts my lower back."

"There's other things that hurt worse," said Riggazi.

Reeder lifted a hand and Riggazi nodded. Taking a small tablet from his coat pocket, Reeder said, "Mr. DeVaron, there's no need to play the open-faced fool with us, because you're no fool. Let me tell you some of the things that we already know about you: you served in Vietnam, served seventeen years on the Memphis police department, achieving the rank of lieutenant. You drink. Your first wife was Rhonda Huddleston, who now lives in Teaneck, New Jersey. You hang on to life by being an erstwhile private investigator. You currently see a lady named Janice Nixon. You own a white Chevrolet Caprice and an old Ford convertible under whose seat you keep an emergency bottle of George Dickel. You frequent a bar called Segregarious." He shut the tablet and replaced it in his pocket. "I could go on and on, but it would be an exercise in superfluity. May we talk now?"

Jesse licked his lips. The kitchen looked to be a million miles away. God, for just one jolt of George and Coke right now. But that was a pleasure that would have to wait, for he needed his wits a hell of a lot more than he needed a drink just now. Because right now those wits were divergent strands of a spider's web that were forming a pattern that had his blood afizz. Garman's letter and its strange message, and the little cross that had fallen onto the bar were meshing with Ollie's calling him to Red and Blue which was meshing with this visit from these two Eagle Scout federal assholes. He thought of the line from the Drifter's song, *Now I hang by a thread over the canyon of doom.* . . . It made a lot of sense and no sense at all; one thing that did make sense, however, was that

Charleston Garman's letter was not the work of a deranged mind. Yes, there was certainly excitement to be had from this, maybe money, maybe both. He would stonewall it. Let these two bastards chew all they wanted—they would get a little juice, but he would still be the dog with the meat.

He said, "I'll talk, but it'll be an exercise in superfluity. You be superfluous and I'll be unctuous."

"Very funny," growled Riggazi.

"He's quite witty, isn't he?" Jesse said to Reeder.

"Prattle will avail nothing, Mr. DeVaron. Tell me about Washington Clark."

"I knew him for a few years. He had a nephew named Charlie something. He was a good old man who lived alone. I went to his funeral today because I felt sorry for him."

Reeder and Riggazi looked at each other with the imperious manner of fraternity brothers who have caught a pledge in a dubious activity. The tiniest hint of a smile played about Riggazi's cruel lips, but it was Reeder who spoke: "That was a strange thing to say."

"What was?"

"Here is a man whose life you summed up in a few words, and you mentioned his nephew. Why?"

"Why what?"

"Why the mention of the nephew?"

"Because as far as I know, it was his only living relative. He also had a helper named Donkey Baby, but that's not the kind of thing you'd put on old Popper's tombstone. Jesus, if you guys would just tell me what this is about, maybe I could—"

Reeder interrupted: "The nephew's name was Charleston Garman. Does that ring a bell with you?"

Jesse put on his best deep-thought face and nodded. "Yeah, seems like that might be right, but everybody always called him Charlie."

"Was he religious?"

"How the hell would I know? This city has got four hundred churches, half of which are black. You might want to get out your little tablet and write that down."

"Perhaps I will. How about you, Mr. DeVaron? Are you religious?"

"I often see visions after my seventh or eighth shot of bourbon." They did not laugh.

"How do you feel about Catholics?"

"They have statues and candles and the head knocker is a Polack. There's a joke in there somewhere, but I'm too tired to look for it."

"Did you ever know of Washington Clark or his nephew, Charleston Garman, to make disparaging remarks about priests or about the Catholic religion in general?"

"No, but I'm beginning to get it, I think. The Catholics murdered Popper over something and the nephew is tied up in it somehow. Am I close?"

"Do the names Don Phillips, Emerson Wolfe, or Lengus de Cristo mean anything to you?"

Jesse thought for a moment and said, "De Cristo is Spanish for 'of Christ' or 'to Christ.' I don't know what Lengus means. As for the others, no. The only Wolfe I know is Fowler Wolfe, but he's a farmer over in Arkansas. Maybe he doesn't like Catholics; you'd have to go ask him."

Reeder was looking strained. He ran his fingers through his fawny hair and formed his lips into a little pooched asshole, the actions of one whose thoughts are dark. "There were five white men at the service today. Did you know any of the others?" he asked.

"No," Jesse said truthfully. "Probably customers of long standing, like me. I'm sure they'll tell you they don't know me, either. It's called corroboration."

"We know," said Rigazzi.

Reeder looked about the room like a housewife seeking one last surface to dust. Finally he said, "Well, Mr. DeVaron, I'm sure that you are aware that this little visit was necessary, and I'm just as sure that you'll keep it to yourself. We may have to visit you again, but I think not. Have we been fair with you?"

"You've been fair, and I hope I've helped in whatever it is you're dealing with." *God, I'm a phony sonofabitch,* he was thinking.

When they were gone Jesse went to the kitchen and looked at the clock radio. It was just after eleven. He fixed a George and Coke and went back to his living room. He sat down. It had been a long day, a time-slice of wonder and terror and confusion and sadness. Days like that come into every life, but seldom with such diversity.

He took a healthy pull from the glass, grimaced, almost vomited. He was almost at the puke-drink stage, that stage that a lifetime of talking to rummies had assured him was coming, that stage in which one buys that one pint in the morning, every morning, takes the first drink and pukes it up and, having done so, can kill off the rest of the bottle. An old barfly had once told him that an alcoholic is a person who sculptures his own perfection of being with a chisel of booze. Jesse mulled the statement and found that it made sense, up to a point; however, the barfly might have added that in the end the sculpture falls apart every time. Yes, Jesse DeVaron was going to quit drinking, first thing tomorrow. Yes, things were going to change.

Things had already changed within five minutes, the whiskey having floated up to where it massaged his mind and allowed him to see clearly just what had happened today.

The money that he had gotten from the doctor had changed from being a monstrous amount to something paltry and embarrassing.

Janice had changed from being a ninety-foot goddess in his jealous fantasy to only another woman who yet wanted him.

Rosa's death was a change from sense of family to sense of orphanhood.

But Popper's funeral and the call from Ollie and the visit at Red and Blue and the subsequent visit from the FBI were change within change. Votan lives. Within those two words Charleston Garman had changed from simply probably insane to dangerous.

Four hundred thousand dollars was a change in anybody's life. He had become a rich man, with a rich man's arrogance, a rich man's ease of thought, a rich man's purposes and demeanor. He looked about the apartment and felt trapped whereas until now he had always felt homey and secure, and he looked at his clothing and dishes and furniture and felt ashamed of them.

After making another drink, stronger this time, he went to the window and looked out at the city. The minimum-wage unwashed were out there sweeping and polishing and guarding and hauling away, maggots and carrion eaters for the well-to-do like himself.

He returned to his chair and thought of the things that he could now have, things that heretofore had been dream objects: Cadillac, townhouse, M-1 rifle.

Votan lives. What did it mean?

Hip Willis and Donkey Baby had said that Popper was acting paranoid. Now Popper was murdered. Now Jesse had the letter from which the little cross and the little letter and the soft voice of God had fallen. Now Ollie Colbert had said, *What have you been up to lately?* and Jesse had smart-assed him and stalled him. And now the FBI had visited.

Votan lives. Tomorrow he would find out just what or who in hell Votan was, even if he had to tear the goddam library apart.

"Rest easy, old man," he said, lifting his glass to Popper's spirit, hoping to feel something. He felt nothing, and nothingness made him feel good.

Thirteen

A fine, misty rain drifted into the foothills of Louisiana just as darkness fell. The pines quickly turned from dark green to black and the highway was no longer gray but became the shimmering dourness of lightly polished onyx.

Vernon "Cowboy" Cameron was not at all displeased by the soul-shrouding change in the weather; indeed, he could not have been happier. It was a happiness that was cloaked in sinister garb, however, for on this night Cowboy had a mission that was not at all alien to his nature. He was about to murder someone. Someone who, as his benefactor in viciousness had advised him, "deserved killing."

Yes, he was thinking as he turned on the truck's windshield wipers, you had to hand it to the Order, these men of God were good—no, *great*—at rooting out the hidden vipers who dwelt under the great rock that was the Constitution of the United States. Emma Lazarus and her poem be damned! The huddled masses were unhuddling in ways that made the attitudes of Caucasian Christianity a thing laughable, vulnerable, impotent, and the ship of state was listing to port, port being left, left being . . . Communist! One had but to put things in such perspective and read between the lines to see who was behind it all. Someday when the CIA and the FBI and the Order all came together the way God and George Washington had meant for it to be, well, Vernon Cameron would be counted very high in that great Roll Call. When that wondrous day came they would summon him up for recognition and then they would tell how at one time he worked for both the CIA and the Order, his innate deftness in these matters allowing him to perform his machete ballet on two stages that were two in illusion only. *E Pluribus Unum*, it said on the coins. One from many.

In the haze a distant ochre glow caught his attention and he slowed the truck. Rolling down the window, feeling the almost tastable air with its heavy water content, he listened to the sliceslush sound of cars out on the two-lane blacktop. The glow materialized into a light bulb hanging out over the facade of a country grocery store, an unpainted and dreary place with front porch, Pepsi box, and gas pumps in front on the gravel driveway. Above the porch roof, like an ugly woman wearing a beautiful diamond ring, a gaily-etched sign of red and white proclaimed Huong Grocery. Behind the place was a shack with window boxes, and an old bent-fendered Buick.

Cowboy left his motor running, stepped down into the damp gravel, felt the kiss of night mist at the back of his shirt. Opening the truck's tool box, he took out the machete, thought better of it, dropped it back into the box. After all, the Mormon women had been *white*, and this Chink that had offended Cowboy's friend named Cartwheel did not deserve to drink out of the same bottle as the white women, much less die on the same blade. Now a heavy gauge flashlight caught his attention. Weighing three pounds, its round globe beginning to rust from disuse and cavalier relegation to the tool box, he dredged it up and hefted it, made little chopping motions with it. Two years ago he had taken it from a policeman who had swung it at him, a swing that had been quite ineffectual, since the policeman's trousers had been locked about his ankles as he staggered from the squad car amid the screams of the woman who had lain there in the seat with him. Cowboy had whipped the man soundly, had told him that his consortion with harlots was not in the best public interest. He had been angry then, but now he smiled.

He went onto the porch, opened the screen door, and smelled the rush of scent that hovers forever unchangeable in country grocery stores. Behind the counter stood a short male with gray-black hair, his eyes expressing that unrelenting sorrow that is the way of the unsmiling Oriental. He was a very small man, perhaps five feet four inches, perhaps one hundred pounds.

"I help you?" he asked.

Cowboy nodded to the tiers of cigarettes behind the man. "Pack of Camels," he said.

As the small man turned, Cowboy swung the flashlight and heard the dull pop of bone. The man's head shuddered as if from electric shock, the gray-black hair leaping from either temple and resettling as quickly as a cobra might strike and recoil. Blood dribbled onto the man's shoulders as he sagged behind the counter, went to his knees, collapsed onto and into himself as an emptied sack might.

Cowboy now had the strangely peaceful sense of standing outside himself and watching himself, the thinking entity separated from the physical entity. The thinking self watched as the performing self walked of its own volition behind the counter and continued to beat on the head and face of the Oriental. The beating continued until that roundness at the top of the torso was reminiscent of something that had been exploded and overlain with cherry pulp. After a time that might have been two seconds more or two minutes more, the performing self rose up, casually rubbed the stress from its back, jerked a sack of potato chips from a steel rack beside the cash register, and began to eat. The thinking self started to speak but was halted by memory: Never say anything to a person with food in his mouth, he'll choke.

A car sloshed by on the dark and wet highway. The thinking self heard it but the eating self continued to stare away at some object at the far side of the store.

Cowboy rubbed his eyes. He was very sleepy. The squeaking cadences of the windshield wipers were protesting against the dryness of the windshield. He was in a small city, but he could not remember what city it was; neither could he recall why he had come to it. Now he saw that he was wearing a light blue shirt, a curious bit of personal trivia, and made more curious by the knowledge that he had worn a tan shirt out of Texas this morning. Too, there was a bundle on the floor on the passenger side that had appeared as a rope of light passed from a streetlamp and illuminated the interior of the cab. A scorch of fear stung his cheeks, caused them to feel as if he had shaved with ground glass.

At the outer fringe of the city was an all-night gas station, one of those ugly but necessary blots on the landscape that are forever managed by someone very young or very old and unhappy to be there. It would be here that he could get his bearings, Cowboy reasoned, and he could do so without telegraphing his confusion. The sign read HEP-UR-SEF. He drove in off the highway, inserted the nozzle, activated the pump, and went inside. The man who ran the place was about sixty years old and his face was mottled with blackheads and he had no left arm.

"Korea," the man said.

"How's that?" Cowboy asked.

"Folks always want to know how I lost my arm but they never ask. I just say the word 'Korea' and you can see the question marks drain out of their face. You gonna fill up?"

"Yeah. What's the name of this town?"

"Magnolia."

"Louisiana?"

The man shook his head. "Arkansas. You passed the Louisiana border some forty miles back. You must've been on the road all day. It does that to me, too." He looked at Cowboy's hands. "I used to be a painter myself, a good one, too, before I lost my arm."

"How's that?"

"You got red paint on your fingernails. Turpentine is the best thing goin' for gettin' paint off."

Cowboy paid the man and went back out to the truck. Removing the nozzle from the tank spout, he squirted a bit of gasoline on his hands and rubbed them together. Before he pulled away into the night he looked again at the bundle on the floor. It was his tan shirt. Jutting from the rumpled cloth were the bent and bloody flashlight and a potato chip sack. Two miles from the gas station he stopped the truck at a little concrete bridge on whose abutment was a plaque: WPA-1939. There was a dampness on the shirt as he grasped it, a crusting and slightly odiferous dampness. He crossed the highway and threw shirt and contents into the little stream. The bundle hit the water in an area that was dappled silvery-white by the moon. For a moment the shirt hung heavily in the water, refused to move. And then the flashlight fell away and the shirt and the small sack drifted out of the dappled area and went on down the stream to where great trees shadowed the dark water even darker.

Fourteen

"Somewhere there is truth, but I haven't found it yet," said Brylette. She rolled over onto her stomach and felt the coolness of the sheets against her breasts and thighs.

"A good woman always likes to be thought a whore and a whore always likes to be thought a good woman," said Ellen Harrison Rogers Talbott. She kissed the glowing and fine and almost-invisible hairs at the concavity of Brylette's spine and allowed her left hand to wander down to the woman's hips. "The wife of a GM vice president once said that to my mother at a lawn party and my mother asked her to leave." Her hand went further and she felt the slick dampness that was mostly her own spittle.

"Is that a truth?" Brylette asked.

"Yes, I think it is," said Ellen. She lay back on the pillow so that she might look up into Brylette's eyes, those incredible green eyes.

"I've noticed that truth is a luxury that is the province of sophomores," said Brylette. "The word *sophomore* is Latin for *foolish wisdom*. Did you know that?"

"I may have read it somewhere," said Ellen, "but my original question was, 'Can a person be true to oneself and true to society at the same time?' "

Brylette took Ellen's left hand, kissed the wedding ring. Licking the two-carat marquisette diamond suggestively, she asked, "How true are you being to him?"

"True enough. If nothing is expected, then nothing can be awarded, nor can it be diminished." Ellen hoped her words were poised, polished, precise.

Brylette smiled. "I think that's just another way of saying that what he doesn't know won't hurt him. It's a tired old adage, but a good one. You and I are both living by it right now. Night before last in Mazatlan we took on three Korean businessmen, I for money, you for . . . whatever reason. I know why they were there and why I was there, but why were you there? For some sort of truth?"

Ellen shrugged, her shoulders reddening slightly, as did her temples. She had wanted to exhibit a keen and facile mind to Brylette, but the woman was taking her into treacherous intellectual waters. She wanted to say a retaliatory thing, which is the wont of the rich who are bested by the intelligent, but her sexual need and the passion that she was beginning to feel with this woman made her remain silent. Brylette, with the red hair and the eyes of incredible green, had by now lain her head on the pillow and was lazing, or perhaps dozing, in that precious nothingness that follows orgasm.

Feeling that numbing rage of those who are sexually cheated, Ellen eased herself off the bed, went into the bathroom and rinsed her mouth and chin. She studied herself in the mirror for a long while, paying special attention to her tongue and lips. They looked the same. She had imagined that burying her face between another woman's thighs for a jaw-cracking thirty minutes would have left some indelible mark, perhaps a scarlet *L*, for lesbian. But there was no *L* for lesbian, nor was there an *S* for Sappho, just as there was no *P* for pervert. Could it be that she would suddenly develop chest hair, muscles, deep voice and swagger? Holden Caulfield had said somewhere in *Catcher in the Rye* that he kept expecting to suddenly turn into a flit. She recalled that the other girls in class had laughed when she had asked what the word meant. Now she was waiting to turn into a dyke, to assume the characteristics of dykehood, right down to boots and rodeo belt. No, it was not to be, for here in these last two weeks of her twenty-ninth year she had learned a truth about something that had bothered her since adolescence, that truth being that no matter what mothers say, the use of the human body for sexual purposes does not leave a mark; rather, it washes away the mental marks left by prepossessing, cold, steely-eyed mothers who closed their eyes and endured on their own wedding nights. The black man named Garman had left no smudge marks on her belly; the Mexican bellhops had marked her with no brown effluvia (semen from both had been pearly, abundant and, it was to be hoped, nonfattening); the Koreans had contorted her into a *ménage à quatre* that defied most laws governing human physiology.

It was the Koreans who had introduced her to Brylette, the latter being admitted to the room as Ellen lay naked and too exhausted to move, or to think of moving. In halting English the fat Korean had told Brylette that he was sorry that they had not needed her again on this night, that the beautiful blonde American on the bed had come to them in the lounge and had embarked on overtures that were unquestionable in any language, that they hoped that she understood and was not angry with them. They had bowed and left the room. Brylette had gotten a warm washcloth from the bathroom and laved Ellen's body, cooing and nodding as the blonde said repeatedly, "I want to leave here, leave here." An hour later, Brylette driving, Ellen asleep in the back seat of the Mercedes; they had headed eastward out of Mazatlan. At sunrise Brylette had stopped the car and they had changed seats and the hegira away from the secret occurrence in Mazatlan had continued, Ellen driving all day, crossing into Texas at about noon. At nightfall Brylette had awakened and it was then, after sharing little more than a washcloth and an automobile, that the two women had begun to talk. Brylette was a Ph.D. in Fine Arts at a small college in northern Florida, had been to Mexico for two weeks, had always wanted to turn a trick, had done so with the Koreans for five hundred dollars, felt no guilt, dreaded the coming fall semester. Ellen had said very little, preferring to remain enigmatic and thus stimulating, for she had known back in Mazatlan while being washed that she and this unknown woman with the coppery hair and the incredible green eyes would be lovers. At Port Arthur, Texas, they had staggered sun-dulled and road-beaten into a motel, had showered, slept together. Nothing more, until this morning.

Ellen returned to the bed and sat, the sudden list of the mattress causing Brylette to sigh and open her eyes. After looking at each other for a time without smiling, it was Ellen who said, "I want you to know a truth, but it will violate a trust. Will you share it with me?"

Now Brylette smiled. This pretty blonde woman named Ellen was but a child in many ways, and this was a child's way of endearing herself. The licking of the diamond and the subsequent words had opened a curtain of symbolism that had embarrassed them both; however, Brylette hoped that her own embarrassment had not shown, that her placing of her head on the pillow had been interpreted as nothing but laziness. It would not do to play mind games with this one. Accept a bit of love, give a bit of love, leave smiling.

"Yes, angel, I'll share with you."

She watched with bemusement as Ellen donned a robe, grabbed her car keys, and hurriedly left the room. These were the zealous actions of a little girl overwhelmed by the need to share a great secret with mommy. She tried to imagine Ellen's mother, conjured a face that was adoring, benevolent, nurturing, a blonde lady like Ellen with skin flawless and eyes the soft blue of iris petals. She flexed her fingers in parody of massage. Yes, a massage would do it, massage being the best ice-breaker employable by those who wish to give love. She had been loved well, and the time to return it was at hand.

"Is this what I think it is?" Ellen asked. She closed the door behind her and reached into the pocket of her robe. The object presented, dropped on the bed, was a square of vaguely yellowish-ochre. Embedded into its face were approximately forty perfectly straight lines of something that resembled tiny pin pricks, scratchings, delineations the size of mites; indeed, Brylette was at first reminded of an orderly procession of almost invisible insects marching with military precision across a citrine rectangle, this rectangle being wafer-thin, four inches by six, and quite heavy—three pounds, perhaps four.

"Gold," she said quietly.

"I thought so. The weight, the dullness of the color. But I wasn't sure."

When Brylette looked up at Ellen the green eyes were troubled, preoccupied. She placed the object on a pillow, went to her overnight case, came back to the bed wearing eyeglasses that were *academe* at its most pronounced; the lover had become a professor, the bed of passion had become a laboratory. Ellen instantly wished that she had not introduced the object, for all warmth had gone from the room. She felt somehow deserted, uninvited, relegated to secondary importance.

"Tell me about this," said Brylette.

Ellen told of the black man in Hermosillo, of his begging, no, *commanding* her to take whatever it was to Memphis, Tennessee, of his caveats of calamitous occurrence if this fell into the wrong hands, of her unawareness of what it was that she was transporting. "Until the night before last, the night we met," she summarized. "Up to then it was sort of a game, something that was . . . well . . . dilletantish in a sexy way." Her eyes clouded. "I was caught up in a fantasy of being involved in some sort of intrigue, like a spy, maybe, a carryover from my Nancy Drew days. And then night before last in Mazatlan, just before I met those Koreans, and you, I couldn't stand it anymore. I had to look, in spite of what he had told me. I knew that the whole Mexican sex trip was over, that I was going home. But I didn't want to get caught at the border with . . . something. Do you see why I had to look, why I had to violate his trust? I don't know why, but it scares me; it scares me more than coming to the border yesterday. The guards saw the Mercedes and you asleep in the back seat and they just waved me through. I couldn't believe it! It was almost as if they knew not to bother me. Does it mean something, or nothing? Am I being paranoid?" She smiled awkwardly; it was a smile in which fear and self-effacement and confusion were melded.

"Pandora lives," said Brylette, continuing to peruse the pinpricks. "There's Greek here, and something that looks like Arabic. And these feathered serpents and sundials are Incan, or maybe Mayan. Strange, four or five cultures seem to be represented here. How many of these are there?"

"Twenty."

"And Hebraic-Phonecian." She moved her fingertips slowly along the tiny lines for two minutes and then said, "It seems to be a very intricate code of some sort. Two letters in Greek followed by one Mayan symbol, followed by Arabic. Strange. But the sequence is not repeated." She gazed again, immersed herself in the quest for something formulable. At last she looked up and said, "I have found one word, that is if I remember my Greek alphabet. The rest is hieroglyphics."

"Oh, what word is that?"

"Patmos."

Ellen shook her head.

"It's an island somewhere off the coast of Greece. I don't know what the significance of all this is, but unless I'm wrong, this is very important." Again she studied the strange markings, laid the object on the pillow, and removed her glasses. "Tell me again about the black man," she said.

"I've told all I remember."

"And who did he tell you to take these things to? Someone in Memphis? Who was it?"

Ellen felt herself backing away mentally; these questions were rearing up from all sides as vipers in strike rage. It was time to lie. "I don't know. He said a man would meet me at . . . a certain place."

Brylette handed the golden plate over to Ellen. "Put it back," she said. "Put it back in your car and take it to Memphis to that person and then go home."

Ellen said nothing. She went outside, was gone for less than a minute. When she came back Brylette was in the shower. By some innate impulse, Ellen started to open the door and join her lover there, to wash her back, soap her feet, make soapy circular motions on her flat stomach, exhibit an obsequious manner that would re-create the mood of thirty minutes before. But she did not; rather, she doffed the robe, let it fall directly to the floor the way beauteous wantons did in the movies, and lay on the bed. She fluffed her blonde hair with her fingertips and waited. The sound of the water ceased, the toweling process was finished, and at last the door opened. Ellen felt herself quivering involuntarily, and she despised herself for it.

Brylette came and lay beside her. "Will you take me as far as New Orleans?" she asked. "I'll pay you."

"I'll take you anywhere that you wish to go," said Ellen. She touched the other woman's slightly-dampened hair and was amazed at the wonder of how precious it could feel.

"New Orleans will be adequate," said Brylette. "I know that you'd take me all the way to Florida, but that would open a chapter that neither of us is ready for. This is your first time, and certain boundaries have to be established. Besides, you're carrying something that little girls shouldn't carry. You're involved in some form of smuggling—God, that's an ugly word—and you should get rid of that gold as soon as possible. If it *is* gold, that is."

Ellen whispered, "I said I'd take you anywhere, and I meant it."

Brylette laughed coyly, rolled over and patted Ellen's stomach, her hand stopping, coming to rest between navel and pubic hair. "We're on divergent wave lengths. I'm thinking of your safety and you're thinking of love. We must do this my way, angel of mine, for I am older and wiser than thee." She patted again, this time letting her hand rest nearer the navel; the teasing process had begun.

Partially frustrated, partially curious, Ellen asked, "You said 'boundaries' and 'first time.' I don't understand."

"You're one of us now, and there are certain tacit laws that we abide by, not the least of which is that you never pull anyone from the closet. 'Evil and the appearance of evil' is Biblical, but it also applies to the gay community. At home, at the college, I am Dr. Brylette Fender, a pillar of society, a worker of good deeds, a committee member par excellence. 'Oh, Dr. Fender isn't married,' they say, 'but that's because she's superior to us and her mind is such that we mere mortals see, do, feel, and experience things that are beneath her; she doesn't need a man.' And they are right, of course—I don't need a man. That's why about every other weekend I trot down to Miami or over to Tampa. The greatest hypocrisies of humankind are surrounded by short and curly hair, dear, and don't you ever forget it."

Ellen kissed her on the forehead and said, "I love you."

Brylette scratched Ellen's tummy playfully and said, "Angel, you love me because you are now eating of the tree of reality for the first time, and I'm not belittling—I'm explaining. From this time forward you will always be in love, and you will always be afraid. The love you feel will be more intense because of the distance at which you will have to keep your lover, or lovers. Distant fires burn brighter; I don't know why that's true, but it is. We are all led by our sex organs more than by any other, and this subservience makes us ashamed, fearful and, at last, secretive. And it is from the secretive that passion and intensity grow. We who have feelings for our own gender are most secretive of all, and therefore most passionate. Do you understand me?"

"No," Ellen said quietly. "Am I *really* . . ."

"Yes, you are *really*. Some of us start asking that question early, some late, and some never know what is 'wrong' with themselves. If I were Queen of the World, the first thing I'd do is outlaw all euphemisms having to do with sex and love. 'Certain needs' is one, and there's the old standby 'tenderness.' Show me a woman who says she needs tenderness, and I'll show you one who could use the soft touch of another woman's tongue and hands. The problem is that they don't even know what they're asking for, and that they're too blinded by convention to hear themselves asking for it. God, the waste."

"But those men in Mazatlan, those Koreans, you—"

"I did it for money. And, admittedly, for a perverse giggle. One woman's naturality is another woman's perversity. That's my message; be what you are, but be safe doing it. There's an old song by Stephen Stills that contains the line, '. . . and there's a rose in the fisted glove, and the eagle flies with the dove . . .' and so forth. It's a summation of the purity and sanctity of self-knowledge. Not surprisingly, the song is called 'Love the One You're With.' "

Ellen smiled and said, " 'Love the One You're With.' That's not such a bad idea." She pulled Brylette to her, guiding the face that contained the lilting green eyes down to her breast. The mouth that had heretofore expounded the philosophy of Self now nursed gently, wetly, silently, and the hand that had teased now moved down to the base of Ellen's stomach, toyed with the soft and curly filament for a moment, and then moved beyond.

Fifteen

Emerson Wolfe sat in the lobby of the Hotel Peabody in Memphis. People were feeding popcorn to the famous Peabody ducks. There was much giggling and laughing and boozing. Wolfe wondered why people made such asses of themselves over ducks, for Christ's sake. He also wondered who cleaned up the duck shit at the end of the day when that skinny, pompous, wizened old black man led the ducks away with such ceremony. Among the other things puzzling him were whether he should get on this uncle of Garman thing or wait for Cowboy to drive up from Texas as had been planned, whether to kill Cowboy now or go ahead and use him and then kill him, whether to have Cowboy kill Don Phillips on sight or wait until later. Yes, Phillips would show up, probably, because whatever it was they were after had been sent to Memphis by Garman, probably. Probably—God, what a word. Probably the Company was by now swarming all over Northern Mexico looking for the three of them. Emerson Wolfe sweated, and thought of the word *probably*.

One hundred miles to the south of the Hotel Peabody, Ellen Harrison Rogers Talbott drove the Mercedes into an Exxon station in Grenada, Mississippi, and went to the rest room while the car was imbibing fuel. She wiped her reddened eyes with a bit of toilet tissue, saw that this did nothing to brighten the haggardness there, bent over the sink and rinsed her face. Applying rouge and lipstick, she momentarily felt human again. Eight hours ago the crying had begun, and it had been at times so intense in her northward journey that her lungs now ached. The placing of a God-sent treasure such as Brylette in a New Orleans bus terminal was tantamount to placing a nosegay in a slaughterhouse. But it was what Brylette had wanted, demanded, along with the admonition that Ellen was never to call or to write her. A bus terminal! God, how demeaning! And just as demeaning was Brylette's implication that these golden plates that lay beneath the mat in the trunk of the Mercedes were dangerous. Good! The more dangerous, the better! She would show Brylette, would send her a detailed letter of just how cleverly she had handled the delivery of the plates to one Washington Clark. Then Brylette would know that this was no common personage with whom she could trade off passion and then desert.

Ellen was barely out of the service station's driveway and back onto the great northward interstate before she began to cry again.

Two hundred miles to the southwest of Memphis, Vernon "Cowboy" Cameron was eating a hamburger in a Hot Springs, Arkansas, restaurant called The Embers. Something caught his eye and he left the table, walked to a greeting-card rack near the cash register and pulled out a sheaf of post cards. Depicted thereon, a blonde woman with a greatly exaggerated ass was turning and winking at the viewer over the caption: GET TO THE BOTTOM OF THINGS IN ARKANSAS. Cameron counted them: nine.

"How much are these?"

"Fifty cents each," a waitress replied.

He handed the woman a five dollar bill, tore the cards apart, threw them into a small trash can. "Little kids see them, makes for filth and degradation," he said.

The waitress said nothing; she only watched with mouth agape as the handsome but strange man in the cowboy garb went to his table and continued with his meal.

* * *

Well over a hundred miles to the northwest of Memphis, Dr. James Wagstaff drove the rented Oldsmobile off the highway and into a field that lay just outside the city limits of Mayfield, Kentucky. The tent was halfway up and the stacks of chairs had been taken down from the truck whose massive trailer bore the crudely painted words: EVANGELIST. REVEREND ORLISS TRIBBLE. HEALING THROUGH THE POWER AND GRACE OF OUR LORD AND SAVIOR. SERVICES NIGHTLY.

"May I help?" Dr. Wagstaff asked.

"Who you?" a boy of about twelve inquired. His T-shirt, once white, was a torn and filthy gray, and his blue jeans were matted at the thighs with grease.

"You from the law?" a voice called from behind the great trailer. "We got permission from the man owns this place." The speaker was slender and bald and middle aged. He wore a blue shirt, ragged gray pants, and black string tie. His shoes were scuffed white at the toes from use and neglect.

"No, I'm not from the law," said Dr. Wagstaff. "Just saw you here and wanted to help."

"You saved?" the bald man asked.

Dr. Wagstaff nodded. "I am now," he said.

Seventy miles to the northwest of Memphis, unaware that he had jumped ahead of his prey, Don Phillips threw a bottle across the bar and barely missed the bartender's head.

"No nigger in Union City, Tennessee, or anywhere else I can't whip!" he screamed. "Three goddam times I asked for another beer and three goddam times you said, 'Just a minute.' "

"I'm comin'," the person behind the bar said tremulously. A black head appeared, followed by a short black body. The bartender was humpbacked and as he opened a bottle of Miller and placed it on a tray Phillips noticed that the man's puffy little hands were fingered by stubby little outcroppings that resembled dog turds. It made him wonder why there seemed to be an inordinate number of deformed black people in the South; the farther he got into Dixie, the more freaks he encountered. Too, there wasn't enough IQ or education down here to fill a foot tub. He had read of the South in James Baldwin and Erskine Caldwell, but this was even beyond what they had caused him to believe. This very tavern was little more than a tarpaper shack with Nehi signs on the outside, and he hated it.

When the bartender left the beer, Phillips picked it up and walked to the door. He drank without tasting and looked out at that evening sun of song and story and was filled with a dreadful sense of melancholy. By God, before he left Memphis he would fuck a white woman and kill a white man. That would show somebody . . . something.

Six hundred and twenty miles to the southeast of Memphis, Dr. Brylette Fender stepped off the bus with eleven other passengers in Tallahassee, Florida. She was pleased that the journey was almost over, was even pleased that the bus company, in its infinite wisdom, was making her change buses after three hundred miles across the Gulf Coast and only fifty miles from her home. The rationale behind this happiness at being disturbed was the man named Rolf, a garrulous sewing machine salesman who had shared a seat with her all the way from New Orleans. Alas, he was employed by a company whose frugality demanded that he *ride a bus* to a sales meeting in Miami, and who are you and what do you do and, finally, do you fool around, ha ha. Well, she would have to put up with this jackass no more, for he was one of the passengers that this bus would carry south on its veerage from the terminal after the rest stop or, as Rolf had put it, "piss call." Ha ha. Men!

Rolf went to an enclosed phone booth, removed a credit card, read the number to the operator.

In Alexandria, Virginia, Vaughn Biddle picked up one of the three phones on his desk and said, "Yes?"

"Mr. Biddle, Rolf here."

"It's about time. Where the fuck you been?"

"Riding the Gulf Coast, just like I was supposed to be. What's got your nose out of joint?"

"Nothing, except it's Friday and the rest of the free world has got the jump on its boat races and john barleycorn. What have you got?"

"Okay, here it is: this Dr. Brylette Fender is clean from this end as far as I can tell. I don't think she knows shit."

"Yeah, from what we've got here it looks that way, too. Did you get any pictures?"

"Yessir. Fifteen or twenty, two of which might be of interest. The Michigan blonde came out of the motel this morning early and got something that looked like a piece of square metal out of the trunk of the Mercedes. I got a closeup of it. Maybe it's something, maybe not. One trouble with our little lashup is that they never tell us peons what it is we're supposed to pay attention to."

"Quit bitching, you're doing a fine job. Turn that roll of film over to the Tallahassee office and I'll handle it from there."

"What about this Dr. Brylette Fender? We just gonna let her go on?"

"Don't ask so goddam many questions, Rolf. Have a good weekend."

"Yessir." Rolf hung up. Now he had to ride the goddam bus in a deadhead back to New Orleans, pick up his government car at the bus terminal, and drive back to Houston. Hell, it would be well into Saturday before he got home.

Brylette waited for thirty minutes and at last the jerkwater bus company that would take her home called her aboard. There were only nine passengers, none of whom were amorous males. One was nice looking, but he wore blue jeans, work shirt, and carried his belongings in a box that had originally been the home of a three-pound tub of Crisco. Good. With fifty miles to ride, she would nap, recall Mexico, recall her session with Ellen, get off at home and none there would know that she had been turning tricks, sunbathing, eating pussy, being herself. It had been a good vacation and she was happy.

The grungy passenger with his belongings in the Crisco box sat four seats back and watched as Brylette fell asleep. He wondered who she was, what she was about, what this whole thing was about. But it was not his place to ponder. Biddle had told him to watch her until she got off and, by God, watch her he would. The Bureau really knew how to fuck up a Friday.

Unaware that things in Union City, Tennessee; Hot Springs, Arkansas; Tallahassee, Florida; Grenada, Mississippi; Reston, Virginia; Mayfield, Kentucky; and the Hotel Peabody in Memphis were converging on his life like ferrets in a labyrinth, Jesse DeVaron parked the old Ford convertible at a gun shop on Summer Avenue.

I wonder how long it will take him to say "Rotten, lousy," he was thinking as he looked at himself in the rearview mirror. *I'll bet I can get him to say it within thirty seconds.*

He stepped from the car and noted that a distant bank clock displayed the time as exactly 5:00 P.M. The hamburger place next door offered a violins-and-clarinets version of "Twilight Time." Their timing was all wrong and it irritated him. Two hours from now, when the sky was lavender and mauve, the song would be perfect. Now all it did was to fight the sounds of the traffic. I'm a purist he thought, closing the door of the old car. He wondered how the vehicle would look a month from now, when he had put a couple of grand into her refurbishment. Having money was going to be even more fun than he had thought.

He went into the gun shop and was instantly seized with the smells of Cosmoline and neat's-foot oil and bluing compounds and all those other ponderous olfactory presences that artillery exuded.

"How's the gun racket, Miller?"

"Oh, hi, Jesse. Tell you the truth, it's rotten, lousy. People come in here and look and leave," said Miller Bass.

Jesse smiled. He had done it in less than ten seconds. "Haven't seen you over at Segregarious lately. You on the wagon?"

Miller rubbed his belly and said, "A case of the summer flu. Can't seem to shake it." He turned sideways behind the counter and said, "Can you tell I've lost weight?"

"Yes," Jesse lied. But the truth was that Miller was the same portly, brown-eyed, brown-haired, round-faced little man with mustache and eyeglasses that Jesse had been drinking with off and on for two years over at Segregarious. All Jesse really knew about Miller Bass was that he liked an occasional drink, had emigrated southward after retiring from a post office job up north a couple of years ago, and that he liked him, liked his avuncular, countrified, no-bullshit way of looking at life. Miller Bass was an alloy of Burl Ives, Gomer Pyle, and Franklin D. Roosevelt, something taken from all the good parts of good America and placed into this round, kindly body.

Miller was looking at his visitor somewhat strangely. "Uh, what are you doing here, Jesse?"

An odd question; Jesse wondered whether Miller was taking too much of his flu medicine. The old man seemed addled, threatened, a bit irked. "Miller, baby, I'm here to buy that M-1 rifle we've talked about for the last year or so. The soldier in me wants to feel that heft again."

Miller's look grew bland and kindly again, "I got it. Come on back."

Jesse followed him into the back room. There were Pythons and Diamondbacks, Smith and Wessons, Remingtons and Marlins, shotguns, rifles, and pistols and racks for holding them, and gun cases and bluing kits and cleaning kits. Marveling at it all, Jesse estimated that there were enough weapons to kill everybody in Memphis in a matter of hours. It all made him feel at once quite secure yet slightly intimidated, an ambivalence that was not unlike meeting a very beautiful and very dangerous woman for the first time. But he dispelled all this by asking, "What are you going to stick me for it?"

Miller leaned down into an elongated box and withdrew

the M-1. It was cleaned, the strap was taut, and it was beautiful. "Eight hundred dollars American," he said with an impish smile. "I cleaned her up just yesterday, and you get that free. I'll also throw in two clips and fifty rounds of good old thirty-thirty ammo. That's cause you're my pal."

Jesse felt that he was being had, albeit lightly, and he also knew that the easy down-home demeanor with which Miller was greasing him gave him no way out. They went back to the front of the shop and Jesse wrote the check.

Thrusting a form at Jesse, Miller said, "You gotta fill this out, Jess." As Jesse wrote the older man asked, "Just for my own information, nosiness, if you want to call it that, what do you need with an M-1 rifle?"

"Nostalgia," Jesse answered. "I walked all over Fort Polk, Louisiana, with one of these things a few years back, carried it into Nam. Then the army, in its infinite wisdom, went to those goddam M-16 bastards that jam after two shots."

"Yeah, I know what you mean.

"Yogi Berra once said, 'Nostalgia ain't what it used to be,' " said Miller. "Old Yogi ain't as dumb as people give him credit for. He also said, 'You can observe a lot by watching.' I've been watching you, Jesse. You feel rotten-lousy about something. What is it?"

Jesse shrugged. "Women, business pressures, traffic lights, the whole ball of wax."

Miller looked at the rifle. "You aren't gonna do anything . . . *final,* are you?"

Jesse laughed and said, "No, not to myself, anyway."

"Can I ask you something else, then?"

"Sure."

"Why did you happen to buy this rifle just today, I mean just right now?"

"I came into some money, Miller. That's between me and you. And, too, like I said, I've always wanted one of these beauties." He picked the rifle up, opened the butt plate, saw that bore rod and cleaner tube were in place, closed it. Picking up the box of ammunition and the glassine bag that held the two clips, he said, "It's been fun, and you worry too much."

"In this rotten-lousy business I have to worry. Some of the people that come in here browsing, hell wouldn't have 'em."

"Next time you're over at Segregarious, I'll buy you a drink."

"The way that cheap bastard Muley mixes 'em, it would take six for me to get a buzz on."

"See you, Miller."

Jesse left Miller "Rottenlousy" Bass, placed the rifle and its accoutrements into the trunk of the Ford, and drove west on Summer. Memphis was winding down from Friday daytime and winding up for Friday nighttime. At a traffic light he snapped the hasp over the windshield, touched the button under the dash, and put the top down. Two teenage girls yelled from a Corvette in the next lane and an old couple in an Oldsmobile glared at him. All this made him aware for the thousandth time that people who come into the presence of an open convertible *must* say something, do something, exhibit something to the convertible's driver. As the light changed and he drove away he felt contempt for all the idiocies of humankind, but down where the moon did not shine in his soul he knew that the contempt was for himself and for the rifle that he had wanted for twenty years and for the fact that it did not make him as happy as he had hoped. He felt like a fool, felt that the world knew that he had just paid eight hundred dollars for a toy, a whim, a panacea that could not cure whatever it was that was the source of some unnamed distress. He had known disgruntled wives who bought clothing only to hang it unworn in closets until rummage sale time, and he hated them and he hated himself for having this afternoon become one of that ilk. God, what if they were right after all—what if money really did not buy happiness?

At the corner of Peabody and McLean he drove into the five-acre parking lot that skirted the great Memphis Public Library, parked, went inside. He felt swamped, overwhelmed, incredibly ignorant, small.

"Where are your religious books?" he asked a nice black lady.

"Books on religion?" she said, tweaking his grammar.

"No, religious books. Books that have seen the light, been baptized. Books that roll in the floor with the spirit and go on TV and ask for money and have gleaming teeth and lacquered beehive hairdos."

They laughed together. It was a uniquely American moment in which total strangers were bonded by bullshit. When the laughter was done she directed him to a well-lighted area that struck him with a sense of solemnity. There were dozens of shelves, thousands of books. He was alone. Sitting at a small reading table, he drummed his fingers for a time and wished that he had taken a nip from the fifth of Dickel that was now a million miles away in the parking lot. God, the top was down, and what if someone looked under the seat and stole it! Get hold of yourself, Jesse; get hold of yourself and go to work.

Votan lives. Who or what was a Votan?

Popper is dead with an axe in his head. Rhyme.

The FBI and Ollie Colbert acting hinky. Reason.

Rhyme and reason. Charleston Garman was not crazy, because there was rhyme and reason. Get hold of yourself, Jesse, and go to work.

"Uncle Popper, do you remember when we laughed at the name Cowdery? You called it cow-dairy . . ."

". . . the truth lay there, but we did not know it . . ."

". . . this thing is dangerous . . . they will try to stop it . . . the greatest war of all time will result . . . they will kill you as I am sure they are going to kill me . . ."

Bits and pieces of the letter circled in his mind like fearful ducks hovering over a frozen pond of conjecture. Jesse closed his eyes and pulled a book down. He opened his eyes and saw that the title was *God's Plan for the Coming Century*. It was dull, desiccate, defamatory, demanding, dogmatic, and damnable. No wonder there were so many crazy preachers; after a few years of

THE VOTAN TREASURE 137

reading this boring stuff anyone would become a stiff-haired drunk or pervert. He whisper-sang, ". . . it could be the Good Lord likes a little pickin', too . . ." a line from Tom T. Hall's old song about Clayton Delaney. He tried to imagine God tapping his foot. It did not work; he could imagine the Foot but not the Face.

A tall and slender young man came into the God section, strode matter-of-factly to one of the shelves, withdrew a book and sat at one of the reading tables. He wore white shirt and black trousers and had minister written all over him.

"Could you help me?" Jesse asked.

"Yessir." The voice was crisp, alert, accustomed to yelling.

"Does the name Cowdery mean anything to you?"

"Yessir."

"It *does?*" Jesse almost choked on his own question.

"Yessir."

"What about Votan?"

The young man's chagrin was apparent. Looking away for a few seconds, he shook his head. "That one got by me," he said. "But the other I can help with." He went to the third shelf down from the tables, paused, took down a medium-sized book whose binding was navy blue. He came back and handed the book to Jesse, and there was a sadness in his eyes.

"Thank you," said Jesse. He looked at the cover. *The Book of Mormon. Another Testament of Jesus Christ.*

"Are you of that cult?" the young man asked, a touch of viciousness in his tone.

"Uh, no. Just need to read up on something."

"Good. That's a filthy rag, and in need of burning. So is the Catholic Bible. You aren't Catholic, are you?"

"Latter-day hypocrite," said Jesse.

The young man smiled. "So many people are, I'm afraid. Ours is the only church mentioned in the Bible. 'The Churches of Christ.' I cannot see how supposedly educated people can overlook that one glaring fact, but they do. 'Speaking where the Bible speaks, remaining silent where the Bible remains silent.' That's our credo. It cannot be improved."

"That's . . . good," said Jesse. He wanted to strangle this little bastard but fought the urge.

"Immersion, redemption, salvation," the young man said.

"My feelings exactly," said Jesse. Just as all incredibly beautiful women ultimately proved to be bitches, all preachers ultimately turned out to be demented. Not only was this asshole a candidate for poster child for Planned Parenthood, he was more of a threat to religion than all the bootleggers in Appalachia.

The young man tapped the book in Jesse's hand and said, "All the Cowdery and Nephi and Moroni lumped together would not make dust fit to be trod on by my Lord and Savior's sandals."

"Nephi and Moroni?" Jesse asked.

"It's all in there, but your time would be better spent with that." He pointed to his Bible that lay on the reading table.

"I'm just boning up," Jesse said.

"Praise Him," said the young man.

"I will."

The minister gave an abrupt nod of his head and sat down at the table and began to read.

After waiting for a moment to determine whether he had been dismissed, Jesse sneaked down one of the book aisles, recalling, as Ollie had once said, *They ain't got 'em all locked up*. At the far end of the shelves the place opened into yet another reading area and Jesse saw a cupboard-shelf that was crowned by the sign DENOMINATIONAL PAMPHLETS. He went to the one designated "The Church of Jesus Christ of Latter Day Saints," subtitled "We are the Mormons," pulled out three: *What the Mormons Think of Christ; Christ in America;* and *What is the Book of Mormon?* Satisfied that he had enough to chew on for now, he returned to the front desk, checked out *The Book of Mormon*, and went out into the night.

As he drove back up McLean and turned left onto

Poplar he reached under the seat and groaned with satisfaction as his fingers felt the neck of the George Dickel. With booze, books, and blunderbuss, he could read a while, drink a while and then shoot out the lights. In his young soldier days the barracks talk of a perfect weekend was to be screwed, blewed, and tattooed, but that had been an innocent time, a time in which whiskey produced hangovers and cries of *never again*. Now, booze produced a yearning for just one more and the wrenching question *when next?* But, hell, he wasn't an alcoholic any more than one who followed the sports pages was a frustrated athlete.

He pulled into a liquor store and bought a pint.

Halfway between the liquor store and his apartment, he impulsively pulled over to a curb and put the top up. After rolling up the windows he sat for a time and stared at the traffic. Threat was in the air, a threat born of apprehension that was in turn born of intuitive reasoning. He looked at the book and the pamphlets on the seat and knew instinctively that he had entered into a thing that was about to endanger his life. Whatever Popper had taught his nephew years ago in the boy's formative years had flowered in the mind of the nephew as a man, and whatever the man had seen or heard or had come to know was enough to cause murder. And now the FBI had visited, a thing that the FBI does not do in a common murder case. Yes, Charleston Garman had been right on target with whatever it was that he was babbling about, and the name Cowdery was damned important, possibly lethal. The letter was the key and Jesse himself had the letter, and the letter had led him to *The Book of Mormon*.

He pulled back into the traffic, drove a few blocks and slipped the pint under the seat with the fifth. Now that he had two emergency bottles, he felt security underscored by self-loathing. Without really knowing why, other than to clear his head, he drove across the new bridge and over into Arkansas. The dog track was doing a banner business and the eight thousand cars in the parking lot served only to depress him: A good sixty percent of the bettors were the dark and poor of Memphis. Turning up onto an overpass, he crossed over, looped back down onto the interstate and headed back toward the bridge and Memphis.

An hour later, with shoeless feet propped on his coffee table, tie loosened, he opened *The Book of Mormon*.

"An account written by The Hand of Mormon upon plates taken from the plates of Nephi."

". . . written and sealed up, and hid unto the Lord, that they might not be destroyed . . . To come forth by the gift and power of God unto the interpretation thereof . . . Sealed by the hand of Moroni, and hid up unto the Lord, to come forth in due time by way of the Gentile . . . The interpretation thereof by the gift of God . . ."

Jesse read and reread the two paragraphs, saw Nephi and Lamanites and Book of Ether, which was "a record of the people of Jared, who were scattered at the time the Lord confounded the language of the people, when they were building a tower to get to heaven . . ." The next page was headed Introduction. This page was more comprehensible:

> The Book of Mormon is a volume of holy scripture comparable to the Bible. It is a record of God's dealings with the ancient inhabitants of the Americas and contains, as does the Bible, the fulness of the everlasting gospel. The book was written by many ancient prophets by the spirit of prophecy and revelation. Their words, written on gold plates, were quoted and abridged by a prophet-historian named Mormon. The record gives an account of two great civilizations. One came from Jerusalem in 600 B.C., and afterward separated into two nations, known as the Nephites and the Lamanites. The other came much earlier when the Lord confounded the tongues at the Tower of Babel. This group is known as the Jaredites. After thousands of years, all were destroyed except the Lamanites, and they are the principal ancestors of the American Indians. Mormon completed his writings . . . delivered them to his son, Moroni.

Jesse read on, saw that:

> ... on September 21, 1823, the same Moroni, then a glorified, resurrected being, appeared to the prophet Joseph Smith and instructed him relative to the ancient record and its destined translation into the English language ... in due course the plates were delivered to Joseph Smith. ... In addition to Joseph Smith, the Lord provided for eleven others to see the gold plates for themselves and to be special witnesses of the truth and divinity of the Book of Mormon. Their written testimonies are included herewith as 'The Testimony of Three Witnesses' and 'The Testimony of Eight Witnesses' ...

He turned the page. There, under a paragraph of testimony, were three names: Oliver Cowdery, David Whitmer, Martin Harris. At the bottom of the page, beneath a shorter paragraph, were eight names. Cowdery's name was not among them. The paragraphs were the hagiolegalistic verbiage of persons who had seen "the plates of which hath been spoken, which have the appearance of gold; and as many of the leaves as the said Smith has translated we did handle with our hands; and we also saw the engravings thereon, all of which has the appearance of ancient work, and of curious workmanship ..."

"Oliver Cowdery," Jesse said to himself, "Cowdairy." He imagined the young Charleston Garman's laughter as Popper had mispronounced the name years ago.

He read the three-page account of Joseph Smith's being visited at night by Moroni, of his subsequent finding of the plates near Manchester, New York.

"A Brief Explanation About The Book of Mormon" was the heading on the following page, and the text read, in part:

> The Book of Mormon is a sacred record of peoples in ancient America, and was engraved upon sheets of

metal. Four kinds of metal record plates are spoken of in the book itself:

The plates of Nephi, which were of two kinds: the Small Plates and the Large Plates. The former were more particularly devoted to the spiritual matters and the ministry and teaching of the prophets, while the latter were occupied mostly by a secular history of the peoples concerned . . .

The Plates of Mormon, which consist of an abridgement by Mormon from the large plates of Nephi, with many commentaries . . .

The Plates of Ether, which is a history of the Jaredites . . .

The Plates of Brass brought by the people of Lehi from Jerusalem in 600 B.C. These contained the five books of Moses, and also a record of the Jews from the beginning, down to the commencement of the reign of Zedekiah, king of Judah; and also the prophecies of the holy prophets. . . .

Now Jesse turned to the First Book of Nephi and great weariness fell on him. There was no way that he could ever get through it. This book was a Matterhorn of convoluted and archaic words and his mind was the tiniest of shovels; there was no way that he could ever dig through. But he could dig *around*. He turned to the back, saw that the book contained 779 pages. He looked at the index, could not find Votan. Flipping back toward the front, the word PEOPLE popped up and he read *1 Ne 5:18 brass plates go to every* . . .

He found First Nephi 5:18 and read, *These plates of brass should go forth unto all nations, kindreds, tongues, and people who were of his seed. 19. Wherefore, he said that these plates of brass should never perish; neither should they be dimmed any more by time. And he prophesied many things concerning his seed.* Twenty and twenty-one spoke of commandments and records and twenty-two stated *Wherefore, it was wisdom in the Lord that we should carry them with us as we journeyed in the wilderness towards the land of promise.*

* * *

Jesse awoke with his head lying forward on his chest, his neck perspiring. *The Book of Mormon* was yet on his lap. He looked at the clock radio. 1:56. He had dozed off while reading, had been out for the better part of two hours. The Dickel and Coke that had looked so good over ice was now brown water in a glass; he had forgotten to take even the first sip.

He stood, laid the book aside, took the drink to the kitchen and poured the fizzless mess out. Rinsing the glass, he thought of making another drink, but, for some weird reason, booze just did not appeal to him at the present. He leaned over the sink, sloshed his face and neck, dried with a paper towel. Something made the kitchen seem to tremble and he stood still in the kitchen and waited for it to happen again. There it was; distant thunder.

Going back through the living area, he opened the fly-specked and slightly dusty French doors that led to a totally unused concrete veranda. On moving in two years ago he had thought that it might be nice to put a chaise lounge here, one of those myriad things he hadn't gotten around to doing. A bolt of lightning illuminated a towering wall of clouds that stretched from Helena to the Missouri bootheel. Memphis was about to be one very wet city. The storm was still some twenty miles out in Arkansas and it would take it a half hour or better to arrive.

He went back inside and stripped down to his shorts so that the wind might better tease and caress his body. This oneness with nature was a godly thing and an erotic thing, a juxtaposition of senses that were ostensibly at war with each other. Somewhere down the line the human mind had decreed unto itself that God could not be involved in orgasm, but Jesse had for years felt that the nearness and purposes of God *were* orgasm. Truth be told he believed all thinking people probably had the same thought at one time or another but, like sexual fantasy, it was one of those things that no thinking person could ever divulge.

A blast of cool air came through the French doors and

blew papers about in the room, some of which were the almost-forgotten catechisms from the library. He picked one up, saw that it was the *Christ in America* pamphlet. Certain that he was onto something that was at best theistic, at worst diabolical, he idly turned to the first page and read: *The Great White God of ancient America still lives! The divine personage that emerges from the discoveries and writings of archaeologists and historians now stands out as an unassailable reality. . . . According to the findings of scholars, he came to America long before the time of Columbus. . . . He taught the ancients his true religion, raised some of their dead, healed many of their sick. . . . He came suddenly and left suddenly in a supernatural manner. . . . And that he promised to return in a second coming is an acknowledged fact, well attested by historical accounts.*

Jesse moved to his chair and sat down. Turning the page he read: "So convincing is the information now available concerning the White God as he appears in the legends of the Aztecs that Paul Herrmann was induced to say in his book *Conquest by Man:* 'Carefully considered, this leaves no other conclusion open than that the Light God Quetzalcoatl was a real person, that he was neither an invention of Spanish propaganda nor a legendary figment of Indian imagination.

"This being, known as Quetzalcoatl in parts of Mexico, primarily in the Cholula area, was known as Votan in Chiapas and Wixepechocha in Oaxaca, as Gucumato in Guatemala, as Viracocha and Hyustus in Peru, as Sume in Brazil, and as Bochica in Colombia.

"To the Peruvians he was also known as Con-Tici or Illa-Tici, Tici, meaning both Creator and The Light. To Mayans he was principally known as Kukulcan.

"In the Polynesian islands he was Lono, Kana, Kane, or Kon, and sometimes Kanaloa—the Great Light or Great Brightness. He also was known as Kane-Akea, the Great Progenitor, or Tonga-roa, the god of the ocean sun. . . . He was frequently described as a tall white man . . . bearded . . . with blue eyes. He wore loose flowing robes. He came from the heavens and went back to the heavens. . . ."

Turning off the lamp, Jesse sat in the darkness for a long while and let the storm's breezes huff gently against his bare skin. The occasional lightning flashes were nearer now, and the illuminated buildings in the distance were thrown starkly against a backdrop of direst black by the recurrent flickerings.

"Votan lives," he whispered.

Now the rain started. He walked onto the balcony and let himself become soaked, occasional shivers coursing through his body as wind and water and lightning assaulted the city.

"Votan," he said again. "Cowdery."

Could it be?

Yes.

The thing that Charleston Garman had spoken of was now apparent.

Joseph Smith. Oliver Cowdery.

Mormons.

Plates.

"Good God," said Jesse.

Sixteen

There were lavenders and scarlets over Rome as the glistening black Cadillac moved through the Palazzo di Fontana. The undersecretary of state of the United States, Amos Fielding, looked at the sunset with fatigued eyes and smirked at the obvious contrasymbolism of those colors. Lavender and scarlet, the universal colors of homosexuality and sin. In his Iowa youth he had often joined the congregation in singing an old hymn that contained the line "tho' your sins be as scarlet, they shall be as white as snow. . . ." And now here he was in the city that was the crux of the greatest church in the Western world and lavender and scarlet were the abiding hues. He rubbed his eyes, looked back toward the front of the car, saw the fluttering pennant that was attached to the right fender and quickly forgot colors. From his vantage point in the rear seat Amos Fielding could see that his driver, a taciturn but pleasant man named Antonio, was very adept at maneuvering through the suicidal Roman traffic whose Vespas, Fiats, and occasional Lamborghinis were hell-bent on destroying themselves and the city all at once. Satisfied that the sheer weight of the Cadillac would serve as a rolling fortress against their mayhem, he opened his briefcase and began to review his notes.

For the tenth time he read the one that he had received just today. Carefully couched in diplomatese, the missive said, in effect, that he was to drop a name. Following the name was the caveat, *This will be sufficient in and of itself to engender contemplation that will effect the desired result. Codicil will be unnecessary and would cause gravest adversity.*

In other words, Amos Fielding said to himself, I'm to let him know that we know something but he's not to know how much we know. It was an obvious scare tactic, but one that had come from Deep Six. And anything that came from Deep Six had a hell of a lot of weight in the White House, in Foggy Bottom, and God knew where else.

One would think that the undersecretary of state would know who Deep Six was, but the labyrinth of American politics in the latter quarter of the twentieth century was about as enlightening as looking at the intricacies of a computer's inner workings. When he was fourteen years old Amos Fielding had worked in a cannery during the summer and had endured a foreman who had offered but one abiding dictum: Do your job and keep your mouth shut. Now, nearly a half century later, someone unknown was saying the same thing. It made Amos feel as if he had spent his life climbing a spiral that had led up to an erudite nothingness.

The car stopped and Amos Fielding looked up and saw that they had arrived. It was totally dark, and Amos reached up and switched off the limousine's reading light before placing the notes back into the briefcase. Antonio came around, opened the door, and Amos stepped into a softly lighted doorway whose ancient stonework was bracketed by two Swiss guards. The men clicked their heels, presented arms. Amos walked past them without acknowledgement. Never smile at the so-called little people, his predecessor had said, because they do not really want you to be one of them.

A potbellied little man in black vestments made a half bow and said, "This way, please." Amos followed him down a short hallway, stopped while the man rapped softly. "You may go in," the little man said. He made an obsequious bow and left.

The bedroom was unsensational to the point of being austere. Lamp, reading table, mandatory crucifix on the wall, a short bookcase with reading materials. The bed's headboard was of wrought iron with cherubs chastely desexed with intertwined ribbons. It came to Amos that, without the crucifix on the wall, the place could be a cribroom in a whorehouse. The thought made his neck hair stand up and tingle. There were two chairs at the reading table, an indication that the tenant was accustomed to holding forth impromptu in these familiar and easy surroundings.

The door opened and the tenant entered. What there was of his gray hair was wet and a towel was draped over his shoulder. He wore white pajamas. Extending his hand, he said, "Welcome to my house, Amos, such as it is."

Amos smiled and said, "Yes, sir, thank you. It's very nice."

"Call me John," said the tenant. "Now that we're alone and those people with cameras are out in the real world somewhere, let's be at our ease, shall we?" He offered one of the chairs and sat in the other. "What may I do for you tonight?"

"When we talked yesterday I told you that the situation in Londonderry was improving. I also hinted rather broadly as to why it was improving. The Irish Republican Army has recently received two thousand M-16 rifles. The Protestants know this and consequently there hasn't been a rock thrown in two weeks."

John was perturbed. "Weaponry. When will it ever end? Who supplied these rifles?"

"Israel," said Amos.

John shook his head slowly. "The Jews are arming the Catholics to kill the Protestants. And the Jews got the arms from the most heavily Protestant country in the world. And this is who God gave dominion over the universe." He rubbed a hand over his damp hair and patted his palm dry on the towel. "I've just returned from Australia. Why can't the world be like Australia?"

Amos was slightly annoyed by this and said, "I don't know, but it isn't. I saw where you dressed down that priest in Sydney, so things aren't perfect even there."

John acquiesced by nodding. "When churchmen are

given to making political statements, they cease to be churchmen. It was, is, and shall be. Your visit yesterday was mostly social, Amos. Every paper and television receiver in the world saw us paying homage to homage. I tend to feel that tonight's rather clandestine visit is more portentous. Am I correct?''

Amos nodded. "We want those rifles out of Londonderry," he said.

"I see. And how do you propose to get them out?"

"I don't. You do."

John's face reddened. "I have nothing to do with the IRA. They are a terrorist group. True, they are Catholic, but if you think that the Church condones their activ—"

"We know that the Church doesn't condone their activities, as such. And, as such, the rest of the world doesn't think the Church condones them. But the world has been fooled before. Look at what has happened over the last few years: Watergate, Cambodia, Tonkin Gulf, Reagan's Irangate. The world rose up and raged as one. What I'm saying is this: a world accustomed to being fooled is a world that will believe anything about anyone, about any situation."

John rubbed the fabric of the towel and looked away. "Amos, I've known you for six years. This is the first time I've ever had the feeling that you're asking me to do something of a political nature. Certainly, I hope that I've misread you. My allegiance is to God first, the Church next; there is no third, except mankind as a whole. You want those rifles out of Londonderry, and so do I. I'd like to see Londonderry and the universe devoid of all weaponry. You seem to think that I can push some buttons in the Holy See and certain priests or cardinals will order misguided parishioners to surrender some arms. If people were that universally docile, we wouldn't need priests and cardinals.

"Now that I've said that, let me say this: you are supposed to be a man of peace. And a moment ago you said that rifles had stopped chaos in Londonderry. So if the rifles stopped chaos, why remove that which stopped it? Wouldn't it begin again? The inversions of logic here are such that I cannot answer them, and neither can you. You may tell whomever you report to that I have no knowledge of any connection between these rifles and the Holy Order. You must believe me, Amos, because we are friends, and because I have told you the truth."

Amos picked up his briefcase, removed a slip of paper, read it slowly. As John watched, he tore the paper into little bits and dropped them into the briefcase. It was high theater: here, the shredding said, was Amos Fielding telling his friend John that no edict of power from afar could cause a rift in their friendship. Now was the moment in which to spring the trap, but to do so in such a way that made the hunter appear more magnanimous than the hunted.

"I know that you can't do anything about the rifles, John. It was just our hope that American weapons would not be used in a conflict that was, for once, thank God, not of American involvement. It was simply our hope that *something* might be acceptable to the lowerarchy, if you will, of the Mother Church. We're doing everything in our world to bring about peace."

John smiled sadly and shook his head. "Amos, as you say in America, it won't wash. The sciatic nerve of modern democracy's financial survival is the sale of arms. At one time it was the sale of consumer goods, and now the Japanese have bested you there with the positive of their own hard work and the negative of your labor unions. And then you hoped to rely on your agricultural exports and promptly proceeded to depress the prices of farm goods so that your American farmer will be a creature of the past by the millenium. You know these things and so do I. It is a matter of historical record that Henry Kissinger gave billions of dollars worth of American arms to Middle Eastern countries in the 1970s if they would promise to cease hostilities! Think of it! To bribe warring countries to stop fighting, he gave them all arms! And you have come to me to ask if I can help rid Northern Ireland of two thousand rifles?"

Amos squirmed. He had lost control of the conversation by staying too long, by saying too much, by the totally inane remark about world peace. He had forgotten that this was one on one and not a thing being said and done for the cameras and the papers. He had long ago learned that the best stalling tactic is the downward turn of the head followed by the pursing of one's lips, a ploy meant to indicate introspection. Actually, he was now doing this in order to clear his throat quietly.

"John," he began at last, "you and I know that most of what you say is true. We've got Nicaragua and Honduras, you've got Londonderry. There is also Chile and Argentina and Iran and Angola. The imperiled sciatic nerve that you mentioned is suffering from Third World ganglia that are just now awakening. The body of humankind is awakening, and it is ill indeed. America can save it, and the Church can save it. The correlation is goodness as your church and my country perceive it. Yes, we use arms to gain certain ends, just as Lengus de Cristo stands to achieve certain ends for the Church."

The two men looked at each other for a time. At last John gazed up at the crucifix and said, "His word endures."

Amos found this to be a cryptic statement. He had done as the note had instructed, had mentioned Lengus de Cristo. He had hoped that John's words would be somehow more revelatory. Dammit, it would be nice to know what in hell was being accomplished here.

"Yes," Amos said, breaking the silence, "His word endures."

John said, "Helen Keller once wrote that a thing done for beauty is never lost. To paraphrase her, a thing done for good is never lost. Do you agree?"

Amos nodded. And waited. When he was convinced that John was going to reveal nothing, he stood and said, "It has been a good evening, John."

"Yes it has. You are always welcome. Tell me, can you do me a favor, Amos?"

Amos said, "I'll try. What sort of favor?" He held his breath. Perhaps the clue to what Lengus de Cristo was about was now to be revealed.

"In the fall of 1965 my predecessor visited Louisiana

and brought back some of the most marvelous coffee. It was called chickory blend. Do you think you might send me some?"

The two men began to laugh and it was a beautiful moment. The small room seemed to dance about them.

"I'll see what I can do," said Amos. They shook hands and Amos retraced his steps down the long hallway. The Swiss guards came smartly to attention and Antonio opened the door of the Cadillac.

En route back to the U.S. Embassy, Amos turned on his reading light and made some notes. They were really just words, catch-phrases that would have been gibberish to even the most astute of lexicographers. Tomorrow he would address the Italian cabinet, but these notes would not be in evidence there, for these personal hieroglyphics were remembered bits of what had just transpired with the man who had smiled serenely and said, *Call me John.* At the bottom of the scribblings he wrote the words "reaction not notable." He hated writing them, for they were an admission of defeat. The paper that had been shredded as a stage setting back in John's bedroom had contained nothing more than a complaint from a lower-echelon foreign service worker stating that his car had been impounded by the *carbinieri* after he had gotten drunk and run it into a fountain.

Reaction not notable. Add to this Lengus de Cristo, and it was no wonder the world was fucked up. Nobody knew what anybody was saying or doing. Nobody knew who was in command or what was to be accomplished. Do your job and keep your mouth shut. This whole hour had been devoted to dropping on John the words Lengus de Cristo and observing his reaction. Reaction not notable. Maybe in this crazy, topsy-turvy world the words meant victory. Hell, who but Deep Six could tell?

He switched off the reading light and watched the city ease past his window. Face it, Amos Fielding, you are an errand boy, he was thinking. You don't know for sure that there are rifles in Londonderry, and from John's adamant posture on the matter you are convinced that even if there are, he did not know about them. So if this

Lengus de Cristo thing was supposed to contain a heavyweight threat of some sort, it just did not work. And what John said about farmers and labor unions and arms was dazzling not in spite of its simplicity, but because of it.

Amos Felding rubbed his eyes and wished that he knew whether anything had been resolved for the good of Democracy on this night.

Tomorrow night Amos Fielding would fly to Zaire to meet with Mobutu, then on to Brussels to meet with NATO foreign ministers. These would be described in the press as "meaningful and sometimes pungent dialogues." The press always described them this way. In fact they would be nothing of the kind. They were but public relations drumrolls to offset the trumpetings of Gorbachev's recent trips to Angola and Bucharest. When Russian wheels roll, American wheels roll. This was done on both parts to illustrate to the peoples represented by their governments that their leaders were peripatetic and dynamic and concerned with the betterment of humankind.

"Focus of chain-bound Influence." "Meaningful and more ascendant directions." Amos thought of these two new catchphrases before he got to the embassy. It was too late and he was too tired to turn on the lamp and write them down. They would keep until tomorrow.

Seventeen

The man's name was Foster St. John, and as he stepped from his tub on this Saturday morning and toweled off his bald head, his heart was on a golf game but his mind was elsewhere. From Pearl Harbor onward it seemed that anything involving national trauma had to be resolved or at least attended to on a weekend. He studied himself in the mirror as he lathered his face and tried to count his wrinkles, a foolish activity, since so many big ones were fed by tributary wrinkles which were in turn leeching off stream wrinkles. Hell, he was thinking, at sixty-one years and with forty years of government service behind him it was a wonder that the corrugations were not even more pronounced. He had entered adult life at five feet and nine inches, and two of those inches were now gone, camouflaged, as it were, by a tendency to stoop and thus to look even older than he was.

But this nondescript appearance belied his professional role: he was a person whose position in government was the essence of attention itself, for Foster St. John was Deep Six, the President's code name for the man who knew where all the bones were buried. In this aura of codes, intrigue, confidentiality, and acrosticity of initials from the six major information-gathering eyes and ears of the highly developed American sensory device, St. John's words were at times the very scales with which the President weighed the possibilities of nuclear holocaust.

But just now his words were these: "Hey, Potter, where in hell did you put the deodorant?"

Agnes Potter St. John stirred in bed and groaned, "We're out. Use some of my roll-on."

"You know how I hate that stuff. It makes the hair in my armpits icky all day."

"Icky or stinky, make up your mind."

"I'll go with icky, but I won't like it." He opened her side of the medicine cabinet, took out the icky and grimaced at himself as he rubbed it in. Now he shaved, patted his face with shaving lotion, dressed in tan slacks, blue pullover and tennis shoes, leaned over the bed, and kissed Agnes.

"Where are you off to?" she groaned.

"I may or may not be at the course later in the day. I'm going over to Alexandria. Business."

"Pick some deodorant up on your way home," she said, patting her pillow, rolling over.

He went downstairs, reset the door latch, went into the garage, and started the Toyota. Say what one might, these damned Japanese cars were good; if the little bastards ever got into the deodorant business they'd probably make a can that would warn with a beeper when it was about to run out. He tapped the horn twice, backed out of the garage and into the street. Georgetown was still mostly asleep, and the only person on the street was a jogging senator from a western state. The senator would not have known Foster St. John from Adam's pet goose, but Foster St. John knew that the senator was involved with the wife of a congressman from the South. There were times when the nation's capitol was little more than Hollywood with the stars and stripes over it, but just now there were other things to think about and other things to do; with the fate of organized religion in the Western world standing at the brink of disruption, the orgasms of a senator and his concubine were petty stuff indeed.

The streets were silent and the traffic lights were with him and it was a good drive. Someone had recently told him that an early morning weekend day was the best time to drive in Washington because, as the wag had stated it, "The Democrats are in bed, the Republicans are in Palm Beach, the blacks are in jail, and the Mexicans can't get their cars started." He smiled at this and sped on across the Potomac.

The garage in Alexandria had been his own idea several years ago, and in his world of paperwork and verbiage it was good to see something structural even if it *was* this decrepit, unpainted, two-story monstrosity. The lone mechanic who worked the garage was mostly a monitor of trivial radio broadcasts, and when a legitimate customer pulled in for a repair the man pushed a button that enlivened a bank of recorders. Easy and happy work, it paid the man thirty grand a year from the government and all that he could take from his grease-monkey work. The bastard had it made.

Foster parked the Toyota, unlocked the office door, relocked from the inside and went up the stairs.

Vaughn Biddle stood. "Good morning, Mr. St. John."

"Mr. Biddle." Foster nodded and sat down in a padded swivel chair at the front of Biddle's desk. His eyes took in the room and he was happy to see that the map was already on the wall behind Biddle's desk, complete with pins. The southern tier of the USA was shown in soft pink. A study had shown that soft pink was the hue least likely to incite anger in convicts, that prisons with pale pink cells had the lowest incidence of riots. He tried to imagine what the study had cost.

"Feed me, Vaughn," he said.

"You want a program of the players or do you want the plot?"

"Plot me," Foster answered, leaning back in his chair, trying to get as comfortable as was possible.

"I know you like it short at first, so I'll keep it short at first. About a week ago we lost contact with three Company men in northwestern Mexico, two blacks and a white. The blacks were named Garman and Phillips, the white, Wolfe. We sent three operatives in the area up to investigate. With the help of the Mexican police, for what it was worth, and a bit of nosing around, they found that Garman is dead and that the other two are bugouts."

Foster looked at the wall to the left of the U.S. map

and saw a map of Mexico. It had no pins. "Go on," he said.

"The Bear is not involved, but this may be something worse than that," said Biddle. He took a red pencil from his desk and waved it toward the map of the American South. "We've got well over a hundred people involved in this one, from SSGs to full-timers." He pointed the pencil at Memphis. "There's the crux city. There's where it's going to culminate. Memphis, Tennessee."

"When do you see culmination happening?" Foster asked.

"Forty-eight to seventy-two hours."

"Have your people on it coordinated things?"

Biddle nodded. "We've got a thing working that is going to keep our asses covered. At least we're hoping it will."

"Bad phraseology," said Foster. "We don't hope anything."

"True, but it's a contingency plan that may flower from its own soil."

"The main thing right now is the bugouts. Have they been accounted for?"

"Yes. But I told you that last night on the phone."

"I like hearing it. Now, I've got the short: give me the long."

Vaughn Biddle reached into the deep bottom drawer of his desk and removed a bundle of manila envelopes. He came around the desk and handed part of the bundle to Foster. Within two minutes they had opened all and placed the contents on the floor to Foster's immediate front. Biddle arranged them in such a way that the players in the production were properly separated for Foster's understanding. Photographs, some obviously surreptitious, some frontal-facial, dominated the room's atmosphere. As Biddle returned to his desk Foster studied several and was again amazed at how commonplace the faces of trouble could appear. He picked up the sheaf of photos from the envelope marked, in government grease pencil, ELLEN HARRISON ROGERS TALBOTT, and whistled.

"I take it you're looking at the blonde named Talbott," said Biddle.

"Who wouldn't?"

"Yes, who wouldn't, indeed. A very strange and sexy lady. But we'll get to her later. Are you ready?" He picked up a yellow legal tablet, flipped through the first pages and looked up at Foster.

"Fire both barrels."

"Then hang on—here we go. This whole thing has to do with the potential disruption of religion in the world as we know it. And if you think religion is not a political firecracker look at Beirut, India, the Golan Heights, abortion, et cetera."

Foster nodded. "I comprehend."

"Here's what our operative, code named Chief, has come up with from Mexico: this agent named Garman is now dead, killed by Phillips and Emerson Wolfe, the other two agents. Garman was onto something that the other two wanted a piece of. A bit of legwork has divulged that Garman stole the object under scrutiny from a church in the Mexican village of Lengus de Cristo. That's where your pretty blonde lady on the floor there came in: she's carrying it in the trunk of her Mercedes right now. She and Garman had a slight fling and he apparently asked her to do him a favor. The odd thing is, for whatever reason, she didn't bother to know what it was until just a few days ago. The only other person who was involved up to that point was a Mexican national named Octavio Diaz. Chief says that Diaz was terminated with extreme prejudice—"

Foster interjected. "Company-ese can be suspended between you and me."

Biddle smiled and continued: "Diaz was killed. In Ciudad Juarez. That's when the thing began to come apart for the other two agents, Wolfe and Phillips. One headed for Texas, that was Wolfe, the white one, and the other headed for God knows where. Not to panic, we picked up his trail in New Haven, Connecticut. *He's* trailing a Yale Divinity professor by the name of Wagstaff, and we're trailing *him*. Wolfe's boy is the one we're most worried about right now, though."

"Wolfe's boy?"

Biddle pointed over the top of his desk. "That one off to your right. Vernon David Cameron. A nonpolitical, but a psychopath. A very bad hombre, a jack-Mormon, someone who has fallen from grace with the Mormon Church. Wolfe is getting this Cameron to do his dirty work for him."

Foster picked up the photos from the Cameron envelope. Idly flipping, he saw Cameron and Wolfe sitting at a restaurant table sipping what appeared to be milk shakes, Wolfe and Cameron talking near the balletlike blurs of an ice-skating rink, Wolfe and Cameron near an old pickup truck in the tunnelway of an underground parking lot, Cameron alone going into a restaurant.

"You say he worries you the most, this Cameron. Why?"

"A real crazy. Slow, droll, quiet, but a viper that strikes without rattling. Our backtrace work indicates strongly that he probably killed two old Mormon missionary women in Phoenix a couple of weeks ago, hacked them to death with a machete. A real humanitarian. Too, he recently aligned himself with this neo-Nazi group that calls itself the Covenant, the Sword, and the Arm of the Lord."

"He probably needs to be taken out of the picture," said Foster. "I can see why you're worried: he's the kind that would make some waves with the free and unbiased press in this great country of ours."

"He will be, but now is not the time; it would tip Wolfe that we're on to him. So far Emerson Wolfe thinks he's pulled a slick one, that we think he's a political and that we're watching all the Bear's dens. He should have known better, but greed does funny things to one's sense of comprehension."

Foster nodded and said, "This Yale Divinity person. Tell me about him." He picked up a photo of an elderly man emerging from behind a truck's trailer. On the side of the trailer was EVANGELIST. REVEREND ORLISS

THE VOTAN TREASURE   161

TRIBBLE. HEALING THROUGH THE POWER AND GRACE OF OUR LORD AND SAVIOR. SERVICES NIGHTLY. The man appeared to be carrying metal chairs toward a tent, a look of spiritualistic acquiescence on his face that the telephoto lens had caught from a great distance.

"Dr. James Ellmon Wagstaff, Ph.D. We lucked on to him, you might say, which in turn lucked us on to Phillips. The back trace on Garman took our operatives to Yale, where Garman was a so-so student of divinity at one time. Coincidentally, his assistant, one Michael Ellis Morton, was found dead. The New Haven police think it was a robbery attempt gone sour or a racial killing— Morton lived in a heavily black area. We tied that to Dr. Wagstaff's sudden bugout from New Haven and that was what put us on to Phillips. Blind luck, but the ball bounced our way."

"And Phillips killed this Morton?" Foster asked.

"Sure."

"He'll have to go. Any reason it can't be done right away?"

"No. He's not the kind to talk, being a Company man, and we honestly don't think he has his own operatives like Wolfe has his crazy cowboy. With Phillips, it has been a one-man show all the way. The only reason we've given him this much rope is that we're letting the bees head for the hive. Phillips was in Union City, Tennessee, yesterday afternoon getting drunk in a dive. Small town, I think we should let him get to Memphis before he . . . terminates."

"Good enough. With all the cattle in one pen the process of selection will wrap without any loose strings. Now, this Yalie, what's his purpose?"

Biddle rubbed his chin and tapped the pencil on the tablet. "It's my feeling that he has seen the light, as the fundamentalists would put it. Our preliminary findings show that he is a widower who's never made waves sexually, politically, or theologically. The only real problem is that he's from Yale. Oregon State Teachers

College or Alabama Tech wouldn't pose a problem, but Yale might."

"How so?" Foster asked, puzzled.

"Simple. Xenophilia lives. So does provincialism. So do largesse and status. A cretin from Harvard can cut through to a big salary ten times as fast as an Einstein from an unknown school in this country. Sad, but damned true. The Ivy League takes care of its own. What I'm saying is, this Wagstaff has the old school tie thing threatening his very existence, unbeknownst to himself, Yale being Yale. I've studied those pictures you have in front of you and have seen a man who's paying homage to a God that he hadn't really seen to now."

"Any suggestions on what we should do with him?" Foster asked.

"Let him go. We've busted our buns doing a personality profile on him over the last few days and he's not dangerous, except in the sense of being where the news media love to roam. He's a man of analytical mind, so either he'll never divulge his fool's errand of coming to Memphis or he'll babble about it as if it were a rumor. Which it is."

Foster thought this over for a moment and then said, "Maybe he'll drift, and maybe not. It will be the decision of Deep Six." He studied Biddle's face for apparency of recognition and saw none. Vaughn Biddle had no idea that it was Deep Six sitting across the desk from him, and it caused Foster to feel treacherous, patronizing, slightly hypocritical. "So tell me about the delicious blonde," he said.

"Ellen Harrison Rogers Talbott," Biddle said in a sprightly tone. "This is one for the books. She's twenty-nine, the daughter of Michigan automotive blue-bloodery, a nonpolitical. But sexually, this baby is the stuff of which dreams are made, or nightmares. The best schools, the best people, the best of everything, and decadent as Satan's asshole. We picked up her trail in Acapulco where she had a gang-bang session with a couple of Mexicans. From there she went northward to Mazatlan, spent one night, made some strange friends."

"Strange friends?"

"The lab boys found traces of semen on the sheets, and hair samples that proved out to be Oriental. Not only that, but while doing three Koreans, she became more than friends with a female college teacher from Florida."

"Good God."

Biddle laughed. "Yeah, it gets even better. We were able to strip the sheets from a bed in a motel in Port Arthur, Texas. The lab samples indicate nonmasculine sexual activity. This lady bats from both sides of the plate."

Foster moved the Talbott envelope next to the one marked Brylette Fender. There were three photos of the dark woman, all of which had been snapped in a bus terminal. As for the Talbott series of photos, there was a diversity of settings: one displayed her in a housecoat opening the trunk of a Mercedes at a motel; two fairly close facial shots at what looked to be a border check point; the remaining four made outside a bus terminal as she and the dark woman talked and embraced. Twenty years ago this might have titillated Foster, but now he found the whole thing to be the stuff of analysis, nothing more.

"The blonde showed the brunette one of what we're looking for. This Fender woman could prove dangerous. She's no fool and her sexual proclivities could leave her open for blackmail, and you know as well as I do that a blackmailee will bargain with any handy chip. I think she has to go. Your opinion?"

Foster meditated. "I just don't like killing people. Sure, in a country of two hundred and fifty million, people disappear all the time, and it would be easy. I vote no, and you vote yes. Deep Six will have to throw in the tie-breaker." As Foster St. John he had given Dr. Brylette Fender life; as Deep Six he knew that he would vote for her demise. There was no belligerence between these two personalities within himself, it was just that one was a human being who thought one way and the other was a pruning machine that thought not at all. He looked at the pin in northern Florida and mentally bade it farewell.

"Now for the gentleman in Memphis, the hub of this little wheel," said Biddle, tapping the tablet with his fingertips. "Jesse William DeVaron. An interesting dude, the party who's the rock that will break this fishbowl. A while ago I said something about a contingency plan that will keep our asses covered."

"Is he one of ours?"

"No sir. An ex-cop. Got riffed from the Memphis P. D. for drinking a bit too much."

"I already don't like him," said Foster, a teetotaler.

"Maybe you will, in good time. Served in Vietnam with the American Division. Rose to the rank of corporal, was busted for striking an officer, escaped a court-martial by the skin of his toenails. That was because on the night of March 27, 1970, he drew down behind a machine gun and wasted an entire company of NVA regulars. It got him the bronze star, and the army does not like to court-martial medal-holders."

"So?" Foster asked. "What makes him so exalted a personage?"

Biddle smiled and said, "His personality profile. The man is a time bomb. It exploded once, and it's about to again."

"So he killed a bunch of North Viet Army regulars. It was a combat situation. What's so explosive about that?" Foster asked with exasperation.

Biddle pointed across the desk with both hands, thumbs and index fingers making little-boyish pistols that fired silently. "After he killed the Viets he left his machine gun, ran through the wire, and cut the heads off every one. He had to be restrained by the troops and that's when he socked a captain. Not your typical altar boy, this Jesse DeVaron."

"I can see why he drinks," said Foster.

"Look at his photographs and tell me what you see," said Biddle.

Foster picked up the envelope designated *Jesse DeVaron* and removed the photos. A handsome man, taller and thinner than Foster had imagined him to be, Jesse DeVaron was pictured going into a gun shop, coming out. There was a rifle braced in his hands in one of the photos, and as he stood at the rear of an old convertible he stared down a heavily traveled city street like a hunter who has just killed, or perhaps like a man who might be about to methodically put a round through someone's windshield. Other photos revealed DeVaron walking up stairs into an apartment complex, coming and going from a liquor store. Taken together, the pictures were a summation of a person in deep throes of loneliness, introspection, self-imposed exclusivity. This DeVaron was a tortured type; the photos divulged this in candor that was uncommon.

"That rifle photo was made just yesterday," said Biddle. "I'm thinking that our little snipe hunt is beginning to head this bird DeVaron toward the sack."

"Oh? What sack is that?"

"If we can get Deep Six to go along with us, this DeVaron can do the scullery work in this matter. He—"

"I don't like it," Foster interrupted.

"Please let me finish. DeVaron is now a private investigator, a man accustomed to slipping in and out of things without a trace. DeVaron is also not averse to mayhem, as the army records prove. DeVaron knows that he is onto something that has brought in the FBI and he's not sure of what it is. Agents Reeder and Riggazi paid him a stage-setting visit recently and got his wheels to turning. He knows, but he doesn't know. He's afraid, but he doesn't know the exact shape of what's frightening him. When the time comes, this man will react."

Foster put the pictures back into the envelope and placed it on the floor. When he raised up there was a glint of anger in his eyes. "Now let me tell you something, Biddle," he said, biting the name off, "you handle the internal, I handle the external. If it goes on inside the borders it's your baby and you get to rock it. But my job as liaison to Deep Six puts me one up on you, so I'm about to pull rank. I know things that would make the average American vomit with fear if he had the slightest inkling that they exist. Two weeks ago a Russian submarine was aground in sixty feet of water for two days off

Ship Island in the Gulf Coast not forty miles from Biloxi. We let him slip away because John Q. Average would have been rioting in the streets over how the Big Red Fish got there in the first place. Fifty people in the country know that, and now you're number fifty-one.

"Forty-eight hours ago the number two man in the Kremlin passed blood from a kidney infection. A sample of that blood is in Tokyo right now. Don't bother to ask how it got there, just rest assured that it did.

"We've got a man in India who does nothing all day but check grass and cowshit for traces of strontium.

"We've got a man in Finland who does nothing but check reindeer tracks; a tank can go just where a reindeer does.

"Dag Hammarskjold was as queer as a pink parrot, and we've got ten pounds of files on who was screwing him, people who are now heads of state.

"We've got Navy frogmen off Diego Rivera Island in the Indian Ocean gathering shit samples from the ocean floor; that's how we know that less than a month ago a Russian submarine crew had a run of dysentery."

Finding that he had leaned forward until he was almost across Biddle's desk, Foster paused, composed himself, sat back in his chair.

Vaughn Biddle's face was a mixture of reds and grays; he looked down at the tablet for a moment and then up and away, as if to dispel this wrath by ignoring it. Finally he said, "I don't see what this has to do with—"

"I'll tell you what it has to do with, Biddle. For the first time in our history we're outgunned, outmanned, outpoliticized, and damned sure outshouted. America is a nice guy who started off facing one bad guy. But the bad guy has gathered dozens of little bad guys around to help in his dirty work. Good guys do not band together; bad guys *do*, if I've got to keep it simple. This country has enough turmoil from outside its shores, and certainly doesn't need any more from within. You sit there and act like a prima donna with your personality profiles and tell me how this character in Memphis is going to jump through a hoop in this thing and make you look good.

This DeVaron is not to be allowed to do our work for us except as is expedient to our purposes. If you want to play animal trainer, go join a circus. Do you read me?"

Biddle answered hoarsely, almost inaudibly, "Yes, sir."

"Last night on the phone you told me that this thing was a threat to religion as I know it, as the world knows it. But you did not elaborate. It started out with the defection of three Company men, period. Now you've placed the cast of characters on the floor in front of me, and it's obvious that the thing is burgeoning, whatever the thing is. You say that it will be resolved in Memphis. Let's stop playing mind games and get on with it."

Vaughn Biddle's face had by now returned to its natural state of soft ruddiness. Like all who have ever endured a scathing and scorching tirade from a superior, he had experienced that wondrous phenomenon that causes the pride and the spirit of self to dissolve, only to reappear magically intact, after the words have torn through the outer perimeters of self-esteem; he had put his dignity on hold, and it had held well.

Foster St. John listened carefully as Vaughn Biddle began to read aloud from the tablet. Over a twenty-minute period Biddle read of Joseph Smith, of the origins of the Mormon Church, of Mormon beliefs which held that Jesus Christ had reappeared incarnate in the Americas after his crucifixion. The distillation process began as Biddle began to read names that were exotically Mayan-Mestizo-Andean, names such as *Quetzalcoatl, Viracocha, Hyustus, Bochica, Votan.*

At last he put the tablet down, massaged his eyes with his fingertips, looked up at Foster St. John, saw that Foster's gaze was directed at the map of northern Mexico.

"My God," said Foster.

Vaughn Biddle said, "Here is what this is about, and why Deep Six must know." Biddle smiled. "I know how you feel. To loose this thing on the world will instantly result in hundreds of thousands of deaths, religious war, the inevitable extinction of either the Mormons or the Catholics and God knows who else who takes sides.

When I told you on the phone last night that this was a thing that would make or break religion you didn't believe me. And now you do."

Foster thought of this and said, "It already has, Vaughn. You just said a magic phrase, a vengeful phrase: 'You didn't believe me.' It's another way of saying, 'I told you so.' Multiply that by the some two billion people who practice Christianity and your allusion to upheaval blossoms to full fruition in the mind."

"So now you know why I had to see you."

Foster nodded. "I see why you had to see me, and then some. This is bigger than all the Russian subs off our coasts right now, bigger than anything that's happening in Moscow." He rubbed his eyes and stared at his fingertips, the act of a tired man. When he looked up it was again at the pink map of the southern states. Restful pink, taxpayer-convict restful pink. The irony of it piqued his sense of the absurd and he smiled. When the thought passed he said, "Do you belong to a church, Vaughn?"

"Episcopal."

"What would your little flock think of this?"

"It's too chaotic to contemplate."

Foster nodded. "So we're in agreement. Anybody having to do with this thing, anybody who has real knowledge of what it might be about must be . . ."

"Terminated with extreme prejudice," Vaughn volunteered, the tiniest hint of smugness in his voice.

Foster gave him a perfunctory smile and said, "The DeVaron idea makes sense now. How do you plan to work it?"

"We've got several people in Memphis, people DeVaron wouldn't suspect in a million years. Two of our SSGs have talked to DeVaron in the last few days, unknown to him, of course.

"These SSGs, are they good folks?"

"One is the best. He's been under deep cover in Memphis for two years watching a certain lady who's been laundering mob money. His cover is so perfect, so natural, that he even helps her with her grocery shopping. She doesn't have a clue."

"Deep Six will be pleased. Don't make any mistakes on this one, Vaughn."

"We don't plan to. It's in the works with DeVaron, then, if I read you correctly."

Aware that Biddle was fishing for an apology for the tirade that had riddled the room thirty minutes ago, Foster resorted to diplomatese: "Caution is the husband of perfection. Your facts, now presented, in toto, would indicate that your original scheme was not as ingenuous as previously believed."

Convinced that this was as close to an apology as Foster could maneuver his vessel of rank, Biddle stored the words away for a private gloat in the future and said, "So the lady professor has to go. And Phillips. And Wolfe. And this psychopath named Cameron. That's four."

"DeVaron would make five," said Foster.

"Maybe. But a strange thing has happened to DeVaron in the last few days. He inherited four hundred thousand dollars from a sister who was killed out West. It's all legitimate, and an incredible coincidence in the midst of all this."

Foster shook his head and said, "I don't see your point."

"The point is, money does strange things to one's sense of priorities. Here's a man who never had a quarter in his life and now he's rich. But something happened just last night that convinces me that he's still our man. He bought a rifle, the one you saw in those photographs, and he went to the library." He smiled cryptically.

"And I'm supposed to ask what he did at the library. Right?"

"Right. He checked out *The Book of Mormon*."

For a full minute silence hung in the room. At last Foster said, "So he's on to it?"

"He may not have the needle, but he's sure in the right haystack," said Biddle.

"So the money didn't loosen him from his nosy ways. I smell a man here who would charge hell with a bucket of water if he got mad enough," said Foster.

"Mad is not the word. Scared is."

"Scared?" Foster asked.

"Yes, scared. The profile is classic, bordering on perfection. The head chopping in Vietnam, the drinking, the lonely life style, the death of the old black man, the letter from Garman. And now he buys an M-1 rifle." He looked at the tablet. "Serial number 2885479, to be exact."

"He sounds a bit like that character who wasted all those people in that Oklahoma post office some time back," said Foster.

"Yes, he does, and if the great populace knew how many of those types are walking the streets at any given moment, it would create a general panic. As my instructor at Quantico used to say, we'll never get 'em all locked up."

Foster smiled at this and said, "We don't want DeVaron locked up. We want him dead or free. Now, how is all this going to come about?"

"Our deep cover man in Memphis will handle it, and they'll never know it's being handled. Even Reeder and Riggazi don't know as much as the deep cover man does. All Reeder and Riggazi know is that DeVaron needed to be questioned."

"You're very proud of your deep cover man in Memphis, aren't you?" Foster asked rather offhandedly.

"He's as cool as they come."

"So how come he's never been promoted?"

"The image thing," said Biddle.

"Oh," said Foster. "We both know what that old euphemism covers."

"Yes. Yes we do."

Foster leaned forward, studied the envelopes on the floor for a minute, then stood. Tiptoeing past the lives that troubled his feet and his thoughts, he went to the door. "I'll recommend to Deep Six that this thing be expedited pursuant to your suggestions. See that it goes well," he said.

"It will," said Biddle.

"It had better."

An hour later, in a variety store in a shopping mall, Foster St. John picked up a can of spray deodorant and walked toward the check stand. A massive bookrack lay off to his right and he altered his course and stood for a time looking at a disheveled bin that was filled with Bibles, some with red covers, some with black. Attached to the front of the bin was a crude sign: BIBLES WERE $6.98, NOW $2.98.

The Word of God had been marked down.

Vaughn Biddle's revelatory words returned; and Foster was again overwhelmed by them. Such simple words, such portentous and awesome words: "This will disrupt religion, and humankind, for hundreds of years."

War . . . Butchery . . . Intolerance . . .

Foster picked up one of the Bibles, shook his head thoughtfully, and dropped the book back into the bin.

Eighteen

The sunrise in south-central Arkansas was beautiful. The two ridges that lay twenty miles apart were almost luminous in their oaken greenery, and the waters of Lake Ouachita became chameleonlike as the sun found them, rose-pink swirling to cinnamon, blues blanching into silvers. At the center of the lake, like a platinum needle easing through fine silk, a fisherman's boat wafted lazily.

Vernon "Cowboy" Cameron had watched the beauty of awakening America for ten minutes. Here was the country as God and Thomas Jefferson had meant it to be; no Jews, no niggers, no wops, and no spics. Yessir, one certainly had to hand it to the Man Upstairs, he was no slouch when it came to lakes and sunrises, but when it came to coons and slopes and kikes, well, that was another story.

He started the truck and drove four miles up the gravel road to the north side of the lake. A six-strand barbed wire fence and a sign, PRIVATE, were all that he needed to convince him that this was the place. He turned off the gravel, drove through the gateless fence opening onto a dirt road that led through a pasture and on into the oaks that shaded the camp. There were four small concrete block houses that surrounded a larger house, and in the woods just beyond these he could make out the raw dirt of a rifle-range backdump and a thirty-foot tower, ropes for rappeling practice hanging limply from its top. As he stopped the pickup's engine he was pleased to find that someone in the camp was already awake; the sound of a radio emanated softly from a cinder block window that was overset with dark bars of heavy iron. Cowboy recognized the voice of Earl Grant:

"So . . . much to do . . . If I only had time . . . If I only had time . . . Dreams . . . To pursue . . . If I only had time. . . ."

Earl Grant was a good singer, even if he was a nigger. Cowboy had read in a tract ordered from the back pages of *Soldier of Fortune* magazine that niggers had more highly refined vocal cords and could thus sing better, the result, the tract assured, of thousands of years of having to call to each other during hunting expeditions on the plains of Africa. It was also why they could run so well; with a lion on your ass you move on out or die. But the thing that really bothered him about the song was that Hitler would not allow Mendelssohn to be played *ever*, would not have that Jew's compositions even mentioned in the Third Reich. And here was a nigger singing in the open right here in the middle of a camp of the Covenant and the Sword and the Arm of the Lord. Somebody wasn't doing his job; the place needed discipline.

Simultaneously, two men emerged from different houses, both wearing mottled camouflage uniforms, both wearing pistols in holsters and Marine Corps pisscutter caps. Their combat boots were polished to a high gloss. One was red-haired and blue-eyed, about thirty years old, while the other was older and darker and graying. The red-haired man came to the right side of the truck, and the dark man came to Cowboy's door.

"Peace to the Gentiles," said the dark man.

"And to the Caucasians," said Cowboy. This instant litany made him feel good, accepted, caressed by an invisible hand that knew what and where to scratch, to stroke. A thousand miles from home, he had found Home.

"What's your name and business?" the dark man asked.

"I'm called Cowboy." He smiled and touched the brim of his hat. Something to his right moved, and he saw that the red-haired man had moved to the back of the truck and was looking at his license plate.

"Talk to me, Cody," said the dark man.

"Utah plate. JN-198. It's him," said Cody.

"Let's say it's the right truck, for now," said the dark man. "He could be FBI or he could be the press." He looked back at Cowboy and said, "So what are you? Either of them?"

"I ought to be mad, but I ain't," said Cowboy. "Does the word 'cartwheel' mean anything to you?"

The dark man smiled and extended his hand. "Okay, dismount and come on in. I'm called Rio. This is Cody."

Cowboy stepped down from the truck and followed the men to the main building. Rio fumbled with a set of keys and opened the heavy steel door. The first thing that Cowboy saw was a huge photo of Martin Luther King, his face the focus of the crosshairs of a sniper's scope. Beneath the circular photo was the caption: One Down, Twenty-Five Million To Go. To the right of the photo was a cheap plaster crucifix from which Christ's feet had been broken, and beneath it: *This Was No Jew.* Just beneath the crucifix someone had made a crudely lettered sign: Hitler Had The Right Idea But The Wrong Race, ha! ha! Two long wooden picnic tables dominated the floor and two stacks of metal chairs were at the back of the room. The chairs were bracketed by two flagstands, the American flag on one, the white and blue flag of the Cross of Christianity on the other. The place carried the vacuous smells of coolness and staleness and disuse.

"You're dismissed, Cody," said Rio.

"Yessir," said Cody. "You want me to go on into town and see if they got that zeerox machine fixed?"

"Yeah. Take that old GMC pickup. And put some gas in the goddam thing this time."

"Yessir." Cody went out and the steel door boomed.

Rio took two chairs from the stack, flipped them open, placed them at the end of a picnic table. As they sat he said, "So you are a friend of Cartwheel. Does he still wear that eyepatch?"

"No. I don't know that he ever wore an eyepatch. But you could call what he's got an eyepatch, I guess."

"Oh? And what has he got?"

Cowboy waved vaguely toward the right side of his own face. Ward Cartwright, known to the inner circle as Cartwheel, had a mottled purple birthmark covering the right side of his face. "That," he said. "And you can test me till sundown, if you want to. Can't say I blame you."

Rio nodded and said, "Okay, I guess you'll pass, and no, you can't blame me. The collusion among the Jew-nigger-Catholic hierarchy has drawn the goodness of the FBI right in and made it a twisted, perverted thing. The FBI will be great again someday, the way J. Edgar Hoover meant. Cartwheel says you are good folks, and I can see why, but if you want to stay here you'll have to go paramilitary. I'm the camp captain and Cody is first sergeant. Cartwheel's letter said you could come in as a corporal, but that was just a suggestion. I get final say on who gets promoted around here. If you stay, you'll address me as sir. I run this camp, and that's that. I'm not harsh, but I am damned well a disciplinarian. All that is for openers. Any questions?"

"A few, but first I'll tell you I didn't come to stay. I'm passing through on my way to . . . the East. Cartwheel wrote you because I asked him to. An introduction letter only, not a request for bed and board. He sort of hinted that you might need me for . . . something."

Rio started to speak, but a sound from outside the building drew him to the door. He opened it and watched as Cody drove the old pickup through the camp and onto the pasture path. When the oaks had obscured truck and dust he closed the door and sat down, his eyes registering fatigue and guile. "I need you for him," he said.

"Cody? How do you mean?"

Rio drummed his fingertips on the table for a time and then said, "He's got to be done away with. Cartwheel said in his letter that you might . . . have some ideas."

Cowboy said, "Why don't you do it?"

"I'm known here, and you aren't. He's not known anywhere. He's tattooed riffraff who came here six months ago for a weekend Klan rally and volunteered to stay. It seemed like a good idea at the time."

"So what has he done to get dead over?" Cowboy asked.

In a self-conscious, precise tone Rio said, "This place, this order, caters to a white, Christian brotherhood that sees America as the Earth Virgin beset by those who would infect her with evil seed. Cartwheel says you're one of us, and that's good enough for me, which is why I'm unloading all this on you on blind faith. Cross us, tell off, and you'll die. That's why Cody has to go. Remember that shootout about five or six years ago, where the Klan and the Nazis shot it out with the Commies?" As Cowboy nodded, Rio went on: "Well, Cody was one of the Nazis. He had a feud with one of the other Nazis, got some dirt on him, and turned him over to the FBI. The man is now doing fifteen to thirty in Atlanta. Cody squealed, so he has to go."

"But he didn't squeal against the group; he squealed against one of the group. It was a personal thing."

"It violated the essence of what we're about, man, don't you see that? A man that will squeal yesterday for whatever reason will squeal tomorrow for whatever reason."

Cowboy said brusquely, "So that's why Cartwheel bragged this place up to me, knew I'd want to come here, knew I was on my way to this general area anyway. I'm being used—right?"

"You are being used to perpetuate what we are, what we hope to be."

Cowboy felt bafflement, anger, indignity. "I've been here twenty minutes and you want me to do away with somebody. Do I look like I fell off a hay wagon?"

"No. You look like a person who does things for the good of his soul, his beliefs."

"You said outside that I might be press or FBI. How do I know you ain't press or FBI?"

There was an audacity here that Rio was not at all

accustomed to from other men; however, when he realized that Cowboy was present on a voluntary basis, was, in fact, little more than a tourist, it occurred to him that he had indeed rushed things a bit. But Cartwheel's letter had hinted strongly, albeit in couched and camouflaged verbiage, that Cowboy, should he show up, was the man for the odious job at hand. And Cartwheel was never wrong about his choices for the right man for the right job. Cowboy's exuberance on entering the camp had ebbed into what now appeared to be detachment, disillusionment. Rio's college degree had gotten him some eleven jobs in the previous twenty years, dead-end affairs whose demise was assured when his penchants for racism were discovered, and several of these had been sales jobs. Now was the time to put all his old sales skills up against the fire of the visiting westerner's indifference.

"Look," he said, "the American Nazi Party at this moment has fewer than five hundred members, most, if not all, known to the FBI. The Klan has maybe ten thousand members, same thing. Our group here, the Covenant, began some ten years ago with a tax protest against the Zionists who control Wall Street and thus control the government. We wear different uniforms, but we are soldiers in the same army, Christ's army. There are three camps like this in the whole country, one in Arkansas, one in Idaho, one in South Carolina. I'm a camp superintendent and coordinator, which means that any and all our people look to me to have a place to train for the coming rising of the real people, the Caucasian and Christian people who want America back, who want it snatched from the hands of the welfare nigger and the clutching Jew. The house of purity is Columbia, the gem of the ocean, and the gem has become clouded. We are the essence of what our fathers died for at Valley Forge, what the guns of Old Ironsides fired against, what Robert E. Lee and Thomas Jefferson gave of themselves for. There is enough chaos from without, so we do not tolerate dissension from within. The Nazis know that Cody turned in one of his own. We've got people in Idaho who bombed the house of that goddamned Catholic priest some

THE VOTAN TREASURE 179

time back, and Mr. Butler has nothing but praise for them; he's head of the Aryan Nations now, but someday he'll be president. Do you see what I'm saying?"

There was a time of silence and introspection as Cowboy deliberated. It was almost a certainty that Cartwheel had told Rio nothing about the Mormon women in Phoenix, else Rio would have used it as a trump card in his rantings of the past few minutes; however, it was just as certain that one murderous session was a hundred times less likely to put one on the gallows as were two. Neither Cartwheel nor Rio knew of Cowboy's current commitment to Emerson Wolfe, knew nothing of why he was in this part of the country. Too, he knew what happened to persons who were loyal to more than one cause, loyalty being, as it is, the most jealous and unforgiving of the gods of human emotion. Still, he was convinced that the Aryan Nations, once they came to power, would seat people such as Rio at the right hand of the rulers, and he envisioned himself at the right hand of the right hand.

"I'll do it," Cowboy said.

"Good man," said Rio.

"Where and when?" Cowboy asked.

"Here. Today. Don't you want to know how?"

"I already know how. I've got the how in my truck."

"Do you have a silencer?"

Cowboy smiled and said, "Take my word, you won't hear a thing. Neither will he."

Rio looked about the room, at the flags, at the photos and the doggerel on the walls. "This all looks silent right now, shabby even, but there will be a day when this place will be a shrine. Look at it as I'm doing now, drink it in with your eyes, think of the millions of white, Christian brothers and sisters who will make a pilgrimage here someday. It still makes my skin crawl when I think about it." He looked at Cowboy and said, "You will not be forgotten when that day comes. You have come at the eleventh hour, but your time in the vineyards will be as my own."

Cowboy nodded. He started to speak, but there was a

booming sound from the bottom of the metal door. Rio got up and opened it. A plain woman with stringy dark hair entered carrying two metal trays. As she put the trays on the table, she paid no more attention to Cowboy than if he had been invisible. She turned and left. Rio closed the door, and as they turned to the bacon and eggs and coffee on the trays he said to Cowboy, "My wife. A good woman. She might be first lady some day." Cowboy said nothing.

An hour later, sitting in a grove of oaks two hundred yards beyond the rifle range, Cowboy worked the machete's keen edge with a rat-tailed file. He had removed his boots and socks and his feet cooled in a shallow, rock-bottomed stream. Minnows darted about, paused and wiggled their tails, darted again. There had been an aquarium in Phoenix, in that apartment. After finishing his work there he had dropped a human hand in among the goldfish.

Placing file and machete in the grass by his side, he lay back, his head propped by the root of a great white oak. Beyond the stream were rolling hills and more oaks and cloudless sky. When the Aryan Nation asked what he wanted as reward he might mention this place, and on that hill in the distance he would erect a three-hundred-foot statue of Christ such as the one over at Eureka Springs done years ago by that great Christian patriot, Gerald L. K. Smith. A rabid hater of Jews and Communism and jigs and mackerel-snappers, Smith had come from nowhere in the 1940s to do great deeds, and the press had roasted him, at the behest, of course, of the Zionist press lords. Cartwheel had told him all about Gerald L. K. Smith, had become so emotional in doing so that tears had flowed.

Old Cartwheel. Ward Cartwright. Five months ago Cowboy had written a letter to Cartwright complimenting him on his fine article in *Soldier of Fortune*. The article had been a derogation on the stopping power of a certain Russian assault rifle. A thank you letter, postmarked Ouray, Colorado, Cartwright's home, had started a correspondence that culminated in a meeting. Cowboy's zealous dislike of the vermin that threatened America's health was equal to, if not superseded by, Cartwright's own. In the 1950s a Mormon woman had testified that Cartwright's father was an adulterer and the father had been ordered to leave the Church, an expulsion to which the old man had forever attributed his declining fortunes and, ultimately, his outright poverty, poverty that became so severe the children had actually been sent at times into the streets to beg for food. The father was dead but the tattling woman still lived and was serving as a Mormon missionary in Phoenix, a prunish crone named Bishop whom Cartwright so hated that he had followed her passage through life all these years. "I have a present for you," Cowboy had said following the handshake from Cartwright that had brought him into the Covenant and the Sword and the Arm of the Lord. "It's nothing that will be handed to you, but you'll know when you get it that it's from me."

Now he pulled himself from the oak root and into a sitting position and he looked at the minnows. Yes, the Lord moves in mysterious ways his wonders to perform. The Phoenix thing, juxtaposed with Emerson Wolfe's asking him for help in finding something stolen by a nigger CIA agent down in Mexico . . . well, you just had to hand it to the Good Lord. Bowing his head, he offered up a silent prayer of thanks that the flesh had not urged him into any sexual dalliance in Fort Worth. If God wanted him to fuck a woman, then God would provide him a woman to fuck. God had sent him here to get rid of this Cody, and when he got to Memphis God would show him the way there, too.

Cowboy had barely managed to pull his boots on when the red-haired man came up behind him.

"Rio said I'd probably find you here," said Cody. "He says you're going to be joining us, maybe."

Cowboy stood and dusted off his denims. "Yeah, maybe. I ain't decided yet."

Cody squatted beside the creek, picked up some tiny stones and tossed them at the minnows. "A friendly piece of advice—don't say 'ain't' anymore. You may have noticed that old Rio talks pretty good English. He's crawled my ass more than once about such. Says we need to upgrade our image." He stopped tossing and looked up at Cowboy. "He say anything about what rank you'd have?"

"Corporal. If I choose to stay."

Cody seemed relieved and tossed the rest of his stones, scooped up more, began tossing again. "Thing is, if you're a corporal, you'll be under me, like I'm under him. I'm a fair person, easy to get along with, if you do your job."

"What would my job be?" Cowboy looked at the machete and the file. They were just to the left and just behind the squatting man.

"Different things. Sometimes we work our asses off, especially before a weekend training session. Sweeping, raking the shooting range, checking out the tower ropes. Rio wants to make a transitional firing range. That'll mean digging holes in the woods so the Klan boys and the Nazis can have Jews or niggers spring up to be shot down. Rio wants realism, he says. We live off contributions, and contributors are a funny lot: the ones that send the least are the ones that complain the loudest. Rio wants to build the camp staff up to at least seven full-timers."

"Rio. Is that his real name?"

"No. His real name is Jason Overfield, but we go by nicknames around here, code names. That's why you'll always be 'Cowboy.' It's best to forget real names, and I don't need to tell you why."

Cowboy knelt over the machete and picked up his own handful of pebbles. Shifting them to his left hand, he picked them up with his right, one at a time, like an old person eating salted peanuts. He tossed one, two, three, a slow cadence, a metronomic bit of theater that drew Cody's eyes to the water, to the darting minnows.

The fourth toss never came. The shining blade glinted as it rose. The sudden descent was soundless, except for that millisecond in which there was a minor inflection like a shovel passing through silt. The cap fell to the right and Cody's head went to the left, the stump of neck spurting a great red stream of blood into the creek. The hands on the headless body twitched and were still, waxen, colorless. The minnows darted in pinkness.

Cowboy wiped the machete on the dead man's shirt, picked up the file, and walked back to the camp. As planned, Rio had left a long-handled shovel leaning against the door of the main building. Cowboy put his machete into the truck's tool box, grabbed the shovel and was gone for the better part of an hour. When he came back Rio was eating Vienna sausages from a small can.

"Cartwheel is a good man, and so are you," Rio said.

"Cartwheel is a great man, and so am I," said Cowboy.

"Oh?" Rio was again taken aback by this man. "And how do you come to say that?"

"Because when this thing is done, settled, the people like me and Cartwheel will take in the grandeur. You college boys who're afraid to get your hands dirty always come out sucking hind tit. Show me a dirty hand and I'll show you a man I can depend on."

"I'm not sure I follow you," Rio said slowly.

"You can squirt ink and hide under the cloud until hell freezes over," said Cowboy, "but when you come out on the other side of that cloud, I'll be there."

"Dammit, if you'll just tell me—"

"Okay, I'll tell you, college boy, and you can tuck it into your file with everything else around here! What was just done had to be done, but it was done wrong! I did it so that it would get done, because if I hadn't, it wouldn't have got done! And another thing—when the time comes for credit to be gave, you'll take the credit. I know your kind—you'll use big words and a flashy smile and you'll shake a lot of hands, you'll never get dirty. But what you don't know is this: the order to come will rid itself of its own excess baggage, and right now you're part of that baggage. What I did to Cody an hour ago is what we will do to you tomorrow. We're out there in force, and the force is getting bigger every day! The kike and the nigger and the Catholic and the Puerto Rican and the pornographer and the dope pusher will feel our wrath. There's dirty work to be done before this country is clean, and you ain't the type to get dirty! You'd better learn how!"

The accuracy of this denunciation had reddened Rio's cheeks; blotches of embarrassment formed at his temples. He removed his military cap and wiped his sweat-beaded forehead with it. "I know you're right. I just couldn't do it."

"Learn how," Cowboy commanded.

"I will."

Cowboy looked at the sun, at the camp, at his truck. "The next time you decide to make somebody a corporal, you just make damned sure you got the guts and the know-how to be a captain. Now, I'm on my way, and I'm god-derned unhappy I stopped here. But maybe what's happened here today has put some fire in your ass; somehow I doubt it. They's three of these camps in this country and within five years I hope they's a hundred. God help us if they get run by the likes of you. Have I got through to you?"

Rio nodded. He looked at the ground, at the small can. With a boot he crushed it slowly, as if he were crushing his own shame.

Cowboy got into his pickup and started the engine. "Anything you want to say or ask?" When Rio shook his head, Cowboy backed away and steered the truck onto the little pasture and drove out to the lake road.

He came to the place where he had paused this morning. The fishing boat was gone and the lake's colors had become a sad green. He removed the western hat, laid it on the seat and bowed his head. "Lord," he whispered, "I took your name in vain a few minutes ago. Please forgive me." For a full minute he kept his eyes closed and then the rush came over him, a coolness that he had experienced dozens of times following monologues directed at the Almighty.

Leaving the truck, he walked down to the water and removed his clothing. The water was lukewarm, perfect for a swim. Floating on his back, looking at God's own sky, he daydreamed about the coming time when the Jews and the niggers and all the others who were the purveyors of corruption would be gone. There would be baptisms here in this clean water, and in the distance the outstretched hands of the three-hundred-foot Savior would bless them all.

Nineteen

Deputy Howard Allbred found his mission distasteful. As a deacon in the Mayfield Baptist Church, his purposes on weekdays were supposed to coincide with his activities on the Sabbath, at least in theory, and this one that the high sheriff had ordered was not in keeping with his precepts. But, the real world being what it was, God was God and a paycheck was a paycheck, so for this moment he would put his principles on hold and do as he had been told.

He drove the county car off the highway, down into the dry ditch and through the trampled field weeds to the tent. The flaps of canvas hung like elephant ears in the morning stillness and he was reminded of a circus. Which, in a way, was what the thing probably was, this sort pushing not clowns but Christ. He looked through the tent's distant side, saw the massive truck and trailer beyond, and walked under the canvas. He wondered what the take had been last night.

Three figures were asleep under the aluminum trailer, two in a sleeping bag, a third on a blanket. The man on the blanket had not bothered to undress. All looked as if they could do with a bath.

"I'm looking for a man named Wagstaff," said Howard.

The three stirred nervously, looked at each other and at last emerged from their beds, their eyes puffy with sleep.

"I'm Dr. James Wagstaff," said the man who had been on the blanket.

"He's a good man, Sheriff, a man of Christ," said the other man. He extended a hand and pushed the third party, a boy, behind him.

"I'm not the sheriff; I'm a deputy. And he isn't under arrest." He looked at Dr. Wagstaff and said, "You have a call, sir. I have been sent to ask you to come to Mayfield with me."

"Is it about Mike Morton? I don't know anything about it," said Wagstaff.

"Come with me, sir. I'm to take you to town. That's all I know."

"That's my car over there." Wagstaff pointed beyond the trailer to the rented Oldsmobile. "Will you bring me back?"

The deputy smiled. "Yes, sir, I'll bring you back." As they were leaving together the deputy turned to Reverend Tribble and said, "That boy needs to be in school." He started to say more but it would have accomplished nothing; there were just certain things that years of police work had convinced him would never change, one of these being the ways of itinerants.

On the way back to town the two men said little. Dr. Wagstaff volunteered that in the previous night nine souls had come to Christ. Deputy Allbred smiled and felt nervous. His police radio crackled and he was glad that the sound was there to disrupt the wall of tension.

At the outskirts of Mayfield the deputy drove into the parking lot of the Green Glades Motel. As Dr. Wagstaff looked at him half-smiling, the deputy said, "Sir, you are to go to room number twenty-three. I'm to wait outside." As Wagstaff started to speak the deputy said, "Please, sir, just do it."

Feeling as if he were being coerced toward a surprise party, Wagstaff slowly walked across the parking lot and caught a scent of bacon and eggs from the restaurant that adjoined the place. He had not eaten since late yesterday afternoon and he imagined that hunger had somehow created this bad dream. Well, it had all the earmarks of a bad dream; a deputy takes one to jail or to a courthouse for questioning, certainly not to a motel. This was, at best, one of the more riddlesome things that had happened in a long while. He went to room 23 and knocked.

The door opened and a man motioned Wagstaff in. The man was tall and balding and well dressed, dark suit, dark tie, white shirt. The bed had not been slept in and there was no evidence of luggage.

Holding up a leather-bound card the man said, "I'm agent Dolph Hannah of the Federal Bureau of Investigation. Would you be seated, please."

Wagstaff sat and said nothing. His stomach rumbled, and his hands drifted uneasily onto his lap.

"Tell me about your itinerary for the past few days, please," said the agent.

"I rented a car up east and drove down here on vacation. Please, is anything wrong? I—"

"No, sir, nothing is wrong. Do you know a Michael James Morton?"

"I did. I understand that he has been killed. Shocking."

"Yes, sir, it is. Can you think of any reason that he might have been murdered?"

"Absolutely none. A nice young man. A Christian."

For the first time the agent smiled. "A Christian. Not a Jew, but a Christian. You visited a synagogue a few days ago. Was there any particular reason for that?"

Wagstaff shook his head. For the first time he noticed that the agent had remained standing. The man seemed threatening. "I've visited many religious establishments in the past few days," he said. He wished that the FBI man would at least sit down.

"You live in New Haven, Connecticut, yet on the night that Morton was murdered you stayed in a motel. The next day you rented a car and left the city. Can you see why a casual observer might see juxtaposition here?"

"Mr. Hannah, I had nothing to do with Mike's murder. I—"

"We know that," Hannah said. "We also know that one Charleston Garman was a student of yours at one time and that he had corresponded with you. Did something in Garman's letter create fear in you?"

"No. It created joy." The agent peered at him oddly. Not to be swayed, Wagstaff said, "Yes, *joy*."

"Mr. Wagstaff, let's don't bandy words. This is an official—"

"That's Dr. Wagstaff, Agent Hannah," the older man said softly, "and I know what it is. I think I've known all along that this moment would occur; I just didn't know that it was to be so politicized so quickly."

Palpably baffled, Hannah said, "This is a murder investigation, Mis . . . Dr. Wagstaff. As I've already mentioned, one Michael Morton was found mur—"

Dr. James Wagstaff raised his hand, palm outward. The little room was patinaed with silence. The agent squirmed a bit, looked toward the curtained windows and then looked back at the old professor. There resided in Wagstaff's countenance a benevolence that went beyond anything that Hannah could immediately identify. This avuncular man who sat across the room smiling at him had, by lifting a hand, come to dominate the scene.

"I will speak," said Dr. James Wagstaff. "You will listen. And then we will both understand, and we will go our separate ways."

The agent nodded.

"Your presence here was heralded to me when I was given a letter by Mike Morton; I knew that this moment would come. It is my feeling that your purpose here is twofold: you have come to turn me away from my goal, and you have come to retrieve something that is potentially damaging to the state. I do not condemn you, nor do I condemn the state; Paul's jailer worked for the state, and you work for the state. In all the world and in all of history, the United States of America stands as the noblest concept of what the state and the individual can accomplish in complementary custom. The United States is not perfect—God help it if it ever becomes perfect—but you and I are fortunate enough to have lived in a time when the goal of man's dreams, perfection, is possibly within our grasp. *Possibly*, such a beautiful word, and *perfection*, such a dismal word. But in our shabbiness those two words are all we have, really, that make life worthwhile."

Dr. Wagstaff pulled out his wallet, took from it a bent envelope, handed it over to the agent. When Hannah had slipped the letter into his breast pocket Wagstaff said, "You did not look at the letter. I knew you wouldn't, and I know you won't. You were told not to do so, and your superior was correct in telling you not to do so."

Wagstaff had finished and now waited for Hannah's response. There was no sound from the outside world. The two men looked at each other for a time and then Hannah looked away. At last he said, "You will return to New Haven." It was neither question nor order nor declarative statement; rather, it was offered in something amounting to apology.

Dr. Wagstaff nodded. "Yes, I will return to New Haven. As a tenured professor I have no worries about my rather dubious way of taking a week's vacation. It was a wondrous moment in my life. Perhaps you did not know this, but I was en route to Memphis, Tennessee, to talk to a man about the proof and presence of God. Did you know it?"

The agent shook his head. "No, all I know is that I have a letter that I was supposed to acquire and a promise from you that you will not go on to Memphis. As you pointed out earlier, those were the two things that I was instructed to accomplish."

The agent fumbled with the curtain, but he did not look out. He did not want the older man to see the disturbance his words had caused. Hannah was prepared to dismiss Wagstaff as an eccentric academic, but there was a dignity to the man which made his speech solid and important. "You are dismissed. Thank you for coming," he said.

Twenty minutes later, on alighting from the county car, Wagstaff said to Deputy Howard Allbred, "Are there many such as these?" He pointed to the great truck, to the revival tent.

The deputy said, "Yeah, the South is full of 'em. Maybe the whole country. Makes a person wonder how they live, a week here, a week there. If I was doing my job, I'd run that Reverend Tribble in for not having that kid in school. But I've got other fish to fry. See you."

"Surely," said Wagstaff. He closed the door and watched as the tan car eased out of the field and back onto the highway.

Reverend Tribble and the boy came down out of the cab of the truck. The boy was eating from a can of Showboat Candied Yams. "What was all that about?" Reverend Tribble asked. "You in some kind of law trouble?"

"No," said Wagstaff. He continued to watch until the car was out of sight. Turning to the boy he said, "Is that all you're having for breakfast?"

"Him and me had us a picnic breakfast while you was gone," Tribble offered, somewhat abashedly. "Had liver loaf sandwiches. The boy loves yams. It's his Saturday morning reward. He works hard all week, I always give him a can of yams, don't I, Cecil?" Cecil nodded and smiled.

Wagstaff pointed to the tent and said, "Where do you go from here?"

Reverend Tribble squatted, picked up a bit of grass, and looked at the highway with worried eyes. "I guess down into Tennessee, maybe up to Indiana. Hard to tell nowadays. They's not that much money in America any more, so it's hard to tell where to go to carry the Word. Time was, you could hit the North in summer, the South in cotton pickin' time, you could pay expenses." He waved a hand toward the tent. "All this—truck, tent, chairs, all of it—I got fifteen thousan' dollars sunk into. Sold my cotton farm in Texas to go on the road and do this. Cecil's mama, she left us, couldn't stand the life. Can't say I blame her—she's a woman, wanted security. Funny thing, security is a commodity that's gone out of America. The jobs just ain't there. People are worried crazy. They need the Lord, but I guess they need money about as much. When they get money, they forget the Lord, and the thing just kind of flip-flops. Me, I'm caught somewhere in the middle." He threw the piece of grass down.

"We didn't have much time to talk last night," said Wagstaff. "Your sermon was good. You and your son are doing good work. I just wanted you to know that. I have to leave now. It has been a pleasure knowing you."

Reverend Tribble stood. "Well, sir, when you get to Connecticut, tell 'em all me and Cecil said hi." He laughed and they shook hands.

An hour later, having watched Wagstaff drive away in the Oldsmobile, Reverend Tribble and Cecil set about their tasks of straightening chairs for the coming night's service, of placing their twenty dog-eared song books in every third chair, greasing the big truck for tomorrow's departure to Tennessee or Indiana or wherever. The truck held three-fourths of a tank of diesel fuel and in his pocket Reverend Tribble had less than ninety dollars. As he squatted beside the rear wheels pumping away with his grease gun, he hoped that tonight's offering might bring in as much as fifty dollars. At that instant the handle on the gun came loose and he said to Cecil, "Hop up in the cab, son, and get me those little wrenches. One oughta work, I hope." While waiting for Cecil to return he recalled that Wagstaff, just before leaving, had gone to the truck and spent a few minutes in the cab.

"Look here, Dad," said Cecil. He was holding the wrenches in one hand, a small brown paper sack in the other. Handing the sack to his father, he said, "Do you think he stole this, what with the deputy coming here and all? Maybe we oughta turn it in."

Reverend Tribble looked into the sack, removed the money. Three one-hundred-dollar bills. For a time he looked at the money, thinking. And then he saw what was written on the side of the sack and a great smile broke over his face. "No, Cecil, he didn't steal it. Not *that* man."

Again he read the words on the side of the sack.
For yams.

Twenty

The chifforobe was ancient and mirrored. The bedstead was brass and the mattress was stained and smelled of sweat. The room was dank and almost lightless. As the black woman led the way, Ellen experienced foreboding tempered with touches of a delicious wickedness. This was to be her last time before returning to Michigan and she wanted it to be, if not perfect, at least memorable. Certainly it could not equal in aftereffect what the episode with Brylette had visited on her sense of the exquisiteness of love, but she had been inexperienced then. Now she was no longer a child, nor was she innocent of some of the more esoteric of human sexual activities.

The black woman paused beside the bed, turned toward Ellen and said, "You gave me a hunnerd dollars, baby, so what you want? You just say, baby." She reached out, touched Ellen's shoulder, felt the blonde woman quiver.

"I want you to undress me," said Ellen.

The white frock was belted and buttoned from hem to bodice, a summery bit of *couture* purchased at I. Magnin's for nine hundred dollars. As she watched the other woman's hands touching belt and buttons, she thought of Brylette's eyes and set adrift on a fantasy. Now these were Brylette's hands whose fingertips gently explored the juncture of her thighs, Brylette's lips that taunted one nipple and then the other. As she felt herself being nudged backward onto the filthy mattress the room became a creation of satins and laces and gold ornaments. Her hands felt the crown of the licking head, felt the overly pomaded slickness of the black curls; these curls became the seadampened tresses of Brylette as they emerged from warm sea billows nymphlike, caressing, loving. Ellen was overwhelmed by the love dream. She pulled at the woman's head, felt her own spine arching involuntarily. She trembled, sobbed, sagged back and away, the perspiration on her back melding with the incredible filth on the mattress.

An hour later, in her room at the Hilton, Ellen showered and changed clothing. Rummaging through her purse, she found the name and the address that the man in Mexico had given her: Washington Clark, River Towers. She went down to the lobby, asked directions, found the great interstate highway that looped Memphis like a noose, drove over to the massive tan structure that stood over the Mississippi.

"I'm looking for a Mr. Washington Clark," she said to the doorman.

"He's dead, miss," said Hip Willis. He watched as the woman looked about the place. There was nothing in her face that would indicate compassion, nor was there fear; she resembled a *grande dame* who has just experienced an unforgivable breach of etiquette.

"I was to see him. Are his heirs and assigns to be found in the city?"

"He didn't have no airs and signs that I know of. He had a nephew, but he don't live here. You might see Mr. Jesse DeVaron. He's a lawyer or somesuch. I think he's handling Mr. Clark's business matters." Hip took a pen and a small tablet from the pocket of his uniform coat and wrote a name and address. Tearing the page out he said, "If you can't find him here, you might try a bar called Segregarious. The bar man is named Muley."

"Mu—Muley?" she said, smiling.

Hip smiled back. "Yes, ma'am. You'll find that nearly everybody in the South has two first names or a nickname."

"Quaint," she said.

"Yes, ma'am. I guess so."

She thanked him and left the building. Hip watched her

all the way to her car, a white Mercedes with Michigan license plates. He wondered whether Jesse would get lucky with her.

Three miles away, Jesse answered the phone, talked for a minute, hung up. He looked over at the sleeping Janice and kissed her on the back of the neck. She rolled over and smiled.

"One of your many?" she asked.

"Yes. His name is Hip Willis. He says a beautiful blonde lady is looking for me."

"She'll have to take leftovers," said Janice. "And after the session we had from two to four this morning, I'd bet you don't have that much left over."

"I love you, but you're still a bitch," he said.

She laughed and touched his eyebrows with a thumb. "You once told me that men fall harder for bitches than angels."

"It's still true. A bitch makes the chase element an ongoing thing. Men are by nature chasers. There's something perverse in us that makes us lose interest in malleable women."

"Malleable? How about pliant? It's a softer word."

"See what I mean? Even when I use the right word you have to top it with a better one."

Here was drama and she loved it. "I didn't top it, love; I assisted by use of a better word."

"I liked you better last night when it was pouring rain and you had your legs locked around me," he said.

"It should lightning and pour more often. What inspired you to call me?"

He shrugged. "I was out there on the balcony sopping wet and it got to me. Call it animal tension, I guess."

"Call it a hard-on," she said, giggling girlishly. She reached under the sheet and felt him. The crustiness of herself was on his foreskin and it thrilled her. "Two months is a long time," she said.

"Longer for a man than a woman, believe me."

"Why do you say that?"

"Men hurt more," he answered. "Women wrap the

pain of loss in a cocoon and it hardens in one place, like a tumor. With men, it invades the blood stream and pains with every beat of the heart."

"You don't know women very well, Jesse."

"So I've been told. They claim that they want to be known, then they shut that invisible door on themselves. Woman is a paradox wrapped in a riddle."

"You've been reading Churchill again: that's what he said about China."

"Inscrutable. That's womankind."

"Unpleasable, that's mankind."

"Bitch."

"Bastard."

They kissed several times, bird pecks of adoration. Both were happy to march again in the parade of love.

He pulled her to him and she rested her head on his shoulder.

"It was a waste, Jesse, these last two months. Can you see that I was right?"

"Yes."

"I can't live with a drunk. I love you, and you don't ever have to doubt that, not even slightly. But I won't put up with the bottle and I won't be hit. Not once, not ever again."

"I'm sorry I did it. Why didn't you hit back?"

"Because you would have killed me. You were crazy that night. I danced with a man because he asked me to and you said it was all right. And when he brought me back to our table you were Mr. Hyde."

"He patted your ass."

"Then you should have said something to him, not me."

"I couldn't."

"Why? Were you afraid of him?"

"Yes and no."

"That's no answer."

He rubbed his forehead with his fingertips and grimaced. "Something that happened in the war. . . . Men who have been in combat have seen and done things almost as an afterthought that would drive civilians into the crazy house."

She stared at him, query in her eyes. "I know that you won a medal in Vietnam. Did it have to do with that?"

"Yes. You read about combat psychosis, about this thing called flashback. I call it mental residue. I try not to get mad any more at anybody. I got mad once and . . . did some things."

She thought of this for a time and said, "I think I know why you didn't hit my dance partner. You wouldn't have stopped hitting, would you?"

"I guess that's about it. The thing triggered a hundred memories. You're female, and that's why I slapped you once and stopped. I'm sorry. God, I'm sorry."

"I don't forgive you but I still love you. I think I love you more right now than I ever have. I'm seeing inside you, though darkly."

"It should be kept in the dark. The strangest thing about this is that I did that thing in Nam out of rage at my mother. Those men that I killed became my mother. I guess I sound like that character in *Psycho*." He laughed.

"Tell me," she said.

"What?"

"Anything you want to. Your mind is fucked up over the war, and my mind is fucked up over you. We love each other and we've had problems. Maybe I can't change them, but I can share them."

He moved his arm from beneath her neck and propped up on one elbow. "Very well, kid: you asked, and you got it. I'm scared."

"Of what?"

"Would you believe me if I said the unknown? I know something, but I don't know what it is. Last night I went to a gun shop and bought an M-1 rifle. A deadly nine-pound army job, complete with clips, sling, shells, the whole works. The thing is, there was no way that I *couldn't* have bought it."

The confusion in her eyes was implicit; she wanted to understand but did not; however, to have spoken might have broken the spell of his confession. She tried to smile but it faded from her face.

"Janice, do you believe in God?" he asked.

"I . . . yes, I think so." The question was so strange coming from his whiskey-scarred lips that it stunned her.

"That's why I had to buy that rifle. Dammit, I don't understand it, but somehow God is in this thing. Don't look at me that way."

"What way?"

"Like you just saw a pissant eat a bale of hay. You wanted me to talk, so I'm trying to talk."

Ten seconds passed and she said, "It's just that I've never felt so close to you, or so distant. Tell me all of it, Jesse; I want to share, no matter what it is."

Slowly, he reeled off the phenomenal occurrences of the past days: Donkey Baby and Hip Willis telling of Popper's strange behavior. Popper's murder. The cross falling from the letter onto Muley's bar. The sinister message from Charleston Garman. The meeting with Ollie Colbert at Red and Blue. The visit from Reeder and Riggazi, the FBI agents. The hallucinatory-yet-believable tableau of Votan as offered by the Mormon pamphlets. By the time he had completed the story his arm was killing him and he lay on his back and stared at the ceiling, remembering, sorting, rearranging the dross of his confusion.

Without looking at him, aware that he was slightly embarrassed, Janice said, "I can see potential worry for you in all that, but I can't see God in it."

"Maybe, maybe not," he said. "But when that little metal cross fell onto Muley's bar, *something* slapped the *real* me as certainly as a hand slapping a face. It wasn't a physical thing, really, just a gut warning about a coming turbulence. A warm turbulence, but a turbulence just the same." He turned his face toward her and said, "Am I making any sense at all?"

"I'm trying to understand, Jesse. Perhaps your drinking has . . . affected you."

He laughed at this and said, "An old drunk once told me that sobering up was like standing a pyramid on its head and falling down to the small end. I think at just this minute I have realized what he meant: life is closer, more confining, but the necessary things become more visible, more recognizable. Last night I dived off that pyramid base and called you, and I knew, *knew*, that you'd come. There was no question. And here you are. You were a reward, your presence here is a reward."

She arched an eyebrow and said, "You've called me many things, but never a reward. If I read all this correctly, my need for you last night was God-sent. Somehow the fact of our fornicating like mink does not strike me as something that a Divine hand would pat on the head."

"You've got a point," said Jesse. "It's just that, with your father being a Baptist preacher, I would have thought that you would have jumped right into my simmering cauldron of religion." He stared away and said, "Maybe it wasn't what I read into it. I'm convinced that it was God, but maybe it wasn't."

"I can sum up my feelings for the Baptists in about two seconds: they say they hate hell, when the fact is, they love hell—for other people. The only Protestant sect that is meaner and more malignant in its self-righteousness is the Church of Christ. Those people adore hell—for others."

"So what do you think of the Mormons?" he asked, pleased that she had allowed herself to be drawn into his theistic puzzlement.

"A harmless group of Hare Krishnas who were ahead of their time. They still practice polygamy in some places, although the main church abolished the practice some seventy years ago. I suppose they mean well, but that thing about Votan should have told you something about the sort of persons who embrace such sops to low self-esteem."

She had lanced certain mental boils with her words, truly enough, but in his intuitions some pain remained. He halfway wished that he had forgone the whole foray into religion, for somehow he presently felt weak, stupid, exposed, vulnerable. "So you think I'm off on a tangent with this Charleston Garman letter?" he asked.

"I'd like to think so," she said, "but the visit from the FBI is the part that captures me. Popper was an old black man who shined shoes for a living, and the FBI visits you because you attended his funeral. The situations are so far apart that they've got to be linked. And if they are indeed linked, then the letter is what links them." She looked at him with troubled eyes and said, "Yes, something is going on, but just don't read God into it. The part that really bothers me is your purchase of that rifle."

"A famous football coach used to tell his team before going onto the field, 'Never mind if the horse is blind—load the wagon.' I'm blind enough to know that I'm either the horse or the wagon."

"Could you explain all that?" she asked.

"All that I'm referring to is this: something definitely *is* happening, and I'm part of it, and I don't know yet what my part is, and that letter from Charleston Garman is much more than the gobbledygook of a religious fanatic with brain damage. Now you know why I bought the rifle: the blind horse knows that the wagon is being loaded, and something is going to have to be pulled somewhere."

"Well, when the time comes, just be careful. Have I told you lately that I love you?"

He patted her belly and said, "Not for at least ten minutes. Have I told you lately that you've got the prettiest triangle of kissable curlicues in the world?" His hand wandered downward.

"Not for at least two months," she said.

"Want to ride the magic horsey?"

She kissed him on a nipple and said, "I thought you'd never ask."

An hour later, when they had showered together and she was gone, Jesse walked onto the balcony and let the magnificence of a Saturday sun caress him. He was happy that he had refrained from telling her about Rosa's death and the impending money from the insurance policy.

There were times when money was the least important thing in the world, and now was one of them. Janice loved him and, dammit, fight it as he might, he loved her. When the money came and when this Votan mess put on its true face, they would go to Las Vegas in a new Cadillac and get married. He mulled the word over: married.

It was a good word, a happy word. A sunshine word.

In Alexandria, Virginia, Vaughn Biddle took a phone message, then hung up. He picked up a second phone and dialed a seven digit number, held and waited. At the fifth ring the party on the other end responded.

"Biddle here. Our lady of the blonde hair is on the move in Memphis. She's headed toward DeVaron."

"So let her head," said Foster St. John. "Deep Six thinks you may be right to let this DeVaron do our work for us. I don't happen to agree, but I'm outranked. Make very sure that I'm kept up to date on all this."

"I will," said Biddle. As Foster St. John hung up on the other end, Biddle got up and moved some of the pins in the map. Reaching into a filing cabinet, he took a map headed CITY OF MEMPHIS, TENNESSEE and hung it to the right of the pink one. Now he removed from his desk drawer something that he had been looking forward to using for the better part of a week, a multicolored group of ballpoint pens that were tightly ensnared in a rubber band. Each color represented a person. The red was for Jesse DeVaron, just as red had been the color for Jesse DeVaron's map pin. For the first time in this grinding mess, Vaughn Biddle wondered whether the red had just *happened* or whether it had been an unconscious symbol for blood.

Twenty-one

Northern Florida was overcast, its skies smoky-dark. As he drove the blue Chevrolet into the faculty housing complex that abutted the small campus, agent Wayne Blades of the Federal Bureau of Investigation was depressed not only by the fall in barometric pressure but also by the incredibly bland nature of anything that smacked of being purchased by tax money. Governmental housing just had that stark look that no amount of shrubbery could ever enliven. Tan brick and beige roof here, dark gray brick and light gray roof there. But, giving credit where it was due, the houses were neat, well-built, well-insulated little boxes that kept the rain off and dust out. It occurred to him that perhaps he, like the houses, had become beige and gray in his spirit; certainly he had other plans for this Saturday, such as cleaning out his garage, perhaps mowing the lawn, maybe a steak on the grill at sunset. But his orders had been either vaguely specific or specifically vague by design, the bottom line being that he was to interview one Dr. Brylette Fender for the purpose, as closely as he could determine, of scaring the shit out of her.

He found the address, parked the Chevrolet behind a green Datsun, went to the door, and rang the bell. A dark-complexioned woman answered. She wore denims and a white blouse tied at the belly Calypso-singer style.

"Dr. Brylette Fender?"

"Yes."

He opened his wallet and let her study his credentials.

"I'm Agent Blades of the Federal Bureau of Investigation. I'd like a moment of your time, please."

When they were inside she offered him a drink and he smiled and declined. Accepting a seat on a couch, he looked about the place and found it to be spotless, immaculate; the scents of furniture polish and cleaning fluids were a not unpleasant counterpoint to the dullness of the motor-pool Chevy.

She leaned against a wall and folded her arms. Moving her upper torso, scratching her back piggy fashion, she said, "How may I help you?"

"You recently made a trip to Mexico," he said. "Did anything occur there that might have jeopardized your position here at the college?"

She stopped the scratching. Her cheeks felt hot; she licked her lips. The memory of something that Ellen had said in the Port Arthur motel flared: ". . . the guards saw the Mercedes, and you asleep in the back seat, and they just waved me through. I couldn't believe it . . ." and ". . . It was almost as if they knew not to bother me. Am I being paranoid?"

The FBI agent had not moved for twenty seconds, had refrained even from blinking his eyes. "Dr. Fender, I asked you . . ."

"I heard you," she said. She pulled a chair from beneath a dinette table, turned it backward and sat down facing him, her arms folded across the back. "It was a vacation. I went to Mexico and was there for about two weeks and took in the sun and came home. Any crime in that?"

"No, no crime in that. Now, while in Mexico, did you happen to come into contact with a woman named Ellen Rogers?"

"Yes."

"Did you come to know her . . . well?"

"Not really. I rode home with her. To New Orleans, anyway. From there I took a bus. May I ask what this is about?" The words *jeopardize your position* would not go away; they seemed to lie as great stones on her back and shoulders.

"It is about this: her husband is being considered for a post at a naval hospital abroad. We think it odd that she would go to a foreign country at just this time." He waited for this falsehood to sink in and then said, "This is nothing at all but a rudimentary investigation. You are in no way suspect in any criminal proceeding."

"That's nice to know. So why the question about something jeopardizing my position here at the school?"

He wanted to say *because that's exactly the way I was ordered to say it,* but he answered, "Forgive me, but that's a euphemism for national security. When we say that one's position is jeopardized, we sometimes come off as appearing a bit overzealous. No, this has nothing to do with your place here." The incisions had been made, the fish was troubled by the line; she was off balance and it was time to go. He stood and said, "I appreciate your help in this matter. I can almost give you a brassbound guarantee that you'll never hear of it again. I would hope that my visit remains secret for the good of all concerned."

Brylette walked him to the door and nodded. She was afraid to speak lest she sound hoarse, intimidated, secretive.

Agent Blades backed the Chevrolet into the street and did not allow himself to think until he had driven through the campus and was approaching the freeway that would take him to Jacksonville. He had done exactly as ordered, no more, no less. The ironic thing was that, unbeknownst to herself, this mannish Dr. Fender probably knew a damned sight more about what was going on than he did. The Bureau followed the mushroom theory with its agents more than it did with the general populace, the mushroom theory being *keep 'em in the dark and feed 'em bullshit.* Yes, he had been ordered to scare the lady with a few choice words and phrases and scare her he had. It would make him look good on Monday, but this was Saturday and there was still time to mow, to do the steaks in a Florida sunset. The garage would keep until next Saturday. He loosened his tie, drove into the interstate and turned on the car's radio. A violin and trumpet version of

"My Cherie Amour" was playing. It was good Saturday music.

When the agent was gone Brylette Fender stripped, showered, lay down on her bed naked. A part of her Saturday cleaning ritual had been the changing of the bedsheets, and the cool cleanness of the percale accepted her body easily, caressed it as readily as a known and trusted lover might.

The agent had lied to her. Or had he? And his saying that her *position* was *jeopardized* was suspicious. It had something to do with that bit of weirdly inscribed metal that Ellen had shown her, a bit of metal that, truth be told, Brylette had forgotten almost as quickly as she had forgotten Ellen herself. In the world of the gay female Ellen was as a kindergarten student, albeit a pretty one, while Brylette herself was *magna cum laude*. When she had attempted to draw Ellen into a meaningful conversation the blonde had been almost laughably inept at any but the most superficial conversational mumblings on The Meaning of Life.

But such thoughts were diversions, a mental camouflage against what had now been laid at her doorstep by this either incredibly inept or incredibly ept FBI agent. He had taunted her without taunting her, worried her without worrying her. Well, would the FBI send an agent to her door because she had laid three Korean businessmen for money, because she had gone down *on* and been gone down on *by* Ellen the Socialite?

No.

But the FBI had questioned her, which meant that the FBI knew something, and her own ignorance frightened her.

She left her bed and went to a drawer that harbored the private stuff of her private world. Photographs, old letters, a soft-rubber penis complete with fur straps, *pro forma* memorabilia of a secret and lonely life. Taking the bundle into the kitchen, she dropped it into a garbage can amidst coffee grounds and orange peels. Opening the back door and walking onto her small back porch, she dropped the dark plastic sack that contained her life into a large metal garbage can, bidding it farewell. It did not concern her that she was stark naked. She stood there for several minutes looking at sun and sky and earth.

Now she went into the house and opened a linen closet. Selecting three of her largest heavy-gauge towels, she returned to the bedroom and lay them over the pillow. She stared at an etagere drawer for a long while before opening it, and when she did the short and ugly .32 caliber pistol lay atop a pile of lingerie like a cobra coiled among rose petals. She picked up the weapon and lay on the bed. The towels were a bit too thick for comfort and she removed one, folded it, lay it against the headboard. The thought came to her that all humankind were fools, and she tried to envision the face of the one who would say, *Well, at least she was neat.* Predictable humankind. Poor, stupid, wretched humankind. Others would say, *We didn't know,* and the rest would query, *Why did she do it?*

She placed the short barrel in her mouth, tasted something reminiscent of a lightly oiled beer can, moved her thumb into the trigger housing, and pushed.

Twenty-two

Detective James Oliver Colbert of the Memphis Police Department returned the phone to its cradle, picked up a handful of popcorn and threw it back into the bowl. He had eaten too much already and he was feeling bloated. But it was not his stomach that was troubling him just now; the phone call had been fast and kooky and anonymous. Not good. Not good at all.

As Hazel Colbert walked into the living room Oliver said, "Do me something, Babe."

"What's that?"

"Call Jesse and say these exact words: RB twenty. Say nothing else." Even as he spoke he was up and walking swiftly across the house.

"What's it about?" Hazel asked. "I thought we were going to watch this Cagney movie."

"This is more important. Besides, I've seen Cagney swan dive off that burning oil tank twenty times."

As he slipped into his shoes and shoulder harness in the bedroom he heard Hazel utter the words. He came into the room and said, "Jesse says he'll be there. He even knew who I was. How'd he know who I was?"

"Something that's been going on for twenty years, Doll. Don't ask."

She looked at him with wifely wryness. "I won't, unless it has to do with women."

He laughed, patted her on the hips, and ran out to the car.

The fluctuations of police work are more pronounced

than in any other line of endeavor, he was thinking ten minutes later as he parked his car beside the porno house. *Within a quarter of an hour I have gone from the quintessence of domesticity to the pits of a cum-sticky hell, complete with perverts.* He remembered a Sunday morning many years ago when he had left a double murder and suicide that had involved a six-gauge shotgun, and from there he had gone directly to church. This was almost as crazy as that had been, and surely it was more serious. If Jesse gave him the same kind of shit that he had shoveled on their last meeting here, he would just hit the sonofabitch in the mouth, for old times' sake and out of true friendship. Yes, this was serious.

He went into the place and smelled that strange odor that was partly old carpet, partly cleaning fluid, partly something like ashfall from hell. Porno houses just had that smell that was like no other. He got two-dollars worth of tokens from a black girl. Satisfied that none of this grotesquerie would rub off on him, he went into the booth room and past the loitering queers.

Jesse arrived three minutes later. Colbert motioned to him and the queers watched sadly and jealously.

"Ollie, we really got to find another place to do this kind of thing," he said. "Frankly, we might get a reputation."

Colbert dropped a token into the wall slot and the projector whirred. The two men sat down on the wooden booth. "This time I get to talk," said Colbert. "You shut the fuck up and listen. The last time we met here you cut me off something fierce."

Jesse watched the screen, which was, as usual, a piece of rectangular white pasteboard. "Why is it they always make ecstasy look like a convulsion suffered by an idiot?" he asked. A bottle blonde had her rump in the air and her knees and face on a pool table. A tattooed man was servicing her from behind. Jesse wondered whether her knees hurt, and whether the pool table itched her face.

"I can see that this ain't going to work," said Colbert. "Let's go." He left the booth and Jesse followed.

THE VOTAN TREASURE

When they were in Ollie's car Jesse said, "Okay, you've got me here, Ollie. Now, what's the big stew?"

Colbert backed his car away from the theater, drove one block to the left, turned right for a block, repeated this broken field activity as though eluding ghosts. And while doing so he talked, the words thinly veiling hurt, thinly disguising a plea.

"You're in big trouble, Jess. I don't know what in hell is coming down on your head, but it smells shitty. You and I met at Red and Blue the other night and you stuck it in and broke it off. You malignant sonofabitch, if we're pals, and if we're gonna stay pals, this is it. You have to come clean with me."

"Does it have to do with Votan?" Jesse asked.

"I don't know who he is."

"He's Jesus."

"Jesus, I *know;* Votan, I *don't* know. What do you mean, he's Jesus?"

"Just that. The natives of Chiapas in Mexico called a blonde white man in a robe Votan. The legend went on for a thousand or more years. And don't look at me that way—watch the street. No, I haven't been drinking; haven't had a drop or wanted one in two, three days."

"You got religion?" Colbert asked.

Jesse laughed. "Maybe. The reason I didn't tell you anything the other night at Red and Blue was because I didn't have shit to go on. Now I know a little, and the little threatens to become a lot."

Colbert checked his rearview mirror and, satisfied that they were not being followed, slowed down. Turning onto Union Avenue, heading west, he said, "Tell me a lot."

"Popper's nephew, Charleston Garman, wrote Popper a letter," Jesse said. "Garman had found something in Mexico. I didn't believe in it at first. Now I believe in it . . . and a lot more."

"What was it he found?" Colbert asked.

"A religious treasure. I call it the Votan treasure. The Mormon religion was founded in 1823 because a dreamer named Joseph Smith supposedly found some plates with the word of God, gold plates. You know from your high school history what the Mormons have been subjected to in this country, and elsewhere. They are about as outcast as Jews, though not as prominently so. That's what I think Charleston Garman found: a second set of Mormon plates. The Votan treasure." Jesse thought these words over, then repeated them: "The Votan treasure."

They were on the bridge to Arkansas before Colbert spoke. He looked down at the gray-green waters of the Mississippi and said, "Okay, you've told me what it is you're working on, and it probably ties in with what my phone call was about. This male voice said, 'Tell your friend Jesse that Cowboy and Wolfe are in the city and he'd better be careful.' "

They were off the bridge and a half mile into Arkansas before Jesse spoke: "Cowboy has got to be a nickname, of course. Wolfe could be a real name or a nickname also. Is that all he said?"

Colbert nodded. "That's all he said. Sounded like a man who knows his business, or meant business, if you know what I mean."

"I've got to ask myself why he was being so good to me. What does it sound like to you?"

"One, it sounds serious, deadly even. Two, it sounds like this Votan thing has you at its very center. But that no longer surprises me. The other night when we met at Red and Blue and I thought you were acting like a college boy, snotty and all, that was what I wanted to tell you. Two FBI men were asking around about you. Reeder and Riggazi. I didn't know what in hell you'd done, but I was trying to warn you not to do it anymore."

Jesse gave him a playful punch on the shoulder but Colbert did not smile. "Ollie, you're thinking hard about something. I've known you for twenty years and you always get that bull-in-heat look when you're thinking about something. Let's have it."

Colbert wheeled the car up onto a cloverleaf ramp, drove over, headed back toward Memphis. The light sparkles from the city's great towers were reflected in his eyes as he said, "It was a black man. The caller was a black man. Dammit, I *knew* there was something about his voice that was staying with me. He pronounced your name 'Jessuh.' You know any black people who'd come to your rescue like that?"

"Not over eight, nine hundred. You're sure he was black?"

Colbert looked at the city for a moment and said, "I'd bet a month's pay on it. But what I can't figure is what a black man would have to do with some Mormon plates. All the blacks I know are Primitive Baptist or AME."

"It could be that his interest is not theological but financial," said Jesse.

"It doesn't figure, Jess. Financial how? You don't have any money of your own, and he didn't ask for any."

"You're wrong on one point, Ollie: I do have some money of my own. Rosa died some time back, and I found out this week that she left me some life insurance money."

"Sorry to hear it. I've heard you mention her. I thought you two didn't get along."

"We didn't." Jesse looked away. They were crossing the river again, and he silently prayed that Rosa's raptured soul had found, as the old hymn put it, rest beyond the river.

"But a ten-thousand-dollar insurance policy wouldn't have any bearing on this, that I can see; besides, how would he have known about it? And why didn't he ask for some of the money up front?"

For the first time in a lifetime Jesse realized why money destroys friendships. To have stated at this moment that the amount of Rosa's bequest was forty times the amount Ollie had mentioned would have been a boast enmeshed in an insult. And he was disturbed by Ollie's assumption that the amount was ten thousand dollars, the amount of life insurance that working class people see as the essence of grandiosity. James Oliver Colbert and his ilk were small thinkers and small doers, the drones in the hive of life. Jesse DeVaron, on the other hand, had risen above all that—the pettiness, the worry, the never having enough and never enjoying enough—and he felt a slight detachment toward Ollie. He had known all through their police days together that he was clever while Ollie was methodical, a relationship similar to that between hunter and dog. But now the hunter had emerged from the forest to don a tuxedo and rise into places that knew not of mud and ticks and the woods of mere survival. Yes, Ollie was still the friendly old mutt, the trusted cur, the uninformed pal who would not be allowed to enter the great house of luxury. In his confusion and loneliness, Jesse said, "You're a good pal, Ollie. If something were to happen, I just want you to know that."

Colbert was embarrassed. "Yeah, well, thanks. But don't call me Ollie." They laughed together and Colbert said, "So, what do you make of all this?"

"I bought an M-1 rifle yesterday, that's what I think of it. I *knew* and I *know* that something was, and is, moving me toward this."

"You sound downright psychedelic," said Colbert. It was a word that they had used in their younger days, a word from the sixties.

Jesse nodded. "Reeder and Riggazi nosed around you, then Reeder and Riggazi nosed around me. The FBI is interested in it, that much we know. We also know that the Mormons are in it, and we think we know why. You get a phone call from a black man—you think he was black—that tells me to beware of somebody named 'Cowboy' and somebody named 'Wolf,' probably code names or nicknames." He looked at Colbert mournfully lazily.

"If I read you right, you think you're being led to a slaughter or led away from one," Colbert said. "It's got to be led *away,* Jess. The black caller was warning you to be on your toes. Damn, I wish I knew who he was."

"There's more to it than that, Ollie. Your caller wanted me to be awake, but he did so out of some vested interest that I can't quite put my finger on. He . . ." Jesse snapped his fingers and said, "DAMN!"

"Damn *what?*" Colbert shouted. He had nearly lost control of the car.

"Hip Willis. He called me today and said that a

woman wanted to see me about something. He always calls me Jessuh."

"So maybe it was him that called me at home. Did the woman show?"

"No. And, coming clean, I'd forgotten all about it. Janice was over this morning and that's mostly been on my mind today. But why would Hip call *you* and not *me?* Why, if it *was* him, would Hip Willis call Ollie Colbert and tell you to tell Jesse . . ." He felt his interlaced thoughts becoming a series of knotted conduits through which nothing could pass. Hip Willis was but a doorman at River Towers, a pleasant black face that was always friendly, sometimes helpful—a nondescript black face in a city filled with black faces. Hip's features merged with hundreds of other features with whom Jesse was acquainted. At last it and the others formed a dark eddy that vortexed wildly, pulling Jesse's ephemeral elation down into nothingness. "Ollie, take me home," he said.

"I will. But I want to know more about this rifle you bought. You once hinted to me about what you did in Nam. You're a civilian now, Jess. Just don't do anything stupid."

Jesse watched the traffic and said nothing. He could not explain to Colbert the partially intuitive, partially disquieting and totally undeniable force that had urged him into Miller Bass's gun shop; to have done so would have sent his old partner off on the same antibooze diatribe that Janice had skirted so raggedly this morning. Hell, maybe they were right—maybe the George Dickel had fogged his brain into believing that the hand of God was in this. One thing was for sure: if God wanted Jesse DeVaron to know what was going on with the Mormons and the FBI and Popper's body, not to mention somebody called Cowboy and Wolfe, then He sure as hell had a roundabout way of doing it. *Votan lives and I suffer,* he was thinking as Colbert stopped the car near Jesse's old convertible.

Getting out, Jesse said, "Thanks, Ollie. You're a gentleman and a scholar."

"I'm a clod and an illiterate and you know it, you

crazy bastard," Colbert answered. "Just keep in mind to watch your ass. And remember, if you need me, *call!*"

When Colbert was far down the street and around the corner Jesse fumbled with his keys and opened the car's trunk which emitted a scent of old dust, old dankness. He picked up the open-ended and rectangular metal casings, opened the box of shells, placed eight rounds in each of the clips. Looking about to make certain that he was not observed, he lifted the M-1 out of the trunk and pushed back the bolt. As ever, the metal resisted slightly as he shoved a clip into the chamber, released the bolt quickly, making sure to jerk his thumb upward. *Just like swimming or riding a bicycle,* he was thinking, *it all comes back to you.*

Now he looked down the street and felt the old rush of power. Three hundred yards away was a streetlight that was more yellow than its fellows, a yellow-fellow disrupting an elongated platoon of white fellows. He pushed the safety forward, heard it click on the outside of the trigger housing. Hefting the weapon to his shoulder, making sure that his right elbow was horizontal, he sighted in on the distant globe. The old code word came back: BRASS. An anagram. Breathe. Relax. Aim. Slack. Squeeze. If it fell he would rush forward and . . .

He lowered the weapon, and felt himself sweating.

Twenty-three

Four miles away, at a bar called Charlie Fatback's, Donald Phillips sat at a table and nursed a Heineken draft. He had drunk beer in Germany, in Mexico, in Costa Rica—hell, all over the world—but this one was especially good, especially memorable. After this beer he would make his move on the Mercedes that was parked in its stall at the motel across the street. He hated the thought of having to kill the blonde, but probably it would be necessary to do so. So far he had been compelled to do in but one person, that fat fart up in Connecticut, but as far as the authorities might ever be able to go in tying him to that one, well, no way, Jose.

Two black women walked in and there came a round of catcalls and backslaps, backslaps that drifted downward into assrubs. Hookers, one in lavender dress and heels, the other younger and wearing orange and gray and tons too much makeup. They moved along the bar doing shoulder rubs and dick grabs.

Donald Phillips hated them. This sort of mayhem would never do in Germany. There was a refinement about the Germans, a tacit *noblesse oblige* that was unheard of in America. Too, the Germans did not look at black skin in the same deprecatory way that white America did. During his hitch in Kaiserslautern there had been a milk and honey blonde named Ingeborg Kolb who had turned herself and himself every way but loose during a three month affair, and not once did she ever indicate in any way that he was other than a human being. No references to kinky hair, nor any innuendo about penis size or staying power. Ingeborg, beloved and much missed Ingeborg.

He finished the beer, ordered another, went to the window and saw that the Mercedes had not moved. Returning to his table, he noted that the two hookers had made contact and were leaving the place with a pair of ill-dressed black johns. By their passage the place seemed to become quieter, to drift into a melba-brown melancholy. Someone dropped coins into the juke box and the plaintive voice of Sam Cooke sang about runnin' like that ol' river.

Sing it, Sam. Sing it even from the grave, the grave that the motel lady put you in back in 1962 when you were chasing that Chink across the parking lot wearing nothing but a raincoat. Yes, Sam, it'd been a long time coming, but a change was gonna come . . .

Rubbing tears from his eyes, hoping that none saw, Donald Phillips knew all too well what Sam Cooke was wailing about. Born in the Pittsburgh ghetto, a place of stickball in the streets and smoking Buicks and whores and pushers on every corner, Donald Phillips had gotten out on a baseball scholarship to Ball State, a so-so college in Indiana. The ROTC had gotten him a uniform, and the uniform had gotten him Germany and a taste for cold beer and white rump, and the cold beer and white rump had gotten him a friendship with a white colonel in G-2 who had gotten him into the Company. Gotten, gitten, gatten, begat. He was here in a Memphis bar because he had been begat and begotten by the white world and, though it troubled him, he loved the hypocrisy of it all that had allowed him to live so well, do so much, travel so far in the last fifteen years. We gotta have more niggers, so let's get him and him and him; that will prove to the world that all are equal in this country, by God. The voice of Mister Charlie, a whisper now instead of a rabid shout, but still the voice of Mister Charlie. A black American was not an *arriviste* in his own land, but . . .

"Get down from there!" someone shouted, pulling Phillips up from the black trench of despair. He looked toward the bar and saw that a lanky black youth, a beer bottle in each hand, was tap-shuffling along the bar. There were shrieks of laughter and rhythmic boomings as some of the patrons beat cadence against their tables with bottle butts.

Walking toward the bar even before he knew that he was going to move, Phillips slammed into the youth's legs and felt the angular lankiness fall against his back as shouts and screams roared in his head, sounds pouring down from something high and far away, human sounds that were neither laudatory nor fearful but the passive shouts of people who would shout at a birth or a death or a fight just for the hell of shouting. These were black people acting like niggers and he despised them. As he bowed his back the boy's body bounced off him like a green willow limb, and he knew that all that he and Sam Cooke had gone into for the last ten minutes would forever be the way of the black race in America; yes, drunk niggers would always shout and strut along bars with a beer in the hand and bleary eyes in the head, but, by God, before leaving for Germany he would make his one statement against it. He stood erect, watched as the young man lay on his back staring at him, the eyes, in that darkened atmosphere, like spotted eggs in a tar bucket.

"Hey, man, who you fuckin' wid?" somebody yelled from across the place.

Phillips yelled, "Who in hell wants to know?" He left the bar and walked gracefully into the darkness toward a far corner where black people were already making a way for him, glasses falling over, women screaming, men reaching for pockets that might or might not conceal knives. Whoever had yelled was not there any longer, had moved with the general traffic to get out of the way of whatever it was that the well-dressed stranger had in mind; he stood looking at the empty tables as if his ghostly tormentor might materialize. Unaware of why the skin of his right hand itched, he turned now and faced the backs of all who were going out the door; within ten seconds none were there but the bartender; even the bar-strutting youth had fled.

Now his hand summoned in its pain and he looked and saw that a traceline of blood coursed from just behind the fourth knuckle to the tip of his middle and ring fingers; the wound was like a pinprick, but the itch was by now enraging.

The room swam; he felt nauseated; his throat seemed to close. Phillips staggered to the door of the place just in time to see cars pulling away from the parking lot, their headlamps slicing the night dust of the parking lot as they went to another place to do their drinking, chasing Saturday night, salvaging what part of it was left to them. He looked across the street at the motel, at the Mercedes, a bleary white object now. Strange, he was thinking, how just two beers and a bit of grabass had screwed up his metabolism, made him so incredibly sleepy. He lurched across the sidewalk and into the street, back up onto the sidewalk, his right hand rubbing the back of his left at the place where the itch was by now benumbed against a pain like a wasp sting. Yes, perhaps that was what it was, a wasp sting. Up the street was a furniture store and there were beds and couches in the window. If only he could get to a bed or a couch. He started to move down off the sidewalk but his legs would not carry him; they had jellified—petrified-atrophied; although they held him, they would not move. In his mouth was the taste of ashes and wood smoke. His last thought was of a wood stove that he and his grandmother had stoked and then dampered on winter nights.

Donald Phillips died. But he did not fall. The two black men who had watched his erratic movements for the past ten minutes grabbed his arms before he could collapse and dragged him to a nearby vacant lot. Placing the body face down, one said to the other, "Get his shoe, he lost a shoe on the sidewalk, get his sh—"

"I'm gettin' it, mother fucker," said the other black man. When he came back from the sidewalk with the shoe he lay it beside the body in homage to naturality, the truant shoe resembling in the half light from the street a carp thrown up on a bank by a disgusted fisherman, its mouth agape, natural yet unnatural. He smiled down at it, at the resemblance of a shoe to an open-mouthed fish.

"Come on, it's done," said the other, a man named Bloodheap.

They ran up the street for a block and then turned off the main thoroughfare of boarded-up parts stores and unlighted used car lots into an area of unpainted houses. Both were sweating and both were silent all the way.

At last the one who had been sent for the shoe said, "I wanta know somethin'—how'd you know that man gonna pass out?" When Bloodheap did not respond he said, "You come to me in that bar and you say that man started the fight gonna pass out on the street. How'd you know that, brother?" Still there was no answer. "Okay, I helped you to take care of your passed-out buddy, so can I have my five like you said?"

They stopped in the street and the five was passed from one hand to another. "You don't talk much, do you?" Shoe Fetcher declared somewhat nervously. When there was no response from Bloodheap the other man backed away, started to wave, thought better of it, and trotted down the street.

When Bloodheap was certain that his impromptu helper was gone he walked back to the empty lot, saw nothing in the darkness, walked on past the tavern to a dry goods store. In the anemic moonlight the oily parking lot was as a nocturnal ocean—placid, contemplative, impenetrable.

Moving to the facade of the store, locating there as if his presence in the moonlight might divulge to an unforgiving world what he had just accomplished, Bloodheap leaned back and waited, fully aware that possibly, no, *probably*, he was being watched. Someone is always watching, the man had said to him on hiring him yesterday. Certainly someone had been watching Bloodheap for quite some time, else how did they know that he was a contract killer? Then again, was it *they* or *he*, the hulking black man darker than himself who had approached him last night with a thousand dollars and one of the more specialized weapons that Bloodheap had ever seen? Curious. The whole thing was curious. Had he not needed the money he would have taken the time to check the guy out, to ask where he had gotten the name of Bloodheap in the dark alleys of Memphis's underbelly. As they said it on the street nowadays, you pays your money and you takes your chances. But it was he who had been paid, and it was he who had taken the chance. He shuddered, the rigor of his shoulders against the grasp of an imaginary hand. It was transitory and groundless fear. He relaxed and let the thought of apprehension pass.

"You did good," said a voice from the darkness.

Bloodheap looked and saw a hulking figure to his left. "About what?" he asked.

"Okay, brother, we'll play your game." The large man passed something to Bloodheap in the darkness. It was a folded wad of paper money. He knew not to count it, knew not to act as though he wanted to count it; he knew from the feel that it was ten one hundred dollar bills. "You got the cigar?" the large man asked. Bloodheap reached into his pocket and handed the cigar over. It was not a cigar at all but a plastic tube from which the poison pellet had been fired into Phillips' hand.

"Nice weapon," said Bloodheap. "I'd still like to know who I'm doing business with. You called me and said where to pick this cigar up and what to do with it. Took a lot of faith. How do I know you ain't the man?"

"Maybe I am the man," said the shadowed figure. "From now on, should I ever call you, the job gets done by you and you alone. Who was that brother that helped you to lay the body in the weeds?"

"Never saw him before in my life," said Bloodheap. "Just a guy that helped out." He felt slightly flustered, fearful. The five dollar helper was a witness, but it was to be hoped that the witness knew of a reeling drunk, not of a dying man.

The shadowed man laughed softly. "Bloodheap your real name?"

"It'll do. I used to help my daddy clean out a slaughterhouse. The name stuck."

"I'll remember," said the shadow man. "You don't know this, but you just got a good deal. Don't fuck up and tell nobody nothin'. Who knows, we may call you again sometime."

"We?"

"Move out."

Bloodheap heard threat in these words. He moved away from the place and crossed the parking lot. When he passed the tavern and the grassy lot there was a serenity about the area that belied what lay in the dark weeds. He would be found in the morning and the papers would make little or no mention of it; one more dead nigger. Racism had its advantages, and so did pellet pistols shaped like cigars. It would be nice to know who it was that he had just killed, nicer to know who his dark and hulking benefactor had been. The thing smelled of something heavier than personal vendetta, something heavier than mob vengeance. The cigar-pistol was a neat touch, smelled of CIA. It was not good to question such things.

In Alexandria, Virginia, a phone rang. Vaughn Biddle turned down his TV set and answered.

"Memphis here," said the caller.

Biddle inhaled deeply, happily. "Go ahead, Memphis."

"The black bugout is dead. You can touch your computer, or whatever it is you do, and erase Phillips from the Company roster."

"Did you have any personal involvement?"

"No, sir. That stuff you gave me on a feller named Bloodheap turned out to be as good as gold. He's a good man. Took the money and ran."

"Good. Was the pellet pistol used?"

"Yessir. I hope it all dissolves like you said it would."

"It will. Now, what about the others?"

"Jesse the dick knows that he's being stalked by Wolfe and the crazy cowpoke. He's on his guard good, has his M-1 rifle ready." The caller laughed. "I think the last parties in this will meet someway, somehow in the next few hours."

"Fine. Where's the blonde?"

"In a motel not three hundred yards from where I am. Do you want us to jimmy the trunk tonight?"

"No, dammit, just do as has been planned all along. We don't want some minor glitch in our plan to queer things at the last minute. We want the blonde and DeVaron and Wolfe and the cowpoke in the same basket before the shooting starts. You're a master at getting things rolling with anonymous phone calls, and I'm leaving all this in your hands.

"You still don't want the blonde hurt?"

Biddle rubbed his eyes, let his hand trail upward to stroke the top of his head. "No," he said at last. "Let's be careful. It's brought us this far. Our personality profile on her indicates that she's a little on the stupid and flighty side. And she's rich, and this is still America, and dead rich people make waves. Don't do anything more than see that she's happy to escape with her ass and reputation intact."

"Yes, sir. I think I can bring the whole thing off before sunup. I've got a place picked out for the meeting, a quiet place. Tonight we're on a roll."

"You'd better be," said Biddle. "This one is big. So big, in fact, that I'm thinking about pulling you out of Memphis after it's over. You're SSG, Special Support Group, so officially you are not anything more than a part-time employee; the odd thing is, this is so big and you accidentally got so involved in it that even our special agents aren't to know as much as you do. Reeder and Riggazi don't know you and they had goddamned well better not."

"If I'm so important, then why can't I know what's the thing I'm after?" the caller asked, somewhat mootly.

"Before this night is over you may, which is another reason I want you out of there. You have two objectives: to get metal squares out of the trunk of that Mercedes with a minimum of hassle and to make sure by whatever means that Wolfe and this Cowboy disappear. You say you can handle it, so, by God, handle it."

"This metal in the trunk: how big, how many, how tall or short?"

Biddle rubbed his head again. Dammit, he owed the SSG this much; after all, he had brought the thing to the verge of culmination with almost no help. "Frankly, it will require a good stout box, maybe a wooden box. It will be several thin plates, metal. *You are not* to look at them too closely. They will be picked up from you by a man identifying himself as Top Kick. Got that?"

"Top Kick. Got it."

"As soon as Top Kick has the plates in his possession, you are to call me. Maybe by tomorrow morning I can get out of this damned place and go home like normal people."

"It *has* been a long week. What place are you in?"

"None of your business," said Biddle. He looked about the room, at his cot, at his TV, at the grungy shower and commode in the claustrophobic closet that served as a bathroom. He had not changed clothes since Thursday and his shirt smelled like chicken shit.

"Sorry I asked. If it works . . . *when* it works, I'll call you. I expect to call you in the next seven to ten hours."

"There's a bunch riding on this. Don't turn the wagon over."

"Fear not," said the caller.

When Biddle hung up he went to his closet, took out a clean shirt and laid it on the desk. Placed there among all the paraphernalia of what he had come to think of as The Quest for the Mormon Plates, it was somehow tantamount to seeing a pair of ballet slippers lying within a display of beheadal swords. An apt comparison, owing to Cowboy's penchant for lopping off heads. But the shirt, like champagne iced down in a clubhouse to be splashed on returning winners, had no place in the real world, not just yet. He picked it up from the desk and laid it over the back of a chair.

Yes, as his SSG in Memphis had just commented, it had been a long week. Biddle looked at his tablet, marked through the name Donald Phillips. He turned to the next page and looked at the mishmash of names and places that had formed the order of battle for the nine main players in the Quest. Like all campaigns, those who worked behind the lines greatly outnumbered those who were at the front. Agents, cities, times: Hermosillo, Salt Lake City, Fort Worth, Phoenix, New Orleans, Mazatlan, Jacksonville, New Haven, Union City; Tuesday and Friday and Wednesday and Sunday. Forty-nine agents had been assigned to do this or that, another twenty or so SSGs had handled some of the more pedestrian scutwork here and there, and one could not leave out the Company men in Mexico and the border guards who had served in capacities minor, medium, or major.

Vaughn Biddle knew at this moment what Eisenhower must have been feeling on the night of June 5, 1944, as armadas converged off the coast of France—none but himself had all the puzzle parts and the weight must have been awesome on Ike as it was now on himself. And there in Normandy predictable debacles had occurred: paratroopers falling miles from their drop zones, an entire division landing a mile from its designated beach, confusion, chaos, night blindness, and bedlam. But the Allies had held on and had won.

He threw the tablet on the littered desk and went to a window. Away to the northeast the city of Washington was aglow in the night sky. The ship of state was sailing on—albeit in a probable state of drunkenness, debauchery, dereliction—and he, Vaughn Biddle, unsung, was seeing to it that those people over there, nameless and faceless, would arise on Sunday morning and go to what was laughingly called "the church of your choice." Not that ninety percent of them would, of course, but the "choice" would be there in the morning because of what he and a handful of people in Memphis were doing right now. Vaughn Biddle and Foster St. John alone knew that the God who was mentioned on every U.S. coin, in every presidential inauguration speech, in the Constitution itself, was being set in His place so that the ship of state could sail on. *Sorry, God,* he was thinking, *but if it ever comes out that the Mormons were right on target, You know what shit would result.*

The street below the garage was empty and reposeful and, in its stillness, tauntingly desirable. He tried to open the window and found that it was stuck in its own paint. Leave it to the goddam Bureau to stick him in one of its manifold hidey-holes in and around Washington that were chosen just for their drabness, and leave it also to the Bureau to decree that the place had to be painted within so that some bureaucratic whim could be fulfilled.

Abandoning the room for the first time in nearly seven days, he opened the door and walked down the stairs and opened the ground-level door. The night air rushed in on him and he opened his mouth several times to suck in as much as his lungs would hold. As a boy he had read that only six thousand stars were visible to the human eye, but tonight there must have been six million. In Sunday School his daughter Molly had sung with her mates a song that went, "The angels are lighting, God's little candles, we call them stars . . ." He could not remember the rest of the words. But that had been thirty years ago and now Molly was a Minneapolis housewife with three children of her own.

Vaughn Biddle gasped again, this time because he was weeping. God, the idiocies of mankind! At about the age of six, children find that the Santa Claus who has made himself known with tangibles *does not* exist, while at the same age these same children are told that a Jesus Christ who has presented them no tangibles *does* exist. And at the age of sixteen they learn by the oddly osmotic advents of common sense and sexuality that both Santa Claus and Jesus Christ are as figmentary as unicorns and that elusive and hypocritical thing called Honor. At the service academies they preached Honor, Duty, Country, but in actual combat the distillation always became Cover Your Ass, and in the business world it became Get Yours, Baby.

Moonstruck, nostalgic, weeping, Vaughn Biddle did not understand anything, and he wondered if he ever would.

Somewhere an old Doctor of Divinity named James Wagstaff had been turned away from tangible evidence of God. But it was for the common good.

Somewhere a black man named Donald Phillips lay newly dead, but his death had been for the common good.

Somewhere men named Octavio Diaz and Michael Morton lay in graves, their passings unsung for the common good.

Somewhere in or near the city of Memphis, Tennessee, people named Jesse DeVaron, Ellen Talbott, Emerson Wolfe, Vernon Cameron, et al., were converging and some of them had to die, but it was for the common good.

The Mormons had been right all along, but it could never be admitted, and it was for the common good.

"O, Thou Hypocrite," Vaughn Biddle whispered at the quiet and beautiful sky.

He returned to the stairwell, closed and locked the door, went back up the stairs, switched off the light, and sat in the darkness waiting for the phone to ring.

Twenty-four

Emerson Wolfe was listening to banjo music when the phone rang. Unaware that it was to be the last music he was ever to hear, he went over and turned down the radio.

"Hello."

"Cowboy here."

"It's about time, son. How is it I can be in this city for two days and you're just now making it?"

"I had people to . . . see. Come down to the lobby."

"No. You come up here. I don't want us to be seen together . . ."

Wolfe hung up the phone.

Yesterday, after asking around ever so slightly, he had learned that Washington Clark was dead and buried, the victim of a murderer.

Not only was Washington Clark murdered, he was murdered several days ago. This was Saturday, and the mess in Lengus de Cristo had started last Saturday, exactly one week ago. And Phillips had left for New Haven, Connecticut, on that jerkwind airline out of Hermosillo late last Sunday. So was it possible that Phillips had not gone to New Haven but had come to Memphis instead and murdered the old man?

No.

But, dammit, Washington Clark had been murdered on Monday. The shoeshine boy named Donkey Baby had been sure of it, had said, "I knows it was Monday, 'cause they laid him to res' on Wednesday." And Donkey

Baby had also said, "He had a frien' name of Mister Jesse DeVaron who is lookin' into this."

Mister Jesse DeVaron.

Wolfe had looked up the name of Mister Jesse DeVaron and had found that he was a jack-leg private investigator. Since nearly all private investigators are ex-policemen, it was but a phone call away to the Memphis Police Department to find out some of the quirks and habits of this Jesse DeVaron.

But, being cagey, Wolfe had not made the phone call. You do not tip the cops, you do not ask the cops, you do not involve the cops. You call in someone like Vernon "Cowboy" Cameron, you assign him an exotic code name, since all John Birch-mercenary-*Soldier of Fortune* types are little boys who love code names, and you use the bastard to kill Jesse DeVaron and Don Phillips and this blonde who is somewhere in a Mercedes. And then you kill Cowboy himself and you take the gold and run.

Period.

The main thing was not to kill any of the principals involved until the Mercedes with the gold had been accounted for. This would be easy enough, probably, because Garman would have sent the blonde to Memphis, just like Phillips had speculated—no, *assured*—back in Hermosillo.

But there were perturbing questions about Phillips that would not go away, the major one being, of course, if Phillips did not kill the old shoeshine man who was Garman's uncle, then who did? And why? Certainly Phillips did not kill him, not with the gold still drifting around in Mexico with the blonde. Only one thing was certain—the Company had missed the three of them, and was tearing up every mattress cover and barn loft from Rio de Janeiro to Halifax trying to find them.

Wolfe got off the bed and walked to the window. Down to his right a Continental Trailways bus hissed and farted as it lumbered into a terminal. His own father had run away from them years ago on a bus like that, and it made him feel terribly alone. The loneliness became guilt and the guilt became fear, and from there it was just one step to downright paranoia. Feeling his legs weaken, saying to himself, *Get hold of yourself,* he went and lay down on the bed again, wondering where Cowboy was, why he was so late.

Mists of disillusionment hung in the room. Emerson was a part of his own disillusionment, part of America's disillusionment, a mere observer to other disillusionments. Hell, every pipe fitter in Houston and every housewife in Omaha now knew that the country was in deep shit, that what Lincoln and Washington and the Roosevelts created had been sullied by the heavy hands of Lyndon and Richard Milhous and Jimmy the peanut farmer who should have stayed one. Then had come Reagan, the great cavalryman who was going to pull the country out of its pit and make us all proud of ourselves again.

What shit. Nobody believed in anything anymore. On the CBS evening news yesterday they had done a redux on starvation in Africa, grist for the news mill some time ago, and the people were still dying like flies. What had been done? the report asked. Nothing much. The newscast ended with a three-minute segment on the making of wedding gowns, the newscaster's smile at the last moment before fadeout indicating that, here at last, was the good news and the levity of life that somehow made the whole ball of wax worth rolling for another day.

But it was this very idiocy in the American psyche, this allegiance to surrealistic occurrence, that would give Emerson Wolfe all the cover that he needed. God, the fuckups that were once spoonfed to the American public on a yearly basis were now down to something like a monthly thing: Boesky on Wall Street, General Dynamics and their billion-dollar cost overruns, blatant graft overseen by the military and then committeeized by Congress. Labor unions with direct ties to the Mob. Iran, the most hated country in America's recent history being fed arms by The Great Communicator who, it turned out, was not communicating with the Lieutenant Colonel in the basement of the White House. Swiss bank accounts. What did you know and when did you know it? And the coming food crisis in America, a thing about which John Q. Dumbass Taxpayer was just now beginning to see the first scratches of the handwriting on the wall.

God, when one thought about it all, put it into perspective, was it any wonder that he, Emerson Wolfe, had the Company by the balls in this gold thing? So what was it that had worried him back in Hermosillo? Losing his job? Not likely. If you belong to the right organization in America you can get away with any goddam thing, and get rich doing it. You can even kill and get away with it. You can lie and be believed.

I am Emerson Wolfe, he thought. I am a member of the CIA. The CIA is an intelligence branch of the United States Government and the profit motive for which it stands, one nation, under Greed, with lechery and gibberish for all.

Oh, the fuckups. Oh, the astounding fuckups of the past few years, fuckups so laughable that the miracle was that the Company still existed.

Zimbabwe, where we were able to get four hundred poor misguided fools to lay down their all to help Ian Smith preserve a white government that was starving thousands of blacks to death on a monthly basis. We lost that one.

Dominica, where we were able to get a rabid Ku Klux Klan Wizard from Alabama to try to impose a white supremacist regime. We lost that one.

The Seychelles, where we tried to help that group called the "wild geese" to unseat President Rene. We lost that one.

Angola, where our overpaid mercenaries went into a civil war with just enough backing to get their asses kicked. We lost that one.

Libya, where in 1981 two of our own Company men hired fifty Americans to help support Muammar Kaddafi's madness. Somebody lost that one, but no one to this day can figure out who it was, or what they were trying to accomplish.

The Bay of Pigs.

Feeling a wave of abject self-pity, Emerson Wolfe was

shrewd enough to know that what was coming to America had lying beyond it the ugly backdrop of what was going to happen to his kind after the impending Holocaust Against Columbia. When the Have Nots finally tumbled the Haves, the slaughter of the unrighteous would begin. It was forever true: hell, look at the Ayatollah's bloodbath in Iran, look at Greece when the Reds took over, look at the Philippines, look at everything that had happened as Africa's splinter nations emerged. All who had eaten and drunk well *then* were killed *now*. One had only to look at the covers of *Time* magazine for the last twenty years to see that America's leaders seldom smiled, forever wore aging and worried faces that spoke of an awareness that they wished to share with the American people but could not. Lyndon Johnson knew that Vietnam was a folly that would turn the green machine of American military might red with its own blood, but it was a horse that he had to ride to the end. Nixon had called the clusters of persons waiting for the helicopters in Saigon all but what it was, a rout. Gerald Ford, an interim embarrassment. Jimmy Carter, sending five helicopters against a country of twenty million to get the hostages out of Tehran, and two of the helicopters crashing, well, Jesus, it was too goddamned ridiculous for words. And Reagan, dealing with the motherfuckers behind the back of his own image. Had to, because it was all that they would have.

A booming knock came from the door. Wolfe bounded over and opened it. Cowboy was wearing the same clothing that he had worn in Dallas. He walked past Wolfe and sat in the chair beside the lamp table. Idly brushing a bit of dust from the Gideon Bible, he said, "I got a message for you: a nigger kid down in the lobby said that you are to meet a Mr. Phillips at two in the morning at River Tower."

Wolfe was at once fascinated and alarmed. "This kid, that's all he said? Who was he? What did he look like?"

"He looked like a nigger and I didn't ask his name." Cowboy looked about the place and said, "Nice hotel, even if there is drinking in the open downstairs."

"Yeah, enough of that," said Wolfe. He sat on the bed and tried to sort out his thoughts. This Phillips thing and the black kid disturbed him. "Why would Phillips send a kid with a message; why didn't he come himself?" he asked.

Cowboy waved a hand laconically. "Niggers is all crazy, gutless. Why would you think this Phillips is any different?"

"Phillips is neither, mister, and the quicker you believe that, the quicker you'll get your share of this thing we're after."

Cowboy ignored Wolfe's surly tone.

"Somethin' puzzles me, Wolfe: how'd Phillips know I was with you?" he asked.

"Because I told him I was going to try to get you in on it, that's how. I described you to him." Wolfe should have felt treacherous during this confession, but admissions of his own treachery were quite far from his mind just now; the fact of Phillips sending a child to deliver a message—and to Cowboy and not to himself—was a source of real worry. Something about this stank.

Cowboy was experiencing setbacks of his own. "You didn't have to tell a nigger nothing about me. Not a thing."

"Maybe you see it that way, but I don't. This is one important nigger in your world right now. God, why can't I make you see that? Not thirty seconds ago we had this conversation! Forget that he is black, or, if you've just *got* to think of him as black, think of him as a cobra or a panther, something to be hunted."

"Someday they'll all be hunted," said Cowboy.

"If Phillips sent a kid with a message, then it must mean that he was up to something that has got to be too important to leave," Wolfe announced to himself. "Sure, that's it!" He snapped his fingers. "I told you he was a sharp one. And if he said to meet him at two o'clock, then he knows that somebody or something is going to be there at two."

Cowboy did not share Wolfe's enthusiasm. "Someday you'll learn that a nigger is just a nigger," he said. "That

Chink I killed in Louisiana the other night wasn't much better."

"What the hell, our purpose is to be there at two, just like Phillips wanted. Good old Phillips. He's a real—" Emerson Wolfe heard his voice trail off into the room's stillness. He watched as Cowboy ran a fingertip over a tooth. "What Chink?"

Cowboy looked at his fingertip. Satisfied that there were neither Jews nor blacks there, he looked at Wolfe and said, "Somethin' I did for the Order. It's got nothin' to do with this." When he felt Wolfe's iniquitous glare he said, "Okay, it was after we left Dallas. That's where I mostly went, Louisiana, up to Arkansas, over to here. From here I go to Flor—"

"I don't want an itinerary after you leave here," Wolfe said bitterly, certain that Cowboy was never going to leave Memphis. "I want to know what in hell you've been up to since you left Dallas. It's important!"

Cowboy's eyes glistened with a cruel enjoyment of his memories. He laughed quietly. "You're right," he said after a time, "it is important. Okay, here it is: I've done four eradications. The first, I did in Phoenix, the old women. One in Louisiana, the Chink, was as easy as pie." His words drifted up easily, like flotsam from the depths of a dirty sea. "The one in Arkansas was a cleansing of our own temple, so to speak. Him, I don't even want to talk about. But the Chink was different, a Viet. Ever notice an Oriental, how dismal their eyes look? When I got through with him, he didn't have any eyes, or much of nothing else."

Wolfe looked at him coldly and said, "Why was he killed?"

"Because his daughter was a good speller."

Wolfe blinked his eyes. "What?"

"You heard right. It'll make sense when I explain it. See, the schools in this country are so rotten nowadays with integration that the South has a lot of private academies. Anybody with tuition money can enroll their kids in a private academy, and since white people have the money, it's whites that get into private academies. But this Viet had money, and got his daughter in. She won the local spelling bee, made straight A's, won the parish spelling bee. It just so happened that one of the big landowners in that parish had a son who was beat out by her. He was a member of the Order and asked that an example be set, a warning to the Chink element that would spill over to the nigger and Jew element. See how it works?" Cowboy's gladness at being a part of this was uncontainable. He beamed at the knowledge that his two-minute act of bludgeonry had blasted open dams of chaos whose waters all the Supreme Court edicts in the world could never dry.

Emerson Wolfe's mouth hung open. "My God," he said. An almond-eyed girl in Louisiana was fatherless because she had won a spelling bee.

"We're everywhere, Wolfie," said Cowboy. "And we know everything. Did you know, for instance, that one fourth of the niggers in Cooke County, Illinois, are on welfare? That more than fifty percent of all nigger babies born in this country are born out of wedlock? That twenty-two thousand Iranian students were going to school on American foreign aid in this country while the Ayatollah held our hostages for 444 days? Did you know that there's a Cuban congressman from Miami who's trying to introduce a bill to make Spanish the basic language in Dade County, Florida? Which is why I'm on my way there. I'm gonna cut his wife's pussy out and stretch it over . . . But enough of that: it don't concern you."

With slight sarcasm Emerson Wolfe said, "And I called you in to help me."

Cowboy misinterpreted. "Yes, and God bless you for it. I was doing work for the Order and your call came almost as the clarion of Gabriel. When you said you needed help with this nigger, I knew that the hand of the Almighty had touched me. What other human is so blessed as me? I work for the Order and for the CIA, both at the same time. You can't tell me the Lord don't have a hand in this, no sir!"

And boy did I ever fuck up, Wolfe was thinking. *This*

bastard is one hundred times more dangerous than I ever imagined. Rabid. Obsessed. It's ten million goddam wonders that he hasn't been caught. Charles Manson was caught. Richard Speck. Gacy. James Earl Ray. Crossbreeding, interbreeding, pullulating like sperm dripping from the penis of a malodorous beast raping the American countryside, serial murderers, political murderers, terrorists, splinter-group psychos, Klansmen, Nazis—God, what is America coming to?

A warm look came into Cowboy's eyes. "I've been straight with you, so why don't you get straight with me?"

"Straight?"

"Yeah, straight. There's more to this thing than just killing a nigger." Cowboy held his chin high, like a cat who has just caught a strange scent.

Wolfe was amused that one who was about to die would be so concerned with purpose, then he recalled that Cowboy did not know that he was about to die. He studied Cowboy's features, trying to determine whether the insane really did look different, but was even further raddled by the normality, nay, downright lucidity, on that handsome face. His gaze shifted upward to Cowboy's forehead. *If I hadn't attended his brother's funeral,* he was thinking, *none of this would have happened, I would never have met him, and none of this would be going on.*

"How much more do you want to know?" Wolfe asked.

"All you can tell me. I know that you're CIA, and some things must be kept secret, but you told me in Dallas just enough to let me know that there's gold here in this thing. I don't like playing master and servant. I've been up front with you."

Wolfe sighed deeply. The therapeutic value of getting the thing out into the open might work wonders for his own sensibilities, but at the same time telling Cowboy the story was the equivalent to feeding rich hay to a horse that was about to be shot. One thing was certain—now was not the time to fuck up, to get caught in a lie. Too, as crazy as the story was, Cowboy couldn't possibly understand it. Hell, truth be told, this whole caper was like an old doorless house in which breezes filtered now this way, now that.

"Gold and letters, mostly," Wolfe said.

"Golden letters?"

"No. Gold *and* letters. I'll encapsulate. A Catholic priest in Hermosillo, a Father Colon, was dealing in dope. Charleston Garman, a black CIA man, found from talking to that priest that something made of gold was hidden in the church of a nearby village, Lengus de Cristo. Something very rich. Garman was a religious man and it ran him crazy. . . ."

Ten minutes later, when Wolfe had finished, Cowboy said, "You mean we're here to find a blonde woman in a Mercedes who may or may not even show up in Memphis? And you and Phillips left Mexico just to stop two letters? It sounds crazy."

"Not really. This whole thing was about maintaining secrecy. If those two letters fell into the wrong hands it would have been over before it started. Since we had to come to the States anyway, and since the blonde probably would have gone straight to the old shoeshine uncle of Garman's, it was our logical move."

Cowboy pondered for a time and then said, "You don't even know how much gold it is, or what size or kind. What if this whole thing is about a brass candlestick?"

"Then it will be about a brass candlestick," said Wolfe. "But when that black kid downstairs gave you a message from Phillips, all the lights went back on. Brass, gold, or whatever, Philips knows what he's doing. And that's why we'll meet him at this place called River Towers at two. My guess is the payoff is tonight, that the woman has shown up in Memphis and he knows where she is."

Cowboy pursed his lips, ran a fingertip back and forth across them. "A blonde with a nigger. I'm glad that Garman is dead. And you said his old uncle here in Memphis is dead, murdered. That means that Philips stopped off in Memphis and killed the uncle before he went off to Connecticut. Yeah, for a nigger, this Phillips is a thinker. I like him, but I'm still looking forward to killing him."

With these words, a darkness returned to Wolfe's thoughts. Yes, the old uncle was dead, but Wolfe was convinced that Phillips had not murdered the old man. And if Phillips hadn't, then who had? Was it possible that there really were other forces at work in this thing? And had the Company really not missed them yet at their hotel in Hermosillo? And what of Octavio Diaz, the Mexican farmer? Did he bury Garman's body down there in the sand among the hogs? Like a man holding a tow rope from a ship headed through a nocturnal sea, Emerson Wolfe was drinking in waters that beggared analysis, was being pulled by a power mostly unseen.

Wolfe leaned over and looked at the clock radio. The time was 11:50. "Go on down to the truck," he said to Cowboy. "I'll be down in a few minutes."

Cowboy stood. "I'm in the parking lot out back."

"Fine."

When Cowboy was gone, Wolfe threw clothing and shaving gear into his suitcase. He went to his closet, pulled out his Smith and Wesson .38, placed it in the pocket of his houndstooth sport coat. He looked at the radio once again and saw that the time was 11:55. If everything went according to plan, within two hours or so he would have the gold and be out of Tennessee and on the way back to Hermosillo in Cowboy's pickup. Piss on checking out of Hotel Peabody—he would walk out of this place and be gone; a man with two and maybe more murders on his mind does not worry about an unpaid hotel bill.

He opened the door, folded the pistol-weighted coat over his arm and looked back at his room one last time. The clock read 11:59. He waited. When the digits blinked onto 12:00, he went out and closed the door behind him.

Twenty-five

As Emerson Wolfe left the Hotel Peabody and went out to the truck, Jesse DeVaron was standing two miles distant on his balcony wishing for another rain. Last night's downpour had been most rewarding. Janice was back, and although she was as cussedly female as ever, he was going to marry her. Probably. It was not good to rush into these things, but dammit all to hell, you had to hand it to her—she was under his skin and always would be. The fact of the matter was that had Ollie Colbert not called him some four hours ago and taken him riding into Arkansas, this evening would have been spent with Janice. But that was the way that Saturday night had been dented, and by the time he had gotten out of Ollie's car and fantasized with the M-1, it had been well past ten o'clock.

Janice was not all that was on Jesse's mind just now. Hip Willis had called this morning while Jesse and Janice were in bed and said that a blonde woman had come looking for Jesse. But the woman had not called, nor had she come. And tonight Ollie Colbert had said that a *black man* had called and warned that Jesse had better beware of two characters named "Cowboy" and "Wolf." Although an interlude with Janice would have been preferable to meditations on these matters, they were too weighty to be ignored, too interlocked by chronology to be coincidental.

The streetlights caught his gaze and he recalled that just two hours ago he had sighted on one of them with the rifle. On the night in which he had cut off Cong heads, a young soldier had said, "I know they're out there, Jesse—do you feel it—do you know the feeling of a thing about to happen?" Jesse had felt it. Now, two decades later, he felt it again.

He was thinking of Olan Oldham's words when the phone rang. Believing—hoping, really—that it was Janice, he trotted off the balcony and into the living room.

"Hello."

"Am I speaking with Mr. Jesse DeVaron?"

Jesse liked the lilt of the voice. "Yes, you are."

"My name is Ellen Talbott. I trust you'll forgive this intrusion, but I must see you immediately."

Her voice had quavered on the last word. It told him that it was a well-bred woman who was feigning composure. This one had to be handled very gently and very quickly; years of dealing with all sorts of humanity from puke-crawling maggots to effete thoroughbreds had enabled him to react immediately to tone, mannerism, bearing, breeding. This had to be the Mercedes lady, and she was scared shitless and was trying not to be. Such persons are prone to do rash acts in the hope that all humanity, like themselves, will respond to motive and with a sense of fair play and magnanimity. Not so. "Yes, Miss Talbott. I've been expecting your call. Where are you?"

"I'm at a motel called The Lighthouse Inn. Do you know it?"

Jesus, Jesse thought, the biggest whore hole in the blackest part of Memphis. "Yes, I know it."

"I'm in room number 16. Please come immediately."

"I'll be in a white Chevrolet, and I'll be there in ten minutes."

There was a brief silence. Jesse heard her trying to clear her throat. Her voice had about it that same tremulous sound that he had heard in her first sentence. "Mr. DeVaron, I'm frightened. Can you hurry?"

"On my way," said Jesse.

He hung up the phone, looked about the apartment, remembered that his shirts were at the laundry—a stupid thought; he did not want to die with his shirts in the laundry. Laughing at himself, he went down and into the street. He opened the trunk of the old convertible and took the rifle to the Chevrolet. Before pulling away from the curb he took one last look at the Ford, at the building that had served him so well over the past few years. He did not want to see his own balcony—as he drove beneath it he forced himself not to look. Some things, he concluded hazily, are best left to memory.

The thought came to him as he drove southward, into the guts of the city, that Memphis, unlike most American cities, was not racially divided so much as it was racially mottled. Ten blocks of whites might abut twelve blocks of blacks which were in turn delineated by another cluster of whites. One of these black areas was just to the north of the airport, and it was there that Ellen Talbott had chosen to lodge. As he parked the Chevrolet, Jesse noted that the white Mercedes with Michigan plates was as out of place as a Westminster poodle in a dog pound.

He started to knock but the door opened. "Please come in, Mr. DeVaron," said Ellen Talbott.

He sat in a soiled chair near the bed, noting for the thousandth time that rich people just had about them that glow of wealth and breeding that circumstances could not eradicate; rather than mocking her patrician manner, the dingy room gave it emphasis. Slender, poised, dressed in dark slacks of raw silk and a white lacy blouse, Ellen Talbott was a paragon to the ways of money.

Jesse said, "I know some of this and none of this. I'm Jesse DeVaron and your name is Ellen Talbott. I want you to tell me everything that's going on. And when I say everything, that's just what I mean."

She appeared to relax a bit as she sat on the edge of the bed. "How far back do I go?" she asked."

"As far as is necessary."

"Two weeks ago I left Michigan. I drove from Michigan to Mexico. Nonstop. I came to a place called Hermosillo. Sonora, northern Mexico. I took a room and slept all night and the better part of the next day. I went shopping and then I rested in a small plaza, a place of fountains. While I was sitting on the rim of the pool a man approached me. A black man. American. He said that his name was Charleston Garman.''

Jesse felt the back of his neck burn as if he had been slapped. Two words recurred: *Votan lives.*

Continuing her story in tones partially apologetic, partially defensive, she said, ''I know that you are Southern, that certain proclivities abound to a greater degree in the South than elsewhere, but I found Charleston Garman to be one of the gentlest, warmest, and nicest men that I'd ever met.''

''So you went to bed with him,'' said Jesse.

''You don't seem shocked.''

''Ellen, just as less than one tenth of one percent of Italians are Mafia, less than one tenth of one percent of Southerners are rabid Klan members. Decency does not begin just to the north of the Mason-Dixon line, nor does intelligence. Now go on with your story.''

She closed her eyes, placed her hands over her forehead. ''I'll try to remember it exactly as it happened. We spent two days together. And two nights. On the first night he had a horrible nightmare. He said strange things, words in a foreign language. 'Con-tici.' 'Quetzalcoatl.' 'Gucumatz.' And other words that were garbled. And then he said words in English: 'Cow dairy.' ''

''This nightmare, how long did it go on?''

''For about five minutes. He was perspiring terribly. I awakened him. All this was at about two in the morning. We talked until sunrise and then we slept again. He said some things in that room that made me wonder whether he were sane.''

Jesse was thinking, *My thoughts exactly when I read the letter at Muley's Segregarious bar, centuries ago.*

''Tell me all that he said,'' Jesse commanded.

''He said that he was in league with evil men. Their names were Wolfe and Phillips. He said that a Mexican farmer named Octavio Diaz had told him of a great secret, a thing that would change things forever. He kept babbling about sin, saying that what we had done there in that bed was sin. And then he would talk more about what had to be done so that man would know."

"Man? Which man?"

"Just man. That's what he said. 'So that *man* will know.' I had the feeling that he was referring to mankind. It was part religiosity, part fear, and a great part of it was illusory, or so I believed at the time. He said that this farmer named Diaz had told him the great secret in exchange for the release of a sister who was in federal prison in the United States. I think it was then that I realized what my bed partner's profession was, although I didn't ask."

"This farmer, Diaz, did you ever talk to him? How about Wolfe and Phillips?"

"No. From what I could gather, Wolfe and Phillips were putting some sort of pressure on Charleston Garman to share in the . . . thing. He never used profanity when talking about them; he only called them evil men. This strange, forgiving look would come into his eyes as he spoke of it. He said that they knew of the two letters that he had written, one to Memphis and one to New Haven, Connecticut, that they had tried to stop his spread of the word. He said also that his time was very short. It was then that he begged me to help him."

"And you helped him," said Jesse. "And Wolfe and Phillips know that you helped him."

"Yes, as of today I'm sure of it. Have you ever been watched without being aware of it until after the fact? Today I learned that the old man to whom I was to deliver this thing had been murdered. I've never been so terrified as I've been over the last twelve hours. In my fear I didn't know what to do. I don't know this city at all so I just drove until I found a motel. This motel. I've spent the last hundred years looking out that window every three minutes, it seems. Finally, an hour ago, I decided to call you. Thank God you came."

Watched without being aware of it. Jesse ran her phrase around in his mind. He had for the past few days felt manipulated but not really watched. The faces of Reeder and Riggazi came and went, as did Ollie Colbert's almost incoherent warnings about shadowy phone calls. *Yes, Jesse, you've been watched,* he admitted. *And manipulated. By whom? To what purpose?* He felt foolish, naked, threatened. And, oddly enough, *protected.*

Putting aside his disordered thoughts, he asked, "Why did it take you a week to get to Memphis? Have you been hiding?"

"No. That was part of Charleston Garman's plan. He said that Wolfe and Phillips were very thorough people, that they had been trained by the best in the business, that he would use that training against them. He said that the best way to do it was to send the thing *away* for a time and then let it come to its destination slowly, 'like a leaf hanging on a breeze before it falls,' as he put it. He was elated to know that I was going to Mazatlan, which is far to the *south* of Hermosillo."

"Good thinking," said Jesse. "And then what happened?"

"You won't believe me."

"Try me."

"We left the hotel at about noon, and he spent the rest of the day preaching, speaking of God, of Jesus Christ, saying things like 'wherever two or more are gathered in my name.' And all the time he kept looking behind him, off to the alleyways. Finally, in the late afternoon, he asked if we might get into my car and drive to a village. In retrospect, I get the feeling that he was waiting until near darkness for us to take that drive."

"What was the name of the village?"

"Lengus de Cristo. I remember the way he said the words, with a softness in his voice, 'Lengus de Cristo.' But we did not go into the village; rather, we parked my car on a promontory and waited until well past midnight. He told me to drive into the village, to park the car behind a church. I sat in the car and waited for what must have been an hour. When he came out he was dirty, really filthy. He told me to open the trunk of my car, but to stay in the car. I released the trunk latch and heard him taking my luggage out. The loading took less than five minutes. He came around to the passenger side and told me to ease out of the village, to drive very slowly. When he saw fear in my face he told me that it was not my worry, that I was not to be afraid, that it was something that had to be done. We went out of the village and to a small house about a mile away, up a hill. The smell near that house was horrible. I remember that he smiled and said that it was certain that I'd never smelled hogs, that hogs have a smell all their own. Whoever lived there was not at home. This made him quite concerned. He said, 'I was going to take Diaz with us. I can't leave him to face them alone. I'll have to stay here.' He wrote a name and address on a bit of paper and handed it to me. Washington Clark, River Towers, Memphis, Tennessee. He said that whatever else happened, I was to go on to Mazatlan and that I was not to look at what was in the trunk."

Jesse said, "Let me guess; he sent you away, you went on to Mazatlan, and you looked at what it was the next morning."

She smiled, but it was an unhappy smile. "You're a cynic, Mr. DeVaron. I looked, but much later, days later, in fact, in another setting."

"And it's in your trunk now?"

"Yes."

"Good. I want to see it." He stood and looked out at the Mercedes. Down the street to the left, some three hundred yards away, an orange and white ambulance and two police cars were pulling away, none using their flashers or sirens. Their lack of hurry indicated that one more person had bitten the dust on a hot Memphis Saturday night. There wasn't even a crowd. *Mankind comes, mankind goes,* he was thinking, *and what mankind is all about is right there in the trunk of that expensive car.* Returning to his chair, he said, "The last time you saw Charleston Garman was beside a house just outside this Mexican village. How did you feel at that moment?"

"Terrified. A little lonely for Michigan. When he told me to leave, I left. There was no question of whether he wanted me to return later; I wouldn't have. And I think that he knew it and I also think that he wanted it that way. I was his last chance to accomplish something."

"Have you given me the whole story?" Jesse asked.

All the time that she had talked her hands had remained over her eyes. Now she rubbed her palms together, got off the bed and went to the window. "As far as what is relevant to Mexico, yes. About two hours ago that all changed."

"What happened two hours ago?"

"Two hours ago I received a phone call. Here. In this room. After learning today that Washington Clark had been murdered, I didn't know what to do. I came here. I had just about convinced myself to go to the police, the FBI, anybody, and then get out of Memphis and go home. I was going to ignore you entirely. But two hours ago I got a phone call. That's when I panicked and called you."

"What did the caller say?" Jesse asked.

"It was a male voice. He said, 'Bring it to River Towers at two in the morning. Be there.'" She shuddered as she remembered.

"Black voice or white voice?" Jesse asked.

"It sounded like a white man."

"And that's all he said?"

She nodded jerkily, her head twitching in spasms of fright. "That was what I meant when I asked if you had ever found that you've been watched. One feels so . . . vulnerable."

Jesse thought it over. What a joke this would be, what a hoot, if he got killed just days before an insurance check for four hundred thousand dollars was placed in his hot little hands. Just as life was about to pay off, he was about to cash in his chips, maybe. *You are a real fuckup, Jesse DeVaron, because you cannot stand the thought of not being involved in this. You are going to go to River Towers and there is going to be killing and your blood is hot for it. If you live through it, just remember not to chop off any heads.*

"Well?" she said.

He glanced up. She had been staring at him.

"Who knows that you're here in Memphis?" he asked.

"No one, I think. Except for the people here at the registration desk, and that big black man at River Towers, the doorman."

Two words came back to Jesse: manipulated and protected. They had passed almost unsung in his thoughts a few minutes before when she had related her tale of feeling watched. Watched, manipulated, protected. Shadows were becoming lighted. Camouflage was falling away.

"Well I'll be damned," Jesse said.

"Why are you smiling at all this, Mr. DeVaron?"

Jesse stood and went again to the window. He laughed heartily. The Mercedes was beautiful and the dark street was beautiful. He had been had and he loved it!

"What is it?" she asked nervously, sternly.

"It is this, Ellen Talbott: we can all sleep well, because our great big, fat, beautiful United States of America is awake! God, it's wonderful! Everything that has happened to me this week has been a mishmash of craziness! But it wasn't craziness at all! I thought that God Almighty had a hand in it, and maybe He does! I'm rich and I'm protected and I've been manipulated! And I love it!"

She had begun to slide across to the other side of the bed. It was as if there were an invisible box there in which she might be able to hide from this madman. Ellen said, brusquely, "I don't understand any of this. Please tell me what you're talking about."

He turned from the window and happily announced, "What it is is this—you came out of Mexico with something that somebody wanted out of Mexico! I just accidentally have been given letters and secondhand phone calls about you and your cargo!"

Ellen was befuddled. Her mouth hung half open and her eyes drooped half shut. "Then I have been watched?"

Jesse nodded and grinned. "Probably every step of the way."

"Then you do know something! Tell me!"

Jesse scratched the side of his head and confessed, "Lady, I know something, but I don't know what its face looks like, only the body. But you can bet that I'll know in the next couple of hours. What time is it?"

She looked at her wristwatch. "A few minutes after one: 1:04, to be exact."

He started for the door. "You stay here. My country needs me."

She was already off the bed, her eyes afire with this order from this cur. They stared at each other for a moment, each set of eyes holding a vision tempered by the past and by experience. As for their motives at this time, they were poles apart and yet very similar. Ellen saw him as a servant, a workingman who had impertinently stepped beyond the lines of propriety to tell those of the manor what they must do. He should be dismissed on the spot. On the other hand, his servant's loyalty in trying to protect her had resulted in an unfortunate usage of harsh words. The man meant well, but someone really had to speak to him about all this. What Jesse saw was a human female who was threatened, who needed his street-scarred expertise in wading puke and blood. He also saw in her his sister Rosa, a Rosa who might have been had the self-igniting fires of poverty not burned most of the good years of her life away. Ellen Talbott was his second chance to do well by Rosa, and do well by her he would.

"Very well," he said, "let's go."

As she went to the closet to get her jacket, Jesse stepped outside. The Mercedes sat with its roof lightly dampened by night mist. Road film from Mexico and the highways of several Southern states scudded the lower half of the car. Somehow it did not have about it the aura of that which held the Secret. He wanted the car to glow, to breathe, to emanate subtle hymns, to become a chariot which would bear him gloriously to this adventure.

Ellen came from the room and handed Jesse the keys to the car. As they left the parking area and moved onto the quiet street he looked over and saw that her eyes were closed.

"If you're praying, make it for both of us," he said.

Twenty-six

A heavy fog had risen off the river. The streetlights near the waterfront were as candles enmeshed in lace. In the suffocating whiteness the great structure called River Towers looked as an apparition whose upper reaches, shrouded as they now were, held morbid and eerie purpose. The city had folded in on itself, and there was no movement except for the ineffectual sweeping motions of a searchlight as a barge moved downriver.

Cowboy stepped from the truck, looked at the hazy river, at the almost invisible lights of Arkansas on the other side. Here, at the southwestern end of the asphalt parking lot, he and Wolfe could watch all movement for hundreds of yards. The great street called Riverside Drive, carved into the bluff that protected Memphis from the Mississippi, was almost empty of traffic.

Cowboy walked behind the pickup, urinated, leaned against a fender. This was a good omen, this fog, this dreariness. In Phoenix there had been a heavy rain, one of those gully-washing Arizona squalls that were gone almost as quickly as they arrived, but it had been there all the same. And in Louisiana where the Chink was bludgeoned with the flashlight, well, it had looked almost like this. Yes, the Lord was sending to Vernon Cameron accolade and blessing in divine white vestments. It was to be desired that such weather would be there when he got to Florida, for if such atmospheric conditions prevailed a *fourth* time, well, he might just as well consider himself anointed. Convinced that this wait for

Phillips was fraught with Holy purpose, he was not at all apprehensive. He opened the tool box, unsheathed the machete, lay the blade in the truck's bed. Now it occurred to him that when he had beheaded the man in Arkansas, the sun had been explosively brilliant. For a few seconds this disturbed him, but his versatility in matters of interpretation told him that the sun had been brighter than usual. Which was, of course, yet another way for the Lord to indicate His appreciation.

Entranced as he was by these meteorological signals from God Almighty, Cowboy did not see that Wolfe was studying him from the truck's interior. More specifically, Wolfe was studying the back of Cowboy's head, for it was there that he would place one bullet at the proper moment. As soon as the gold was in hand and Phillips was finished, Cowboy Cameron would be disposed of. In theory, there would be but one shot fired, since the black man would fall to Cowboy's machete. And, because it was the weekend and few cars were in evidence in the parking area, the chances of one shot being heard from the muffling fog were minimal.

Wolfe looked at his watch. It was exactly two o'clock. A stickler for punctuality, poor old doomed Phillips would probably arrive in the next two minutes. Wolfe hated betraying Phillips, somewhat, but business was business.

Wolfe's chest lurched; his scalp tingled. There it was! The white Mercedes, unseen since a week ago and nearly two thousand miles ago! The car eased down Riverside Drive in the fog, a white fish swimming in a white sea.

"He's coming!" Wolfe called. He got out and went around to the rear of the truck. Looking at Cowboy's face, he saw rage there, and something else—a perverse fulfillment. "Remember, don't make any sudden moves until I give the word," he ordered. Then, almost to himself, he said, "The bastard is in the woman's own car. Now how did he do that? Jesus, you gotta hand it to Phillips—he was one hell of an agent!"

"He ain't a 'was' yet," Cowboy said laconically. "But he's about to be." He looked into the bed of the truck where the machete lay.

The two men watched as the Mercedes turned off the street and into the parking lot, slowed, began to ease past the facade of the great building. In spite of the evening's dankness, Emerson Wolfe felt himself sweating. Now the car was at the western edge of the parking lot and it turned south, the headlights causing but minor illumination in the swirls of white. When the car was fifty feet from them, it slowed to a crawl, stopped.

"Something's weird," said Wolfe.

"No, it ain't," Cowboy countered. "He's sharper than you thought. He wants us to walk to him so he can see us better. I can't bring that blade out of the truck. So what do I do?"

"One thing's for damned sure, if we stay here another ten seconds he'll be suspicious. Just stay close to me. Let's go."

They walked toward the car, their steps soundless on the wet asphalt. When they were within twenty feet of their destination Wolfe saw that the blonde woman was a passenger in her own car and that the man with her definitely was not Phillips; however, committed and exposed as he and Cowboy were, there was nothing to do but continue to walk. They stopped at the left front fender and watched as the driver rolled his window down.

"Speak," said Jesse DeVaron.

"Where's Phillips?" Wolfe asked.

"He didn't make it," said Jesse. "You must be Wolfe."

Emerson Wolfe looked at Jesse's face and saw danger. "So where is he and who are you?" he asked.

"My name is Jesse DeVaron. As for Phillips, he probably took it on the lam. The little lady here wants me to protect her from all enemies, foreign and domestic. So how about it, Wolfe, are you her enemy?"

Cowboy approached Jesse's window and said, "You're a liar, mister. Phillips sent a kid to give me a note less than—" He grunted as Wolfe nudged him.

"Cowboy and Wolfe," Jesse said tauntingly. "Funny, I thought you guys would be bigger. Or maybe brighter.

Hell, Phillips has gone over the hill. You've been had, so suck it up and run with it."

Wolfe looked at Cowboy and then back at Jesse. "Then you won't mind if we look in that car. How about you step out and let us search. If we find nothing, she's off the hook."

"She's off the hook anyway," said Jesse. "Guess who's on!"

Emerson Wolfe made a sudden step backward. His right hand moved toward his coat pocket. He watched the car's hood surge downward as Jesse backed away. Cowboy was running toward the truck. The car halted, began its turn toward the street, Ellen Talbott's screams knifed through the insanity of the moment. The car lunged, its spinning tires hissing in the dampness. Wolfe aimed the pistol and fired.

Jesse heard the puff-burst of the window glass, felt the branding iron lancet of pain as the bullet ripped heat across the back of his left shoulder. He steered to the left, knew that this exposed the backs of their heads, turned left again, the dizzying visions of fog and river and buildings and lights melting into a blur. The car rocked and spun and Ellen screamed. The second and third shots blasted out the rear window glass behind his head. He again wheeled the Mercedes to the left, blinding Wolfe with his headlights. Shoving his foot hard on the gas pedal, Jesse aimed the car at Wolfe and cursed as Wolfe jumped across the short concrete abutment and onto the grassy hillock that led down to the river. Screaming, "The rifle! The rifle! Get the goddamn thing into the front seat!" Jesse again whirled the car to the left, this time missing the pickup and the open-faced and open-mouthed Cowboy by inches. The blade of the machete thudded down onto the car as it passed. As Ellen dived into the back seat, Jesse hit the brake at forty miles per hour and whipped the wheel, again to the left. Thinking *I will not lose and I will not run, not now*, he again accelerated. Aiming the Mercedes toward the front of the truck, his transfixions were divided between the truck and the emptiness of the foggy knoll beyond it. Hearing Ellen scream again, he braced himself as the Mercedes slammed into the hood of the truck, the screams overwhelmed by a sound blast of outraged metal and glass, underscored by the tinny resonance of falling chrome.

"Oh, God!" Ellen sobbed.

"Shut the hell up and keep down," said Jesse, grabbing the rifle with one hand, shoving her down with the other. He leapt from the car. His thumb found the trigger housing and shoved the safety forward. Floating on a high of emotionlessness that he remembered from combat, he ran in a crouch past the right side of the truck until he was at the rear bumper. He started to kneel, to look beyond the truck for Wolfe. A tremor in the truck caused him to look up. Cowboy had arisen from the bed of the truck and was poised over Jesse, the machete held high, in classic stance of the headsman. Jesse thrust the rifle upward and the detonation of steel against the butt plate of the M-1 threw him backward onto his hips. The smells of asphalt and scored steel invaded his nostrils. He rolled to his side and was on his feet as Cowboy leapt from the truck, the machete again raised as Cowboy shouted, "Bastard, bastard." Jesse raised the rifle horizontally to a point just to the front of his head. The blade bit into the rear sight, creating a frenzy of sparks. Swinging the rifle from his right, Jesse heard the dull crunch of cartilage and flesh as Cowboy's head snapped backward, spumes of blood and snot spraying from his nose and throat. Cowboy's blood-dappled hat fell to the pavement. Cowboy reeled, staggered backward, tried to focus his eyes as Jesse went into a bayonet stance, swung the heaviness of the rifle again. The crosslatched steel of the butt plate exploded against Cowboy's forehead. The wall of bone splintered, shattered, pierced the brain. The machete fell to the darkness beside the hat and Cowboy collapsed over both, his bloodblinded eyes already glazing in death. Hemorrhaging violently, Vernon Cameron gasped in his own blood and was suddenly still.

Emerson Wolfe was running from the darkness of the grassy hill, his movement vector on a line with the Mercedes. Near to collapse from exhaustion, Jesse went around the rear of the truck trying to lift the rifle, trying to get his arms to respond to command, to outright beseechment. In rage and frustration he saw that Wolfe was going to reach the car first, the other man's gait measured, dynamic, positive in its lethality. With legs as nerveless as latex, Jesse dragged himself and the rifle on, his lungs and mouth fire and sand.

Wolfe lunged on, stumbled against the truck, leaned on it. His eyes contemplated failure, despair, commitment to a final duty that was revenge at the profitlessness that had been his life. Lifting the pistol, aiming at the screaming and dark turbulence in the car that was Ellen Talbott, he looked at Jesse and said, "This is the whore that caused all this."

Jesse opened his mouth to shout, his arms and shoulders drawing from within themselves enough stamina to lift the rifle by its barrel. He swung the M-1 like a club as an orange snout of flame and sound bellowed from the pistol and Ellen rose up and sagged toward the front seat. The bloody butt plate of the rifle caught Wolfe at the back of his skull and he fell to his knees, rivulets of ebony-maroon gore spilling onto his shoulders and back. Feeling himself dying, Emerson Wolfe lifted the pistol and fired directly at Jesse's face.

Jesse felt himself drifting, heard shouts echoing as if from the far end of a dark tunnel.

Twenty-seven

Jesse was cold. The fog was gone. It had been replaced by a soft light and the smells of strange oils.

"Blanket," he said. Drifting in and out of consciousness, he felt the weight of rough fabric being laid over his upper torso. His mother had come back. He was in the sharecropper's shack where they had once lived, and the winds of another winter had come to infiltrate the cracks in the sideboards. Now his mother was washing his face with a warm cloth, taking the blood away and rinsing the cloth in a pan. He felt the blanket, found that it had arm tubes. It was probably his father's hunting coat, a malodorous canvas affair crusted with the blood of rabbits and squirrels. At least they would eat tonight. He began to laugh.

"What's funny?" a man asked.

"I didn't even fire my rifle," Jesse said. "Eight hundred dollars for an M-1, and I used it like a cave man's club." He laughed boisterously now, as if his confession were the most gallingly and happily embarrassing thing that had ever happened. The others in the room were infected by it and they, too, began to laugh. He wanted to hear his mother laugh but her voice was not a part of the din.

Just as he tried to open his eyes the warm cloth was laid over his face. Now he was conscious. Now he remembered.

"Did we win?" he asked. It was a thing that someone had once asked from the floor of a bar following a brawl.

A man chuckled. It was the man who had washed Jesse's face. "We won," the man said.

"It was you all along, wasn't it, Hip."

"Yes," said Hip Willis. "It was me. And you. And a lot of people you'll never know about. Dozens of people. Hundreds, maybe."

"I knew it. I knew something or somebody was setting me up for something, but I didn't know what. Still don't, really."

"Maybe it's better you don't, Jesse."

Touching the cloth, feeling its warmth becoming cool, Jesse said, "Tell me about it."

Hip sighed heavily. "Had to do with religion, Jesse. The oldest and bloodiest story there is."

"I take it you're more than just a doorman at River Towers, like I always thought."

"I'm part doorman, part other things. Everybody is part other things than what we know about them."

"Jesus, I go in for a shoeshine and all hell breaks loose. Remind me never to go to River Towers again. What does the casualty list look like?"

"Cowboy is dead. Wolfe is dead. You did good work with the rifle. And Ellen Talbott is dead."

Jesse winced. "I thought so. She fell heavy when she was hit. After Nam, the look of death is a second nature thing, no nonsense, no questions asked."

Hip removed the cloth, wet it in the pan, replaced it over Jesse's eyes. The fantasy-dream that he had experienced while regaining consciousness had all but dissipated by now, except for two things: there really was a coat serving as a blanket over his bare chest and there really was the smell of strange but not-so-strange oil in the room. He wondered why the smell reminded him of oil; certainly it was not motor oil, nor did it have to do with engines. It was . . . something else. The back of his left shoulder hurt and his head throbbed, especially the area around his left temple. When he reached to touch it, Hip grabbed his hand and forced it away.

"You're a lucky man," said Hip.

"Sure," said Jesse. "My left shoulder is gone, the left

side of my head is on a parking lot somewhere and I've got at least two killings to answer for. My cup runneth over."

Hip chuckled and said, "You've got a three-inch gash in your shoulder, a grazebump on your head and you've killed no one."

"They sure looked dead, Hip."

"Oh, they're dead all right. Only you didn't kill them."

"I didn't?"

"No. The headline will say 'Three Killed in Shootout with Federal Agents.' Wait and see. The public is used to those headlines. There won't be any stink at all."

"So I killed them, but I didn't kill them," said Jesse.

"Let it go, Jesse."

Hip's admonition had none of the teasing quality that Jesse had hoped to hear. Jubilant at the mere fact of being alive, Jesse now wanted to find out what had actually happened, from the beginning. He could not shake the feeling that Hip was serving as both nurse and warden: healing Jesse and watching him carefully.

"I can't stand it, Hip," he whispered, recalling that he had heard at least one other person laughing in the room. "Please tell me what this is all about."

Hip's chair squeaked as he turned and said to someone, "You want to take a look out front." A door opened and closed. "You know most of it already, Jesse. You know, for instance, what it was that we've all been looking for."

"A set of Mormon plates. A second set. Tell me, Hip, were they real?"

Hip mused for a moment and then said, "Who's to say? Some people thought they were. And that was enough. Is the Shroud of Turin real? Lourdes? Fatima? Look what those things have done to people for years."

"Funny thing," said Jesse, "not only did I not fire the rifle, I never even saw the plates. Now Popper is dead, Ellen Talbott, those other two that I killed. Four people dead, and for what?"

"More than four. Lot's more," said Hip.

"Yeah, I knew all along it was a big thing going on.

So are you going to bring me into the inner circle or not?"

There came a long silence. At last Hip said, "Jesse, have you ever heard of SSG?"

"No."

"Special Support Group. FBI agents who aren't really agents, as such, but who serve in a civilian capacity, mostly as intelligence personnel. Three years ago when I went to work as a doorman at River Towers I was put there to watch a lady with criminal leanings. She lives there. Rich, drives a Jaguar, has all that this country can offer and wants to bring it down."

He took the cloth again, wet it, laid it over Jesse's eyes.

"And last Sunday I got a phone call," he continued. "Three men in Mexico had disappeared. One was Charleston Garman. He had sent a letter to his uncle, old Popper. My orders were to get the letter. I did, which was easy enough, since he was a scared old man. I told him I'd help him out. It was then that *you* came in mind. I had an idea and I called Washington and told them about it."

"Let me guess," said Jesse. "I came in for a shine and you decided to give me the letter and make me the Judas goat in this thing. Why me?"

"You were a civilian, you were a private investigator accustomed to keeping his mouth shut."

"And I was *handy*."

Hip laughed again. "And you were *handy*. And so was I. There are probably ten thousand SSGs in America right now, people the public sees every day and pays no mind to—phone men, meter readers, Avon ladies. Eyes. Ears. The eyes and ears of a good country. Anyway, I happened to be where the letter went. And that's how I came to be on this case."

"What about Reeder and Riggazi? They were right up front in this thing. Why didn't they handle it?"

"Reeder and Riggazi knew very little about this, frankly. Which is exactly the way the Bureau works sometimes. They were sent to plant in your mind the awareness of importance. When you read Popper's letter in Muley's bar you didn't look all that interested."

"You mean I was being watched even then?"

"Yes, even then. Don't ask who it was—you'll never know. By the way, it wasn't Muley."

"Good," said Jesse.

"One of the three men in Mexico was a black named Phillips. It was Phillips who had Popper killed. As best we can figure, Phillips flew out of Mexico, called a dopehead named Oaks Scott. It was Oaks Scott who killed Popper. Did you by any chance see in the paper this week where Oaks Scott had been killed in a robbery attempt?" When Jesse shook his head Hip said, "He had it coming. People like him, it's just a matter of time, in and out of jail."

"Sounds very convenient," said Jesse. "Oaks Scott gets killed in a robbery attempt just after he kills Popper."

"Don't push it, and don't ask," Hip said coldly.

Chastened, Jesse said, "Okay, talk on."

"The people you killed last night were just as bad. Especially this Cowboy character. His real name was Vernon Cameron. He was a member of a lunatic splinter group called the Covenant, the Sword, and the Arm of the Lord. We're sure that he killed two old women out West, an Oriental down South, and probably a man over in Arkansas. That sword he swung at you last night has seen a lot of action."

"How did he happen to be with Wolfe?"

"Wolfe was a coward, and treacherous on top of it. Wolfe and Phillips killed Charleston Garman in Mexico, saw that they had screwed up and let the plates slip away. They played a pretty good game, giving credit where it's due. Emerson Wolfe called Cowboy in to kill Phillips. Then he was going to grab the plates for himself. Afterward, he was no doubt going to melt them down."

"This Phillips, where is he?"

"He's been a lot of places, but now he's dead. He went to the Northeast, killed a man there. He was a sharp man, but too sharp for his own good. He was following an old college professor whose name you'll never know. He knew where the professor was going, but he decided to make a game of it, I guess. And that was his downfall."

"How did a college professor get into this craziness?" Jesse asked.

Again, a long pause. And then Hip said, "You've heard enough. Too much, really. I've told you what I have because I know you and trust you. And knowing you, I was pretty sure you'd do some digging on your own. You know enough, so let it go."

Jesse rubbed the cloth along his forehead. When it touched the wound a burning sensation resulted. "You were willing to let me get killed, Hip. That goes against the grain. And Ellen Talbott got killed. How are you going to be able to sleep tonight?"

"Very well, Jesse. You'd have gone into this thing even if I hadn't been involved, and you know it. Here you were, a rich man, and tearing ass around town like a hungry coyote on this caper. We knew we had the right man. We just had to give him a few nudges in the right direction."

"How did you know I was a rich man, Hip?"

"The inheritance from your sister. We knew about it before the insurance agent did. Like I said, there have been hundreds of people on this thing for over a week. Each had his own little bit of the action. It came together beautifully. By the way, it was me who called Colbert last night. If he ever dogs you about it, just say it wasn't me."

"In other words, lie."

"Yes, Jesse: lie. A lie told for good is no lie at all. It is truth wearing a dark gown. Whether those plates be the real word of God or whether they be brass etched in acid, they had about them the stain of evil. They would have been a disruption, creators of chaos in an already chaotic world. They will disappear because they must disappear. I'll never know, and you won't either."

Jesse smiled and said, "The philosopher doorman. And

here all this time I thought you were just a nice non-Caucasian who opened doors and supervised luggage."

"They didn't exactly scrape me off the street."

"Yes, I could tell that you've picked up some education in the last ten minutes. Jesus, Hip, was I an idiot all the way through this?"

"No, just off balance, which is the way they . . . *we* wanted it. We won this one, with your help. It'll make the evening news and then it'll be forgotten. Dan Rather and Tom Brokaw will give it twenty seconds between hemorrhoid commercials. What you see on the news sometimes goes much deeper than what is presented. The American people suspect it, but most take it with a grain of salt."

Jesse stirred, shrugged, began to rise. Hip grabbed his shoulders and forced him back onto the bed. "What's wrong, Hip?" he asked.

"Just a word of caution before you get up. Your wounds are superficial, but we're going to take you to a doctor who's . . . simpatico. What you see here is never to be revealed. I've laid my ass on the line already by telling you any of this. You are about to see somebody you know, and you are about to see a place that you know. It was the only place to bring you so that we could check you out. Not a word to anyone ever about this conversation or this place. Do we have a deal?"

Jesse inhaled, smelled the strange oil again. Tingling with anticipation at being allowed to see the source of the torturous scent, he nodded. "You got a deal, Hip."

Hip helped Jesse off the bed, which turned out to be a cot. The washcloth fell away, hit the floor soundlessly. They were in some sort of storeroom. Boxes were stacked against a wall, and on their sides were familiar names: Remington Arms, Smith and Wesson, Winchester. On the other side of the room was a repair table complete with bore rods, pliers, bluing compounds, saddle soap, neat's-foot oil.

"Well I'll be damned," said Jesse.

Hip smiled. "I told you we're everywhere, Jesse. We're the good guys."

"Where is he?" Jesse asked.

"Out in back. He's going to take you to the doctor. Probably you won't be seeing me anymore. We were with Reeder and Riggazi last night on the parking lot. They already knew about him, but they didn't know about me, which is why I'll disappear. That, by the way, is why Wolfe left the riverbank and started running toward the Mercedes. We surprised him. Bastard nearly stepped on my hand. See, you were safe all along."

Jesse pointed to the side of his head. "Does this look like I was safe?"

Hip snapped his fingers in parody of someone admitting a stupid mistake. "That was my fault. I'd have sworn he had emptied that pistol. We miscounted his shots. Forgive me?"

"I'll work on it, you sonofabitch."

They smiled and shook hands. Jesse eased into his torn and bloody shirt and together they went out the back door. It was still dark, but the eastern horizon had begun to adopt the gray-taupe color of a foggy sunrise. The car was Jesse's own Chevrolet. Hip Willis helped Jesse into the passenger seat and said, "Hang tough, Jesse, you're good folks." Jesse turned to say something, but Hip was gone.

The car was dark and there was silence. Jesse wondered whether there had been a mistake, whether someone had missed connections. A hundred questions went through his mind, things he wished that he had asked Hip. His shoulder and forehead burned. He bowed his head and gave thanks, a thing that he had not done in years. While doing so he made a promise.

The car's left door opened. Miller Bass got in, fumbled with the key, started the engine.

"How's my favorite gun dealer?" Jesse asked.

"I feel as rotten-lousy as you look, Jess. Now do you know why I looked so surprised when you came in Friday and bought that rifle? I was thinking, why Jesus Christ, the jig is up."

"So you're an SSG also. Damned small world, Miller."

"Nope. It's big world full of small people. By the way, I'll have to ask you never to come into my gun shop again."

"Why? Afraid I might blow your cover somehow?"

Miller laughed. "Nope. Anybody that would fuck up a good M-1 like you did yours don't deserve to have one. Dammit, Jesse, you're supposed to *shoot* it, not swing it!"

They laughed all the way down Summer Avenue.

Twenty-eight

In Honolulu, Undersecretary of State Amos Fielding strode across the lawn of a palatial estate with Ferdinand Marcos, ex-president of The Republic of the Philippines. As they looked across Honolulu and to Diamond Head beyond, Marcos said, "This must be handled, and soon."

"It will be," said Amos. "We've dealt with this person before, and he'll respond to reason. One would think that twenty thousand per month would be enough for this place, but we'll pay an extra twenty just to keep the matter out of the papers. You say you've paid these extra monies twice? That's forty thousand that we'll reimburse you. Fair enough?"

Marcos looked at Amos, his eyes seeming to boil with a vicious liquidity. "The pain and suffering that has been endured by us over this matter is much more than that. He doubled the rent exactly because he knew that we would pay it."

"Correction, sir—because he knew that *we* would. So what else is it that you want?"

"How long can your court system tie up these people who are trying to steal my New York real estate, my holdings elsewhere?"

Amos smiled and looked out at the Arizona Memorial. "Forever if need be. How long do you want it tied up?"

"Twenty years at least," said Marcos. "Perhaps longer. The Marcos name will rise from the ashes of the Philippine fire and live again."

"If we did it for Baby Doc in Haiti, we can do it for

your children. But let's give Mrs. Aquino a chance for a year or two. She may work for you more while in office than you worked for yourself."

Marcos said, defensively, "And what does that mean?"

"Well," said Amos, "she brought the Communist guerillas out of the mountains for sixty-day cease-fires twice. If she starts to totter, it can always be said that she was soft on communism. You'd be surprised how malleable this thing called public opinion is. You had a taste of it yourself." He paused to let the barb sink in. "Of course, what has been toppled can sometimes be returned to its pedestal. As long as the thing knows what controls the base of its pedestal."

Marcos looked out at the sea, at the distant horizon, a longing and a sadness in his eyes. "How might that be accomplished?" he asked, wanting not to sound as if he were begging.

"Your country is primarily Catholic. What if the Holy Church were to become involved in its usual tirades against communism, only more so?"

"How would this be effected?" Marcos asked, a glint of old fires in his round face.

"Let's just say that, if needed, the Church would be on your side. Something has been established that makes the Catholic Church quite amenable to whatever we might ask of it."

Marcos smiled and shook his head. "The government of your country amazes me. The American people amaze me. You and I both know that I have four billion dollars of your money, that your country is paying my rent for this palace, that it was your country that took me out of the Philippines when my own people revolted against me in their ignorance. And now you are saying that you can manipulate the Church to put me back in power?"

Amos nodded. Over the Arizona Memorial the banner called Old Glory was touched by a morning breeze and fluttered outward from its standard. "Yes," said Amos, "It can be facilitated. But I'm curious about something. You've got five million times more money than you could spend if you started blowing two million dollars a day right now and lived to be a hundred years old. So why would you want to return to the Philippines?"

Marcos said quietly, "Look at them." He tilted his head toward the twenty-seven people who were stationed about the lawn, security personnel. "By lifting my hand I can elevate or destroy any of them. Multiply them by ten million and it is the same thing. It is a narcotic, this thing called power."

"And because somebody raised your rent you want him broken," said Amos.

"It is more than that," said Marcos. "I simply want this token of assurance from your government that will illustrate its good faith. Yes, I could have paid forty thousand dollars a month instead of twenty but I should not have to. This matter breached a small dike and, as any rice farmer can tell you, it is the shoring up of the small breaches that prevent the large ones. Do you understand?"

Amos understood. He hated kowtowing to this little man in his orchid-emblazoned shirt of raw silk. Marcos was asking that cannons be moved up to kill a fly. It was not the presence of the fly that was most disturbing to Marcos, but the current absence of the cannons. Show me that I'm still viable, Marcos was saying, pass in review. Pay my rent and chastise the landlord. You scratch my ass and I'll scratch yours. Light a votive candle to me.

Marcos said, "I have answered your question regarding why; now I wish to ask you one regarding how. You made allusions to the Church being the method of my possible re-entry into my homeland. How?"

"The current government in your country is weak," said Amos. "The political assasinations have never stopped for a moment. There is still chaos in the streets. We can engender the support of the Church in a dozen ways that will be to your advantage."

Marcos looked at Amos and a trace of a smile crossed his lips. "Your answer, though taken as a positive, has about it the broad-brush approach."

Amos placed his hands behind his back, British-royalty fashion, and said, "We wanted to stop communism in the

Philippines, and it was your place to do it with force of arms. You were rewarded and rewarded damned well. But you let your people starve. You fed the very fire that you were supposed to suppress. Now the person in power in Manila has offered the hand of friendship to the Communists and they have accepted it. In her naiveté she believes that she has ended hostilities, or at least banked the fire for a time. You had her husband killed because an idea of something better had emerged in the hearts of the Filipino people. It was a bit of political sleight of hand that should have worked, but did not. Within two years the insurgency by the Communists will be more vicious and more pronounced than ever. Wait and see. The Reds do not give up. Not ever. It is at that time that the Church will call for a return to the benevolence that you represented. Benevolence being a comparative term. The kaleidoscope of shifting power as viewed by the eye of the world will tire of the current yellow and yearn for a return to blue, you being the blue."

Marcos said, "But what of that other color in the kaleidoscope, the red?"

"Just now they are on hold in the Philippines, thanks to your successor. In Nicaragua and Honduras the woods are afire. Our eyes are there. When Central America is quelled as a hot spot, the Philippines will flare again."

"How do you know these things?"

"Anyone who reads history and thinks knows these things," said Amos. "The human heart and the human belly. Feed both those things that are necessary for physical and spiritual sustenance and those about you become your property. The spiritual is the Church and the Church will respond when the time comes."

"And the belly?"

"This time when you go back—if you go back—the belly will be filled. We do not intend to lose Cavite, Subic Bay, Mindanao or anyplace else because some Filipino child grew up in a tin-roof shack with hunger pains. You've got yours, and you damned nearly blew it. This time, what is sent to *your people* will get to *your people*. I trust that we understand each other."

Marcos's cheeks reddened. "I provide for the belly and you provide for the heart. I still don't understand."

Amos thought of the words *Lengus de Cristo*. The manipulation of something found in an obscure Mexican village had been set tracking on a collision course with world history. The Church would do what it was told, when it was told. Probably. Such things remained to be seen. "I'm not sure I understand either," he said truthfully. "There are so many variables."

"Such power to do all this," said Marcos, "and such wealth. Boundless resources. Where does it all come from? At the very bottom of all this subterfuge, this nullification of power, this granting of power, this house of mirrors called American politics, where does it all come from?"

Amos Fielding looked out at the Arizona Memorial once again. The flag hung limply over the white tomb with its arched windows.

"From the American taxpayer," he said. "And God help us if he ever awakens."

Twenty-nine

A week passed.

On the Sunday following the carnage on the River Towers parking lot, a great many people in a great many parts of the country were experiencing its aftereffects.

In Grosse Pointe, Michigan, Mrs. Gordon Harrison had her maid lay out an Yves St. Laurent suit of decorous black. Since the funeral on Wednesday so many of her *kindest*, yes, really *dearest* acquaintances had exhibited *chez élégante maison*. Ellen's funeral, so someone had said over cocktails after the ceremony, had been *de rigueur*. Perhaps they would utter such things today, and one should prepare oneself for such contingencies. Having thought thus, she vacillated between two white handkerchiefs, one ornate tulle, the other an emphatic braid. The tulle was more feminine, more of a *tuteur* for the eyes. They would see this and they would know, really *know*, that here was a woman whose *élan* in the throes of adversity was Spartan, a mirror of generations of selective breeding, the good and strong broadcloth of the American fabric. She studied her book of French phrases for a time, found one suitable for the coming afternoon, repeated it several times. "*Le mieux est de ne pas en parler.*" The vice president of International Marketing at GM had married a French woman last year, and the trend among the hierarchy was toward *ménage francophile*. There would be a great deal of French spoken today, and with her recent tragedy, her black suit and white handkerchief,

Mrs. Gordon Harrison knew that she would be a veritable *fleur de lis* of *dénouement*. She would show them that propriety, culture, and breeding were not the exclusive protectorate of *les dames gauloises*.

In Bremerton, Washington, a heavyset black man named Hip Willis assumed his second day of duty as butler for Dr. Milos Nialozec, instructor in Russian and Hungarian languages at the University of Seattle. The good doctor's house looked out over Bremerton Navy Yard. The previous butler had left suddenly last week after being offered a position elsewhere at two thousand dollars per month, a heaven-sent windfall. The employment agency had recommended Hip Willis highly.

A pair of high-powered binoculars lay on a table near the great windows that faced the bay. Using his feather duster, Hip went over the table briskly, looked about to see whether his employer had yet arisen. Satisfied that he had not, Hip picked up the binoculars, worked the rotator, zeroed in on the USS *New Jersey*. The team of scientists and Naval technicians who had spent yesterday working on and about the great vessel's guided-missile housing had not yet assembled. This being Sunday, probably they would not.

Hip smiled and laid the binoculars on the table exactly as he had found them.

In Hernando, Mississippi, Donkey Baby awoke in jail. He had gone on a toot the night before and his head hurt him fiercely. He had no idea where his car was, how long he had been here, or why he was twenty miles south of Memphis. Someone had once said that the best Saturday night was the one you were too drunk to recall, a bit of wiseacreage that Donk would have questioned just now.

"Coffee and donuts," a voice said. Donkey Baby heard movement in the cell block as his fellow miscreants shoved toward the bars.

"Watch that shit!" someone warned.

"Watch your own shit!" another countered.

Lying on the floor, his eyes closed, Donkey Baby only hoped that if they fought neither would fall on him.

In Waycross, Georgia, John and Evelyn Fender made preparations to visit the grave of their daughter, Brylette. Sitting on the edge of their bed and sobbing, Evelyn Fender held a childhood photograph of her dead daughter. In the photograph Brylette wore a cowboy suit—hat, chaps, guns, vest—and stood beside a Shetland pony.

John Fender hit his wife on the shoulder with his fist, a thing that he had done at will during the forty years of their marriage.

"Get your ass up and let's go," he commanded. Walking past his gun racks, his bird dog trophies and his walls that were festooned with Marine Corps memorabilia, he went out to his mud-caked four-wheel-drive Ford Bronco and waited.

In New Haven, Connecticut, Dr. James Wagstaff went over his notes for his talk to the congregation of Second Presbyterian Church of New Haven. As guest speaker, a thing for which he had volunteered three weeks ago, he would stress love, compassion, tithing, the simplicities of the Holy Word. It would be a mundane sermon. There were so many things that he would have preferred to tell them, but he could not. Besides, they would not have believed him.

In Alexandria, Virginia, Vaughn Biddle mounted the steps of the garage–office with bucket, mop, brushes, and two cans of Comet cleanser. It had been exactly one week ago today that Hip Willis had called him and advised that the Memphis-Mormon-Votan thing was settled and Biddle had immediately rejoiced and departed for home. But because of the absolute secrecy of what had gone on here, and what would go on here during other inevitable crises that were to come, even the scullery had to be done by Biddle himself. He looked at the phones, at the desk which was now barren, at the pinholes where the maps had hung. Somehow this just did not look like the sort of place in which the fate of religion had been decided.

In St. George, Utah, a cemetery attendant named Kale Webster started his John Deere riding mower and lowered the blade. Driving among the tombstones, he passed a barren bit of newly turned earth that was appended only by an aluminum marker that read: Vernon Cameron. The dates of birth and death were too small to see. As Webster drove on, dust and grass forming a greenish emulsion in the air, he hoped that he could finish by noon. The Phillies were playing the Cardinals this afternoon, and Kale Webster had five dollars bet on the Cards.

In Licking, Missouri, Ollie and Hazel Colbert sat on the front porch of her mother's house shelling purple-hulled peas.

"Some vacation," said Ollie. "We drive three hundred miles to hull peas."

"Hush," said Hazel. "She'll hear you."

"I coulda got more rest in Memphis. I wonder how Jesse's doing."

Hazel dumped a load of hulls into a washtub and said, "Did you ever find out what happened to his head?"

"No. He was kind of sketchy about it." He ran his thumb down the spine of yet another peastalk and let the peas fall into a pan. It perplexed him that for twenty years Jesse would have told him what had happened to his head. But Jesse had changed of late and those days were gone forever.

Looking out at the front yard, at the pecking chickens and at the cattle in the pasture beyond, Ollie Colbert suddenly felt very old, and very lonely.

In a pasture near Renssaleer, Indiana, Reverend Orliss Tribble sat on a blanket under the massive trailer that bore his name. The rain poured and the rattling on the trailer's roof was leading the evangelist toward sleep. Last night's offerings had totaled less than thirty dollars and it would take that much just to fill up the truck for the hump to the next county.

He missed Cecil. On Thursday he had given Cecil a bus ticket and fifty dollars so that the boy might visit relatives in Texas. The money had been part of that wondrous windfall from that kind man who had helped them down in Tennessee, the man who had left the yam money.

Reverend Tribble tried to recall the good man's strange name, but could not.

He lay back on the blanket and watched it rain.

In Reston, Virginia, Foster St. John kissed Potter goodbye while she slept and sneaked out of their new apartment. The place had a racquetball court and he was dying to try the game.

A young, upwardly mobile couple sat on their balcony and watched as the older man walked below. His skinny legs, bowed back, and general milquetoast appearance caused them to smirk good naturedly.

"People come and go from this place like crazy," said the young man. "Who's that one?"

"Probably nobody," said the young woman. "Did you see those blue socks and black tennis shoes? Yuck."

In Phoenix, Arizona, Detective Sergeant Paul D. Lang rolled over in bed and felt his usual Sunday morning depression, a Sabbath melancholy that had plagued him since boyhood. His parents had always saved their fights for Sunday morning, that time of the week when their noncoinciding factory shifts had allowed them time to be together. This morning it was worse. He had been hoping to wangle a promotion to lieutenant out of the murders of two old Mormon women, but a week ago the guilty party, one Vernon Cameron, had been killed in a shootout in Memphis. Leave it to the FBI to come in and hog the glory.

In Fort Knox, Kentucky, Agents Charles Beale and Ira Heinz of the Federal Bureau of Investigation stepped from a C-119 "Flying Boxcar" onto the tarmac of the military airport. They had not spoken to the colonel and the captain who had flown the plane from Memphis, nor had they even seen them. As soon as they had removed the tightly bound box and placed it in the trunk of a waiting U.S. Army Chevrolet, the engines of the great plane roared and the pudgy monster lifted off and was gone.

The sergeant was under strict orders not to engage the agents in conversation and the three men rode in silence. At a tall gate of reinforced steel a stark black and white sign read UNITED STATES GOLD DEPOSITORY. FORT KNOX, KENTUCKY. Two military guards checked the credentials of the car's occupants and the Chevrolet was allowed to enter.

Two hours later, as agent Charles Beale boarded the stodgy Army Buffalo four-seater that would fly him back to his home base in St. Louis, he wondered just what he had done, why it had been done, why he had been chosen to do it. Certainly the FBI had been weird on this one. He had spent four hours with agent Ira Heinz, and knew nothing about the man but his name. They had met with a man in a gun shop in Memphis this morning, a pot-bellied character who said "rotten-lousy" a lot, had taken the box from him, had flown in silence to Kentucky.

Weird. That was the only word for it.

A young captain with sunglasses and a swagger slid behind the controls and said, "Beautiful flying weather, sir. St. Louis, huh?"

Agent Charles Beale smiled at the young man and nodded.

On Danny Thomas Boulevard in Memphis the white Cadillac Fleetwood Brougham eased to the north. It was just before sunrise. Seeing the great bridge to their left, Jesse and Janice giggled like children. They had fallen asleep together eight hours ago after a Saturday of buying new clothing and new luggage. The smells of *new* and *fresh* and *happy* were everywhere.

"One more time, just for the hell of it," said Jesse.

Janice opened the glove box for the third time since

they had left her apartment. As expected, the ten thousand dollars in American Express traveler's checks were still in place.

"Takes a bit of getting used to," said Janice. She ran her fingernails along the burgundy leather of the armrest and sighed with an excess of contentment.

At this hour the great bridge that led to Arkansas and then on to Las Vegas was mostly empty. Jesse drove to its center, slowed the car, stopped. Janice looked at him happily. He got out and took two bottles of George Dickel from under the seat. The bridge was totally his, as was the great river below, as was the world. He walked to the guard rail, threw both bottles, watched them somersault lazily downward and splash without sound. An eighteen wheeler roared by but Jesse neither saw nor heard it.

Jesse looked up just as the bridge lights went off in acknowledgement of the coming day. He walked back to the car, got in, drove westward.

"What was that about?" Janice asked.

"Just fulfilling a promise," he said.

She touched his forearm and said, "I love you."

"Me too you, Janice. And when we get to the Desert Inn, I'll prove it."

"I can't wait that long. How about we get a room for a couple of hours when we get to Little Rock?"

"You're on," he said, laughing.

TOP-SPEED THRILLERS WITH UNFORGETTABLE IMPACT FROM AVON BOOKS

TASS IS AUTHORIZED TO ANNOUNCE...   **Julian Semyonov**
70569-9/$4.50US/$5.95Can
From Russia's bestselling author, the unique spy thriller that tells it from the other point of view.

RUN BEFORE THE WIND   **Stuart Woods**
70507-9/$3.95US/$4.95Can
"The book has everything—love, sex, violence, adventure, beautiful women and power-hungry men, terrorists and intrigue."
The Washington Post

COLD RAIN   **Vic Tapner**   **75483-5/$3.95US/$4.95Can**
A stunning thriller of cold-blooded espionage and desperate betrayal!

DEEP LIE   **Stuart Woods**   **70266-5/$4.95US/$5.95Can**
The new Soviet-sub superthriller..."Almost to plausible...one of the most readable espionage novels since *The Hunt for the Red October!*"
Atlanta Journal & Constitution

MAJENDIE'S CAT   **Frank Fowlkes**   **70408-0/$3.95**
Swindler against con man compete in a plan to bring the US to its knees and wreak global economy for good!

THE GRAY EAGLES   **Duane Unkefer**   **70279-7/$4.50**
Thirty-one years after WW II, the Luftwaffe seeks revenge...and one more chance at glory.

THE FLYING CROSS   **Jack D. Hunter**
75355-3/$3.95US/$4.95Can
From the author of *The Blue Max*, a riveting, suspense-packed flying adventure in the war-torn skies over Europe.

Buy these books at your local bookstore or use this coupon for ordering:

Avon Books, Dept BP, Box 767, Rte 2, Dresden, TN 38225
Please send me the book(s) I have checked above. I am enclosing $_____
(please add $1.00 to cover postage and handling for each book ordered to a maximum of three dollars). *Send check or money order*—no cash or C.O.D.'s please. Prices and numbers are subject to change without notice. Please allow six to eight weeks for delivery.

Name _____

Address _____

City _____ State/Zip _____

Thrillers 11/88